Nothing I Touch Stands Still

JANE SPIRO

Nothing I Touch
Stands Still

CRUCIBLE PUBLISHERS, *Bath*

This preview edition published by
CRUCIBLE PUBLISHERS
Norton St Philip, Bath BA2 7LN, UK

www.cruciblepublishers.com

ISBN 1-902733-04-5

Typeset in 11/13 pt Bell
Digitally printed in Great Britain
by Antony Rowe Ltd, Eastbourne

In the Beginning

Rosa's father spoke gently into the books, as if they could hear him. He told her why Goethe came before Marx and who they both were, and the reason why poetry went on one shelf and essays on another. Only sometimes she opened the books and ran her finger down the crack between the pages so her fingerprints came out dusted and downy grey.

It was on a day like that, a day before Rosa's ninth birthday, when Lola first came into the library. She had sandals that flapped at the toe, being too big: and a cardigan that ended at her elbows, being too small. Lola was the youngest person ever to read books in the library, and she sat in a corner cross-legged with her knees showing, cradling the book in her skirt.

'Are you really reading or just pretending?' Rosa asked.

'I'm choosing one for Father' she said.

'Do you understand them, those big books?'

'Oh yes. I learn the bits I like by heart.'

'I don't believe.'

'Well it's true.'

'Go on, show me then.'

She stood up, smoothed down her skirt, pinned her arms along them at each side, cleared her throat, and began,

Man, proud man,
Dress'd in a little brief authority,
like an angry ape
Plays such fantastic tricks
it makes the angels weep.'

'Oh that's good!' Rosa cried, 'what language is it?'

'English,' she said.

'What does it mean?'

'People are like pigs when they're bad-tempered.'

'Oh no, does it really?! Does it really say pigs?'

'Yes.'

'Oh how rude! What are all the other words?'

'God doesn't like people who shout.'

'Does it say that really?'

'You keep asking the same thing. You ask me everything twice.'

Lola borrowed a book that day. It was a fat book with small writing and thin paper you could see your fingers through.

Rosa thought it would take at least a year to read, so she wouldn't see Lola again for a long time.

But the following Sunday morning, Father called her in from the yard,

'Rosa, your scholar friend is here!'

and she went running into the library.

'Did you learn your book off by heart again?'

'Some bits,' she said.

'Tell me some.'

She stood up in the corner and cleared her throat.

'Gather together all the children of the universe; you will see in them nothing but innocence, gentleness, and fear; had they been born evil, mean, cruel, they would give some signs of it, like when small snakes bite and when small tigers try to tear things to pieces.'

'Oh I love that! Who said it?'

'Mr. Russia, Rousseau.'

'What does it mean?'

'Cats and dogs fight all the time, but children are good.'

'Does it say that really? I know some cats and dogs which don't fight all the time.'

'But they chase chickens.'

'But you didn't say chickens.'

'Yes, it says chickens or anything you like.'

'What else?'

'This is another bit.

People say that men are born the child of the devil, and of evil. Nothing is more untrue...'

Lola was in full bloom then. She was operatic. She mouthed words the way she rolled noodles amongst her cheeks, she was rolling and mouthing when a scream knocked her short. Knocked short by Mother, her feet in socks, waving doughy arms with sleeves falling back to the deep elbow dimples, shouting,

'You don't say that word in this house! Not in this house!'

Lola stopped with her mouth round in the ooo of 'true'.

'Which word?' Rosa began to say, but her mother filled the space first.

'Now see how that child is corrupted! The words that came out of her head! I heard it! Don't you call me stupid! Don't you fool me with your highbrow names. You should clean your mouth, may the evil eye *keneinen hora* not get you first. And it's you!' She swung round to the place of Father, holding his steel spectacles over the pages of a book like a magnifying glass, standing against the window where the light came in on a train of dust.

'I blame you, corrupting innocent children, and look at Rosa, lapping it up like the evil eye would smile to see it.'

Julius Klein stood against the window with Maimonedes' obligations of husbands to wives open in his hands, and let her rant and swirl around him like a wind around its eye.

She snatched Lola's new book out of her hands.

'Now go home, go on, off you go, tell your father to do his dirty business himself. He might let you go bad, but I'm not seeing my daughter go bad too,'

Lola ran out of the house.

Julius rarely raised his voice. He only groaned.

'Books are windows to the soul and in doing this you are stealing the soul,' he said.

Rosa pulled the nearest book she could find off the shelf, and ran out onto the porch. Lola was sitting there, hugging her knees.

'I don't care,' she said.

'Don't you really?'

'No, course I don't. As long as I can do what I want, I don't care who shouts at me.'

'Here,' Rosa said, 'I got a book for you.'

Lola looked at it, turned it round and round, opened the front cover and turned the crinkly front page with its brown letters.

A spectre is haunting Europe,' she read, '*all the powers of old Europe have entered into a holy alliance to exorcise this spectre.* '

'What does it mean?'

'There are ghosts in Europe and nobody likes them.'

'I don't like that.'

'He may not be right. What they write isn't always right.'

Lolinka made Rosa feel better. She stretched the edges of what was possible. She would always do that, for Rosa.

'I didn't know Father had books like that, about ghosts.' Rosa said.

Lolinka squawked with laughter.

'Don't you *read* your father's books? What's the point of just looking at them and moving them around if you don't *read* them.'

'They're grown-up books. I don't understand them.'

'Oh silly, no-one understands them. You just pretend.'

Lola got up and skipped home with the book under her arm. Rosa stayed on the porch, her mother's voice rising higher and higher inside, pulling Father with her like a snake eating a mouse's head.

There are ghosts in Europe, thought Rosa, as she went back into the house. Or maybe not. Maybe Lola was just pretending.

CHAPTER ONE

Sunday Night

Isobel helped Leo change gear at the front while I sat in the back of the van with the antlers. I watched the streets disappear into blue, the way things disappear when there is a lake, everything rings around the invisible thing and looks into it.

The van stopped at the kind of chalet where children are forced to stay on school ski camps. Cleaners in orange uniforms were hoovering the street in dodgem cars with electronic scrubbing brushes on the end. A dog was being pulled on its back legs to a special dog toilet attached to a lamp-post. I saw that the village stopped here, because behind the hostel was a wall of rock that went up plat where sky should be.

As we went through the open doorway, Leo stopped, pulled a handful of jellyfish fingers out of his shorts' pocket, and hung them up on a hook outside the door. They clinked and plinked in the breeze.

'Windchimes,' he said. 'I'll take the antlers,' and went off down the corridor with the furry tips sticking out from under his arm, and Isobel running three steps behind him.

Life Enhancement Group (LEG)
Short courses in life skills and personal development:
life-changing courses in beautiful Swiss lakeside town.
Run by registered members of
the Sri Praphulladatta School of Psychopersonal Training,
Huddersfield

*   *   *

At Basel station I wasn't at all sure which country I was in. The boy in the carriage said that the front of the train was France and the back was Switzerland. I felt quite upset. Geoffrey had written down ten things to remember on the journey. One was never to ask help from people you didn't know, and another was never to look at men in the eye. He said in some cultures, looking at a man in the eye meant you were a prostitute. However, I took no notice until we crossed the Channel. The boy had Eire stamped all over his suitcase, so it didn't count as another culture. Anyway, it is impossible to share a carriage with a person without looking at them.

I couldn't sleep all night. I could hear him zipping and unzipping, and shuffling about inside his sleeping bag

In the morning, I saw his feet with hairs on the toes. A tuft of hair stood up on the back of his head like a baby monkey's, and you could see the creases in the sleeping bag on his cheeks. I had never seen a boy straight out of bed before without even washing.

We both shuffled about making dressing and rucksack and sorting out the bunk noises, and sometimes he made puffing and yawning noises. When he had finished all those, he sat on the bunk opposite with a water bottle in a khaki jacket.

'Want some?' he said.

Yes I did though it was strange drinking out of something rough that felt like a soldier's trousers. His T-shirt made a V with his neck sprouting out like a plant, and round it a silver line as if he was metallically jointed. It was a cross on a plain silver chain. He would clutch it from time to time and shift it round his neck so it hung at all kinds of assymetrical angles.

'Where are you to then?'

'To Pacino in Switzerland,' I said.

'Well, would you believe that for a coincident,' he said, 'for I'm at Pacino too, preparing me poor legs to walk the Jungfrau.'

We both looked at his legs, and then we both blushed. It was interesting the way he had blue eyes: most people I knew had brown eyes or sometimes grey. I wasn't used to that, blue eyes like icicles pointing straight at me.

'I'm Sean Kelly,' he said, putting out his hand to me.

'I'm Laura Cherry.' I said.

'Well, fellow travellers then,' he said, 'well met, and all that.'

The countryside was opening up now, rushing through stations with clean platforms and fields with painted cows and glassy mountains. His tongue kept bobbing in and out to lick away the beads of water from the corner of his mouth: and when he did that his chin came to a point like a pixie's.

'Would you mind me opening the window?' he said, pointing his icicles at me.

'Yes, no I don't mind,' I said.

He pushed the window up and the rumble and gruzzle of the wheels roared in and with it a crisp slice of air like lemon cake.

From outside the window, the place where his head was, I could hear puffs of Irish jig whistled into the air. it was a funny pixie sound, and it seemed to come from inside my head, not from outside his. From the back his neck looked as if it was blushing, and his shoulders looked bony like a coathanger.

When he left to wash his teeth, I put my head over the window too and the ice cream air took my breath away. It moved in a thick band of dew, and I rubbed my face in it, shook my face into the day. I could sing, I could scream and no-one would hear: the train would loose it and throw it away over the fields. At home you couldn't scream, not from the bottom of your toes, not so it was a red O from the middle of your stomach, you could only sometimes scream in tune at choir. But here you could, here you could start at the centre and let it spread out to all the edges and the wind would just whirl it round and round and it would disappear. So I pulled all my breath together and made a fist of sound inside me and heaved it out right through my throat into my head and I could feel it ringing round and round inside me my head was a bell and the sound sprayed out a bright red ribbon into the stream of the wind. 'Fuck you! Fuck you! Fuck you!' it said, someone else's voice, and my own voice sat on my shoulder saying, 'Oh yes! Say it again! I've always wanted to say that!'

When I turned round, I was out of breath with the shock of the air. Sean was back, quietly putting on his boots.

'You've sure a voice on you!' he said, looking up from his bootlaces.

I blushed. I didn't want him to think I swore all the time.

At Pacino station Sean was met by a group of stooped people with wardrobe-sized rucksacks on their backs and white knees like uncooked chickens.

I was met by Leo and Isobel with a big LEG sign.

Sean looked at me as he was led away by the people with the white knees and I was led away by Leo with Isobel attached to him.

The LEG building made me feel I had made a dreadful mistake. My room had a wooden bed with edges like a butter dish. It would cut anyone to pieces who tried to share it. And the pillow was hard as a salami. All round the corridor were rooms like mine with butterdish beds and identical tables and wash basins. It didn't feel like a building where one had an experience.

When I went downstairs for the first Life Enhancement session, Leo was polishing a porcelain Buddha and all along the windows were little blue sticks smelling of old lady's bedrooms.

'It's jasmine,' he said.

*   *   *

'Empty your mind of everything you have brought with you to this workshop' Leo was saying. 'Try and enter into a new open space. For your first evening in Pacino we are going to start with a silence just to gather our thoughts together, to bring our minds into this space. I'm going to light this candle as the darkness falls. You can place the candle at the centre of your mind and focus your thoughts around it. It is a symbol of our light and our coming together.'

Pictures popped up like a pop-up book: Sean with his pixie chin and knees, Geoffrey giving me advice at Victoria Station, the streets that disappeared and the secret lake, a place where things disappeared: and the rock behind the balcony, a place where things stopped.

The more I emptied my mind, the more pictures popped up.

standing outside the party afraid to go in

the room was thrumming up and down with the sounds inside the smoke the zebra lights

Tina was already there in leather trousers and green spray in her hair

but not me I was afraid to go in and every time the door opened a crack the thrum broke out like an animal

then Geoffrey arrived shaking out his fringe and said, 'oh, you needn't have waited' and there wasn't time to say, 'but I wasn't' when he said,

'Well come on, no point hanging about outside,'
and pushed me into the room in front of him

otherwise I might never have gone to the party

I'd have waited outside bits of the animal squeezing belching out the door crack by crack and pawing me

I'd never have smelt the feromones on his neck

I meditated with my eyes open: but everyone else had their eyes closed. I don't know how they could focus on the candle with their eyes closed. I felt like I was watching fish through a glass-bottomed boat: they floated around, in this spooky silence while I watched. Isobel was running her hands through her hair as if preparing to have her photograph taken. There was a thin boy there, whose face was tight as if he had just been slapped. The woman next to me was shuffling from knee to knee and her ankle bands were jingling. Another older lady in velvet trousers began snoring. Leo had a really rude look on his face: I bet he wasn't thinking about the candle. When everyone opened their eyes I quickly closed mine so they wouldn't know I was cheating.

Then we had to go round the group, saying what we felt. Isobel said she felt very conscious of her body relaxing. As she said it, her T-shirt dropped completely off one shoulder, as if by remote control. The lady in the velvet trousers said

'I felt myself floating'.

I didn"t know what to say when it came to my turn.

'I couldn't clear my mind', I blurted out. 'My mind just feels too busy.'

Isobel looked superior, as if *her* mind was never too busy

Everybody hugged after the session: it was strange how thin some people were, or how your fingers got caught in their clothes, or how you would bump noses. I realised I hadn't had enough practice. The more Leo said how we were all part of a happy family, the lonelier I felt and the less I wanted him to hug me.

So I wandered along the corridor and found a new door, on the end wall, that was half open. On the other side there was a sudden gush of air and sudden electric eyes of geraniums all round the edge of a balcony, quietly, sending its face out into the twilight purples and the navy blue night rocks.

I stood there breathing just a second, feeling all the thrill of alone when I realised I was not. Leo was standing on one leg with his eyes closed. Isobel was sitting on the floor, trying to pull her right foot over her left knee like the porcelain Buddha. It was their balcony. Of course.

So I went to bed, but somehow I felt there was something else happening that I was missing: maybe people were talking or hugging on the steps, or doing things with the incense, or walking to the lake in the moonlight. Whatever they were doing would be more romantic and adult and free compared to whatever I was doing. So I wrote my diary.

At the disco Tina was showing her legs and Polly was showing her breasts. Even though I had both, I wasn't showing them because I had been taught not to. I had been taught that nice men noticed your mind. I stood there all evening in my five layers of grunge and nobody noticed my mind.

I stood outside the party while the room thrummed and flashed like a dragon, until Geoffrey pulled me in.

He stroked my hair. It was the first day I could sit on it.

'Never cut it,' he said.

I grow into him and he grows into me like toenails. I can't see any way of us being separate without it hurting.

I thought the future was another planet but all along it was just the other side of the curtain and I could open it with a fingernail open it with a yes.

Grandma covered Geoffrey with blessings and pomegranate seeds. He was her holy grandson-in-law-to-be, he was an offering from her God and she touched his head with her hand, see-through with brown spots.

'You, you will be happy,' she said to me, putting her hand over mine. It was a tiny hand, a flap of velvety skin.

'He is a good match for you,' she said, 'professional, he will have a good salary, he will be a man in the community, a Mensch. You must take care of him, don't give him away to anyone.'

'Why would I give him away?'

'Look closely after him because a good man he can quickly disappear.'
   She is not right.

He will not disappear. I will not cut my hair. One week will make no difference. I will go home after one week and everything will be the same.

Every time you feel alone, grandma said, recite the shema. It's the one thing, she said, that kept me alive.

My daughter, keep the commandment of thy father
And forsake not the teaching of thy mother.
Bind them continually upon thy heart,
Tie them about thy neck.
When thou walkest, it shall lead thee;
When thou liest down, it shall watch over thee;
And when thou wakest, it shall talk with thee.

CHAPTER TWO

Monday

The first session of the course was about Belonging. First we learnt each other's names. We practised them by throwing oranges at each other, then we had to make a shrine to ourselves with pictures, objects or words we cared about. Daphne with the velvet trousers built a shrine made of rocks she had brought with her from Dartmoor. She must have carried them all the way here in her luggage. I drew a giant engagement ring on a piece of sugar paper, and filled it with the faces and names of people in the family. Then we walked round the room, saying kind things about each others shrines. Isobel had traced a line around her own body, and filled it with words to do with body parts. In the part where her heart was she had drawn a man with hair plastered down like a Spanish waiter.

'It's my father,' she said. I pretended I wasn't at all surprised.

When we had finished our shrines, Leo brought us back to the circle.

'Our shrines are the way we see ourselves. They are the places where we belong most of all, the shrine we make for ourselves where we feel most comfortable. Now where in the outside world do we feel that belonging? Where can we put down shrines in our lives?'

We each had to think about what Belonging meant to us: when we had felt it last, why and with whom: what it was like NOT to belong: when we had felt that last, why and with whom. The woman with ankle bangles, whose name is Gloria, cried at that point: we all gathered round and hugged her until she was howling. What was strange was how hugging seemed to make people cry even more: it didn't seem to make them feel better at all. Leo explained that crying was a way of feeling better and an important part of change. Several other people started crying at that point, and Leo hugged them all. Sometimes I felt a little left out, that he never hugged me: however, I wasn't so upset that I was prepared to cry.

When everyone had finished crying and hugging, Leo asked us to close our eyes, and remember a moment in our past when we really felt we belonged. He asked us to remember smells, sounds, sights, people, what they had said, what we had said. When we opened our eyes, we were to write it all down on a piece of paper. I am four and it is 1974.

My story of belonging and not belonging

On the first day at school I had to change shoes for outdoor play, then change back again for indoor play and then back again into outdoor play shoes for going home. My sandals had butterflies cut in the leather and straps with holes you had to punch with a silver buckle and they were brand new with no creases in them.

After changing shoes, they did a thing called Register, and then they did another thing called Sembly. Teachers had all different words which you didn't use in a person's home. For Sembly you had to make a long line so you could all go through a door one by one.

Some of the children, however, did not go into this long line. They went into a short line. I wondered how it was you could get into a short line, and whether you could join if you wanted, just to see what it was like. There was nothing different, or bad about the girls in that line. One girl had her hair tied up with cherries, and another girl had elastic bands round her socks to keep them up, but that was no reason to be in a special line.

They went through a brown door in the corridor and we went through another brown door. Most of the doors were brown, but these doors were a dirtier sort of brown.

There were so many girls in the big room, I thought I had never seen so many people all together except at the station, except these people were neat like in flower beds.

Miss Mavey put a book into my hand. It had soft covers you could squeeze, and gold edges like people's hair when you separated the pages. The pages smelt like mouldy sweets. Polly and Lisa sitting on either side of me seemed to be very familiar with this kind of book. But I had never seen anything like it. There was a picture of a man in a white nightie with brown hair down to his shoulders, and strange brown eyes and there was a lightbulb round his head. He seemed quite nice, but I didn't know anyone like that at all. Polly and Lisa seemed to know him quite well and even knew his name.

As the Sembly went, it became stranger and stranger. The head teacher called a number, and everyone in the room rose to their feet. They seemed to know rules which I didn't. The number made them make all these words, like

cheesy verger
cheesy loves you
mother verger cheesy son

All the words were new ones that I didn't know.

Everyone seemed to know the song: they all sung it in loud voices, as if they had sung these songs every day. I couldn't understand how Polly and Lisa knew the song, when it was only our first day at school. Had there been another pre-school school which everyone but me had attended?

What if Miss Mavey found out I had never been there, and didn't know any of the rules or the songs? What if Polly and Lisa discovered I was only pretending to know the words by making round shapes with my mouth and going UMMM and AAHH.

When Sembly was over, we made another long line again and went through the dirty brown doors and met the other short line girls coming out of their door, and we all joined up and went into the classroom. I said to the one with the elastic round her socks,

'What do you do?'

'Same as what you do,' she said. So I asked Miss Mavey.

'What do those girls do in Sembly?'

'They sing their own songs and say their own prayers,' Miss Mavey said.

It was clever, to make your own songs. In our Sembly we had to sing these other people's songs which I didn't know. It was better to make up your own songs, because then it wouldn't matter if you didn't know anything.

Every day I joined the line for the Big Room, and I held the book with the squashy cover and the gold sticky pages and picture of the man in the white nightie, and I made all the noises and faces the other girls made.

I got to know all the words about cheesy off by heart, and I could hum all the tunes and make mouths like the grown-up girls. I began to quite like it, like swimming practice. The water smelt funny, but you got used to it.

One day, when we were getting ready in our short line and long line, Miss Mavey came and gently leaned over me.

'Laura dear,' she said, 'I think you belong in the other queue'.

I couldn't think what I had done which made me belong today but not yesterday. I hadn't wet myself or put glue on the teacher's chair, and I had had my fringe cut on Saturday. I had got to quite like the long queue and anyway those other girls didn't have a book with pictures to look at. But Miss Mavey took my hand and I had to go with her because you did with teachers.

Through the other brown door was just an ordinary classroom, and the chairs were in circles not in flower beds, and there was room for a chair each. The girl with the cherries in her hair sat next to me. Her ponytail stuck up from the top of her head.

'My mum knows your mum.'

'Who's your mum?' I asked.

'Mummy,' she said.

Then everyone went shush sshh and a senior girl began chanting with her eyes open. Then through the buzz and shushing noises I realised I knew the words she was saying, and it was the first thing I had known since I started school. They were the nonsense words we said at home, and which grandma said on Fridays and Saturdays: *le totty foot hoover ho naffer show bane annie ho.* They were serious words and we weren't to laugh or talk and the words in English made me tingle all over and made my ears go red.

Let these words which I command you this day, be always in your heart, teach them diligently to your children and speak of them in your home

yes and on your doorposts and foreheads I will do what you say and the words will shower down like great walls of thunder

we are from the desert all of us in the room with the baking sand and men with rolling white beards and sticks

inside us we are all wearing white sheets and veils and wash our clothes in the Dead Sea

inside our plaits and white socks we are ancient which means very very very old because Jessie beget David beget Deborah beget Susannah beget Samson beget Daniel beget Hagar beget Rebecca beget Rachel beget Sarah beget Peter beget Jonathan beget Jacob beget Laura

beget means to have a baby

if you were beget you lived in a tent and wore a veil if you were a girl and collected water in a vase from the well

In the other Sembly room they must have had different sorts of grandmas or maybe fathers who wore nighties.

I curled up my toes. Mother and Father, Grandma Rosa and Grandpa Gabor, Hannah in her Saturday socks and patent leather shoes floated into the room and sat on my shoulder. It didn't seem so strange at school after that.

*   *   *

It was a jolt to remember where I was and who with. Leo was saying,

'Now Laura, come and join us in the circle.'

Everyone else was sitting round, cross-legged, and only I hadn't finished.

'Let's go round the group, and everyone can tell us whatever they would like to share about their moment of belonging. Who wants to start?' he said.

'Me,' said Gloria, sitting right next to me so I could smell her velvet trousers. When she spoke she stared strangely over my right shoulder. I turned round to see who was there, but there wasn't anything, and nothing was on my shoulder either. I brushed it to make sure.

'My moment of belonging was recognising my anger towards my husband when he left me, instead of feeling like a victim.'

Everyone nodded, and murmured as if they agreed and understood and had felt exactly the same, even though no-one else's husband had left them.

'He made me feel it was all my fault and I deserved it,' she shouted. Then she began howling like a wolf, with her head back and her mouth open so you could see her fillings and I didn't know what to do, whether you just watched when someone howled, or joined in, or went away so they could be alone. Her howls went on and on while Leo closed in on her like a cat so that when she had finished he was holding her with her hair hanging down all damp and limp against his shoulder. She must have been to lots of these courses before.

'Now look at everyone and see how everyone supports you, and how brave we think you are,' Leo said.

Everyone arranged their faces and I didn't know how to look right when I didn't think she was brave at all but just stupid to have to cry with strangers around.

When she had finished and Leo had unwrapped himself from Gloria, we carried on round the circle.

The boy with the slapped face (Donald) said,

'I felt I belonged when I had my first poem published in the school magazine. I wanted people to think of me as a writer. They did. They began calling me Rag Mags after that.'

I began laughing, then stopped myself because no-one else was laughing and I realised Donald seriously thought Rag Mags was a good name for a writer. Leo said did Donald want us all to celebrate his achievement and Donald said yes he did so we all had to clap and cheer him and he nodded and blushed as if he deserved it. But I know people who have written in school magazines who aren't clever at all.

The older woman who always looks as if she is asleep (Daphne) said,

'I loved early mornings, hearing our sheepdog barking in the mornings , and my husband below lighting the fire. When I moved to the farm I never wanted to leave.'

She had a tinselly voice and long silvery fingers and a long sharp nose that famous people have, and there was nothing messy about her, so Leo passed on quickly to the next person, who was Isobel.

Isobel said her moment of belonging was when she lost her virginity. I didn't dare look at her to see what had happened to her T-shirt. I didn't dare look at Leo in case he realised I was still a virgin. I'm sure he would think I had a problem, and start trying to help. They spent a long time on Isobel, acting out being a foetus and being born and flying. When I've been with Geoffrey in the bedroom, it has never felt like being a foetus or being born or anything like that at all. I suppose that's because there's always a relation about to break in with trays of tea, just as we begin the flying part.

When it came to my turn, I was still thinking about virginity and about having to get married to be allowed alone in a bedroom, so I wasn't ready with my answer.

'I thought about going to the wrong school assembly and not under-standing what was going on,' I said. But it sounded very tame, beside what the others were saying; not like an important moment at all. I could see Leo was a bit put out.

'Do you want to share more with us about that?'

'I went to Christian prayers by mistake, and they were singing about Jesus. I'd never heard of Jesus, except vaguely.'

Isobel laughed. I don't know why she was allowed to laugh at me, but not at Donald or anyone else. I thought they had been much funnier.

'You felt you didn't belong in Christian prayers?'

'No. I didn't know any of the songs.'

'They weren't your songs?'

'No. We had other ones.'

'We?'

'In my family.'

'I'm sure we'd love to hear one of the songs. Have a look at us all. You see, it's quite safe to sing one of your songs here.'

I looked round the circle and it didn't seem safe at all. Isobel was look-ing at me as if I had crawled out of an apple, Donald was staring with his bottom jaw hanging open, Gloria was looking fiercely at the wall bars, and Leo was spreading his shorts in my direction as if he wanted me to cry inside them. Only Daphne looked welcoming, with her long fingers folded on her lap and her silvery smile right into her eyes.

'I don't think I want to,' I said.

'Then just feel as if you belong here in the group, and sing your song if you change your mind.'

We sat for a full half minute, everybody silent, shuffling about a bit, Leo with his eyes closed as if he had forgotten about me. The half minute went on and on. Then Leo opened his eyes.

'Now do you feel as if you belong?'

'Yes,' I said. He had punished me for not knowing the rules and then for breaking them.

When the session ended, we all hugged again. This time no-one cried at all because we were all too hungry.

Lunch was in the big dining room. Leo had put 'shakra' candles on each table, with a label explaining each one. Our candle was orange and was

the 'genitals' shakra. The card said:
  When this shakra is open it leads to deep personal sharing.
  When it is closed feelings and sexuality are disconnected.
  The shakra relates to the sense of taste.
  Sanskrit word: Svadisthana

Daphne and Gloria's table said 'Heart'. I thought maybe I preferred the Heart table, but it was too late to change.

I was sitting with Donald and Isobel. It was a little awkward at first, because we knew each other's belonging stories but nothing else at all about each other.

'Oh I hope it's not that macrobiotic stuff,' Isobel said. 'It just doesn't agree with me.'

She began chewing her hair and looking dreamily towards the kitchen.

'I should have told them I have a really delicate stomach,' she went on. Donald looked as if he too might have a delicate stomach. Next to them, I felt like a horse with a metal stomach.

'What was your story then?' Donald asked suddenly.

'It's not what you think,' Isobel answered quickly, quite sure. 'I belong to the sisterhood of women,'

'Did you go to a convent school?' I asked.

She looked at me as if I was a hermaphrodite, then guffawed.

'You must be joking! Why, did you?'

'Oh no,'

'Well you went somewhere odd,' she said, picking up the end of her hair again.

The meal was an enormous rude white sausage with onions. I had never seen anything so nearly pig. It almost walked. Isobel and Donald began attacking it with a fork, starting at one end so it hissed. I began with the onions.

'What's up. Never eaten Swiss sausages before?' Donald said, his mouth full.

'Does it offend you?' Isobel asked, waving a pink piece in the air. They both began snorting with laughter.

So I ate the sausage slowly, piece by piece like a punishment, to show them I was not odd and hadn't been to a convent school.

On the way to the meditation, Gloria came to talk to me.

'Don't feel bad about this morning,' she said.

'I don't.'

'Well, I don't think it worked out quite right for you.'

We walked on down the long corridor to the gym and our feet clip clipped one after the other.

'Maybe it didn't.'

'I'm an atheist too,' she said. 'I've got reason to be. I'm sure you have too.'

I stopped just outside the door of the meditation room.

'I'm not an atheist,' I said.

She looked at me very slowly, starting from my nose outwards as if she was smelling a cheese.

'Oh, I'm sorry,' she said, as if one of us had made a grave mistake.

I don't know what she meant.

In the meditation Leo told us to empty our minds and focus on the candle. But my mind didn't empy. It filled with pictures.

outside grandma's flat Uncle Michael hunched in his coat with the rain dripping off his nose and inside his coat a lady with a silvery voice and small white hands both of them with the rain running out of their hair and off their noses

'Won't you come in to tea?'

'No Laura not today, and don't tell grandma you saw us.'

Grandma's tea party: honey cake, cheese cake, cream crackers, herring, fried fishballs, boiled fishballs, plaited rolls with black seeds on top, cream cheese, smoked salmon rolled up,smoked salmon on the cream cheese on the rolls

warm apple pie.

outside Uncle Michael shivering with the lady inside his coat.

I wrapped a piece of honey cake in a serviette. Then I wrapped another piece of honey cake for the lady in his coat, and slipped out the door down the steps into the street. The rain was driving so hard I could hardly stand. It was only afternoon tea-time but the street was frightening policeman black

I couldn't see Uncle Michael I ran up and down the street

honey cake was his favourite

but he wasn't there his coat his nose his lady with the wet hair none of it

I slipped back to the tea party and Mother squeezed my plaits and gave me a strange look and said,

'Where have you been?'

the serviette had soaked into the cake and it wasn't nice to eat

I coughed for a week afterwards

Leo struck a little brass gong for the end of the half hour, and it scattered the picture like a broken reflection.

We had to tell a partner whatever images had come to us during our meditation. My partner was Leo.

'Stupahs in Nepal, washing feet in the Ganges, monks walking barefoot in the snow,' he said to me. 'That's what I see. What it must be to control your body so much that you can do that.'

I didn't like the way he looked at me, when he said that. I didn't know what stupahs were but decided not to ask.

'I remember my uncle shut out of the party,' I said.

'Why was it?'

'Grandma didn't approve of his girlfriend. He wasn't allowed in to the party with his girlfriend.'

'Did you approve?'

'I hated him to be outside in the street with the rain coming down not allowed in. I thought about him all through the tea. It must have been terrible.'

'You wanted to belong?'

'I wanted him to belong.'

'Why him, why not you?'

'Why him? Because he was the one who was shut out.'

'A terrible fear for you.'

Why did he keep talking about me when the story was about Uncle Michael? Leo never listened, he just made up his own stories about people.

'OK yes,' I said, because each time I said no he sat nearer to me and if I said no one more time he'd have been sitting in my lap.

When I said yes an icy spike of rain sliced right through me and made me shiver like it had on that street when the afternoon was like night and the honey cake crumbled in my hand.

CHAPTER THREE

Monday Night

In my room, on my own, I practised dancing in front of the mirror. It's one thing I do, wrapped in sheets or net curtains.

There's the dance of the Sister, the Hannah dance. Dance Hannah with the head for carrying books in posture classes and shoulders spikey as set squares. Hannah's arms will be held out to comb hair or clip hand-bags shut and her steps will always be small and useful and go round in circles.

Grandma. She dances full of spikes and her arms are kick, push and enfold. She dances with a train behind her, the length of the Volga, sweeping us up in it and tripping us over. There are so many steps, we'll never learn them, and some of the rules are secret anyway. She would never tell us the rules, but just see if we can learn by copying.

And my duo with Geoffrey. It is a circle inside a circle: I am always inside the ring of his arms, bent smaller by him. When we dance our duo I am always cradled, like a child.

It is the same with my mother's dance. It is very like Geoffrey's, but that in this duo she opens the ring to let me through, her arms are waving me away and drawing me back at the same time, they sweep in and out like the horse's mane.

Grandma thinks I will break out like the horse's mane and be uncon-ventional and spoil my marriage chances.

Hannah thinks she is the bird and I am the tail, flying with her back to the nest and then back to the nest and then back to the nest again. She will choose the worms for me.

For Geoffrey I am a wife-in-waiting. Now I am an unborn wife with my parts not yet fully formed, my grown-upness not yet finished. But I will finish, soon. Here in Switzerland I will finish off nicely.

Mother keeps stopping her own dance, to teach me the steps. She wants me to copy hers, then to send me away to practice. When I return from here, I will be perfect, ready to do the dance in public, with all the family standing in lines applauding.

When I look round, the door has swung open and Donald is standing in the corridor watching me with his jaw hanging open.

'What are you doing?'

'Practising Tai Chi.'

'You look like a ghost.'

'It's the sheet,' I said, and shut the door quickly.

At midnight, when I was wearing bedsocks and writing my diary at the bedside lamp, there was a knock at the door. It was Leo.

'Your mother phoned. She'll call back in ten minutes. You can take the call in the Yin: Yang room.'

It was irritating. I didn't want Leo to know I had the kind of mother who called me on holiday: and I didn't want him to see me decomposed at my worst time of day. But I slung on my jeans and T-shirt and ran down to the Yang room anyhow.

'It's your mother, darling,' said my mother. Her voice was funny: I knew something was wrong.

'Yes, yes. I'm fine, mum. Are you OK?'

'We're all fine, we're missing you. But we have some sad news. Your grandma is in hospital, darling. She had a heart attack earlier today. She's doing as well as she can. We just wanted you to know. Perhaps you could write her a note.'

'Yes, yes.' But my voice had gone tiny and dry like a gull's beak.

I ran back to my room. I didn't want to see anyone. I didn't want to tell them or not to tell them, or to have their pity or not to have it. I just wanted to be alone in my room.

When I got there, I realised I was wearing my T-shirt inside out.

Grandma had been so angry that I was going away. Now this had happened.

'Now why you have to go like this when there was no need is a madness. What do you think, leaving a fianc behind? You think fiances are so easy to find? You think he will be a blind man for you when you are away?'

'What do you mean, grandma? I'm only away a week.'

'You know what is a week? A week and God made everything what you see and time to put up the feet. And to destroy? Not even so much time you need to destroy. To destroy you can do in one second. And you say a week is nothing.'

'It's not a disaster grandma. You always think about disasters. It's nothing, just a week in Switzerland. You worry too much and it's bad for you.'

'There is worry and worry. The first is worry for nothing. The second is worry for something. You know what I call this? I call this sensible.'

'You don't understand Geoffrey, how much he loves me.'

'No, no, I wish it so, I wish I didn't understand you, you know how much nicer this is? Laura, this is a terrrible responsibility to know too much, and please God you stay stupid. What kind of prayers are these that you have on the course?'

'Oh, they're meditations. They teach you meditation.'

'What kind of a prayer is that? You call that a prayer?'

'No, it's not like that. I'll be learning new things I've never done before. That's why I want to go.'

'I know these new things. You think because it's new it's good. Sometimes it's not so good and it's better not to know them.'

'I know you think that,' I said.

'They give you a bathroom?'

'I'm sure they do, of course they do. It's Switzerland.'

'You share with another girl?'

'No. They're single rooms.'

'Rooms too cramped even for one. If I were you I would ask for a bigger room. It's a long way for you to go, to be in a room so small.'

'A single room doesn't mean it's small. It just means it's for one person.'

'Now don't you be a Cherry, always content with the pieces the dustman leaves behind. You know this, take the best and hold on to it like your leg!' and she held up her fist, to show me how to hold on your leg.

'I do hold on to it, but I haven't found it yet,' I said.

'Well you look so hard you don't see,' she said. 'You are still too much of a child.'

'I'm not nearly as much of a child as you think.' I said.

'No, no, it is the opposite. You are more of a child than you think. You have a lot still to learn.'

'You always say that and you never say what it is I have to learn.'

'Well when I was your age I thought the same: and now I wish I knew now as little as I did then. '

She would like to sweep my life into the tail of hers, like a long long dress.

Maybe I had been a bad grand-daughter, and maybe I had said bad angry things about her behind my teeth, and made faces at her when she left the room. But I didn't mean her to leave.

All I could write was this.

Dear Grandma,

I was so sad to know that you are ill and in hospital. You were so well just a few days ago. I do hope they are looking after you very well in hospital, and that you are comfortable there. I wish I was there so I could come and see you.

I have just arrived in Pacino and my course is going well. We have talked a lot about when we were younger and what we did at school. I did the medita-tion and I know some more about it now. It isn't like prayer at all, do you remem-ber, like you said? There are no words.

I liked you living with us last year. I am so sorry I left in a hurry without telling you how nice it was that you were in our house so we could see you every day. You helped me a lot, to study and to get engaged and there are lots of things I would never have done without you. I should have said thank you but I never had time.

We have a prayer on the course (a meditation) and I shall think about you each time, wishing that you will get well.

Thinking of you every minute with love,
  Laura

She came as if I had called her. It wasn't a surprise because I have often seen her there, in all sorts of strange forms and voices. But I had never seen her like this, coming quietly into the room, her cardigan with pearl buttons pulling tight across her chest and her face lantern light with the brown patches and the mole still there on the edge of her chin like a ladybird opening its wings.

'Oh, I'm so glad you're well,' I cried.

'I'm fine, quite well. But it's been such a long journey, and I'm so tired.'

'Did you come on the train?'

'By train, most of the way. By train, on the foot, sometimes I don't even know how I come, I think once even there was a man lifted me up carried me straight on in the carriage you could smell what the horses do in the wheels.'

'The man?'

'I didn't even say to him thank you when he did such a good thing. He knew the route in the dark, and he didn't ask for nothing, not for noth-ing and this was a good thing because nothing was what it was I had. This is a good man like bread in the pantry.'

'I'm glad he was kind to you.'

'Papa, Mama. I worry so much about them. Is there any news, do you know?'

None. I had never heard about Papa and Mama. Not much. Only that Papa kept books in the front room and it became a library for the whole village.

'I know his name was Julius, Yulek.'

'Luba and Marek, Elias and Lolinka, is there any news of them, do you know?'

I looked at her, tried to make some words out of nothing that I had to say, started, stopped, while she waited and grew tired and her face grew papery and empty.

'No news then. My father will be waiting for news too. The letters I send, the parcels I send, but do they ever arrive? I don't know if they ever arrive. In the house he will be sitting at table his head in a book and mother talking talking with the chicken's neck in the soup and fish in the flour she talking he waiting for news. They will be waiting. I must go and tell them I am safe.'

'They will be so glad you are safe. I'm sure they will be so glad.'

'Then what must I do? I must tell them I am safe but Luba is not, Luba is gone, Luba is captured, Luba I meant to look after, Luba is gone.'

Luba I knew

sister Luba

great-aunt Luba whose name I am

'Luba with the long brown plait. How she was proud of her long brown plait. To be wise and good and clever you must work and live hard, but to have a long brown plait you do nothing but grow your head. Oh Luba Luba what good is it now, to be loved for your silky face and hair clips? Even a broom can be beautiful.'

We sat side by side, both of us with our hands in our lap. Any word I said might break the stories. So I waited, breathing quietly so it would not distract her.

'I lost them, Marek and Luba. You know how I lost them, how stupid it was, an accident when you fight like this between yourselves as if this is important some little thing when men are tearing at our world and we have nothing to trust but each other. You know how I lost them like a boat makes small hole and then too late bigger it grows and all the drops fall through every piece of the water falls through all is gone even the boat too. So it was with Marek we made our fight me against him he try-ing to give me the kiss in the dark and he walks away and out into the hill alone his bag behind in the ditch and the light coming up you can see the sky become red. Suddenly I see a shadow falling one side the other side and so quick so quick I see what it is two soldiers in Russian uni-forms. One shouts to the other, then they hit the snow with their rifles, shouts it hurts the heart to hear and I see through my eyes though closed how Marek freezes there and terror in his face lifted up under the sol-dier's arms, marched away under their arms his back lifted up into his neck his chin in his chest and I hold my breath squeezed in my heart and die without a sound to watch it through my closed eyes and even closed I hear them shout and hear the rifles on the snow and hear the screams of Luba as she wakes.'

'I'm so sorry.'

'If she hadn't loved Marek she would be here too.'

I waited in the strange oily light for her to tell me, but she looked at them, not me. I was as pale to her as she was to me.

'But I won't say a word about him, not now. It's too late now, to say a word against him. I should have warned Luba earlier, you could tell he was bad from his nails. Long nails are a bad sign in a man. Take care not to love someone like Luba loved Marek. He was a philanderer. He courted both me and Luba at the same time. But I was the wise one, and did not love him. We were two sisters and God meant us both to be saved.'

'No grandma, God did not.'

'Then I can't understand what He is doing. He has made a big mistake. There are many mistakes now, and they can't be undone.'

'What about the others?'

I didn't know the others, and never before had grandma Rosa wanted to tell me.

'Lola, such a girl born to hold the world in her heart. You know that, she could read in four languages, and no-one knows how she did it. It wasn't her father; he was a simple man. She came often to our library, and recited the books to me, standing on a chair. I loved it, to hear the languages I didn't know. I thought, one day I will learn that English and know that Shakespeare's language.'

Did she learn that Shakespeare's language? Now in our meeting like this I had walked through the veil of language and now I shared hers, instead of her sharing mine, and I felt shamed. I had forgotten how she might be in her own language, that she was not always feeling her way through the broken reshuffled pieces of a language that wasn't hers, that her thoughts had once grown up fully dressed in their mother tongue.

'Elias, poor boy, such a delicate boy. I wonder how he will manage it all. It affected him you know, it changed him, all that study. It went to his head. And now I think he is good for nothing, not good for the world at all, and how he will find his way without his glasses I don't know.'

'Which one was Elias, grandma? Was he one of the boys in the photo?'

'The one with blue rings under his eyes at fifteen.'

'The boy with the blue rings under his eyes, he is just like my father. I always thought he was my father. Jacob as a boy, I always thought he was like that, with the long white neck like a swan.'

'Wherever Jacob is I bless him,' she said. Then she turned to me, and clasped my hands so I gasped with shock at the coldness and her yellow nails cut half moons into my skin. 'Will you tell me if you hear, even a word? They say all kinds of things, I don't know what, but you must tell me, don't protect me, what you know you must tell me, better always to know, with this you can live better than not knowing.' She held my hands until I promised, yes, I would tell her whatever I heard, but in truth I didn't know what she meant.

Then she sank back and her face smoothed out again and the mole fell into place back in its corner.

'There's something about you I trust. Now tell me, will you, what kind of country is it here? What kind of place is it?'

'I don't know it too well yet myself, grandma. It's just a short stay, just a week. '

'Oh yes. I'm passing through too, I shan't stay for long. I'll have to be on my way too'

'Where to, where are you on your way to?'

She sat with her white hands on her lap, so fine I could see the veins like blue leaves under her skin.

'Well I shall see, but perhaps I'll find them all again, you know, if I go.'

She sat there, and her gums were chundering together up and down with the jaw folding in a little where the teeth had fallen back, and they grated together slowly up and down up and down.

'If I go, perhaps I'll find them all again.'

I walked out into the corridor, to follow her, but it was too dark to know where she had gone. There were candles puttering on the window sills and I felt strangely glad of them, like glow worms. Who put them there at night? Maybe it was my eyes, that had passed across the border and I was seeing my own dreams? I could put out my hand and touch her. I could see the dent on the bed where she had sat.

If I squinted in the darkness, the corridor was less real than she had been.

'Laura Cherry, what are you doing up at this time?'

It shocked me, the voice, to the core, not because it was a ghost but because it wasn't a ghost.

'My God, you frightened me!'

'This is a fine late time to be at large in the corridor.'

'You are.'

'Best we both forget that and get to our beds.'

'I was meditating, the way you taught us. I saw things in the candles, I thought I did.'

'But it was just me, a tall dark stranger.'

'No, it wasn't just you. I didn't notice you at all. That's why you shocked me.'

'Does your mother know about you?'

'What do you mean?'

'Does she know you go prowling along corridors at night bumping into tall dark strangers?'

'Usually I don't,' I said.

'Oh, I can see that!' he said. 'Your mum's daughter ought to watch herself,'

and I watched Leo's back, with his shorts frayed around the knees and his long hairy calves, creep down the corridor like a snake loop by loop, creeping into the shadows of the walls as if he wasn't there at all.

I will never forgive Leo. A person who runs a Life Enhancement course should never use a mother's phonecall to tease them. I felt so angry I had tears in my eyes.

Dear Geoffrey

Something has happened. I have seen grandma. Will you believe me, or will you say that just isn't sensible? I know it isn't sensible, but lots of things that happen aren't sensible.

Dear Sean

In your religion, do you believe in ghosts? I think you do, and I know it's somewhere in the borderlands between life and death. Grandma was here, and she is crossing the border. In her eyes you can see she is neither there nor here.

Light candles when evening falls, she said, it is your duty to mark the end of the day.

Blessed are You Who creates the illuminations of the fire

Who separates light from darkness

CHAPTER FOUR

Tuesday

We spent the morning in one corner of the gym, sitting on the criss-cross floorboards with high windows and wallbars around us, on Leo's blue and red Indian restaurant cushions. The room was too big to make a grand entrance, but Isobel tried to, her legs sweeping in first with the cut-off shorts swinging in afterwards, and then parts of her bottom after that. Leo looked at her through his eyelashes, Donald checked the floor for splinters. Daphne was sitting already with her eyes closed and her silvery blue hands spread out on her black velvet knees.

'Today share your first thoughts with a neighbour, just let them out and when it's your turn to listen, just listen without talking, just let your partner say what they need to, no judging, no responding with words, use other ways to respond and show you are interested.'

I saw his eyelashes responding without words. You could tell he was a specialist.

My partner was Daphne.

'I'm thinking of my farm today,' she said 'and I miss it. I miss it not because of today but because of where I might be in a year's time. Now that sounds strange. My son marries, and brings his wife to his home, and takes over the farm. Now where do I fit in?.'

She stopped, and her hands turned into lines of shiny knobs on the dress.

'What would they want with an old grandma there, a young couple starting out in life? They'd be quite impatient with it, if they were at all wise. Life moves on, it has to.'

I opened my mouth to tell her that grandma had lived with us and now I was glad she had, but she touched my hand to stop me.

'It's only fair. The young need their own space.'

She described how her son had grown up and learnt to feed the calves with a bottle and check the sheepdog's fur for ticks. The gloves steamed on the woodburning stove, and the Dartmoor ponies flicked their fringes out of their eyes. You could smell their droppings like rich hot pats along the hedge.

When it was my turn, I told her how grandma had lived with us.

'And I feel bad because she annoyed me, and I never really noticed her properly.'

Daphne looked at me kindly, as if I had said something quite wonderful.

'She made me polite, she made me want to be good so she would praise me. She praised Lucia because her hair curled and she sang in Hebrew, and I hated Lucia for being better than me, and grandma for liking her better, and myself for being dark and slow and dumpy.'

I began to talk more and more, about secretly hating her, to see what Daphne would do. I could have said anything, that I had murdered grandma, and Daphne would have just nodded and said, 'how wonderful'.

'She pottered around outside the door when I was with my boyfriend, and we could never be alone because of her.'

Daphne touched my hand and said,

'I think you loved her very much, whatever you might say.'

The theme of the day was 'rules and rebellions'. Leo asked about the rules we lived by, voluntarily or not. Then he asked us where the rules had come from, and what it would be like to break them. And it was easy, because grandma always made me think about rules.

Grandma and the broken rules

Uncle Michael was my favourite. He didn't seem old, like most uncles. He still had toys that he had when he was young, a car with doors that opened and shut, a man in swimming trunks on a wire that swam up and down when you pulled a handle, and a tent shaped like an Arctic roll that you could put up in the garden.

But two things made Uncle Michael Perfect.

The first thing was, he did impersonations. He could do Grandma impersonations.

'Tak tak tak!' he would do, nodding his head so his hair flopped over his eyes.

'Ach ach!' he would do, shrugging his shoulders so his neck disappeared.

The second thing was, he broke rules. If you liked rules Passover was the best time of year, because there was a rule for everything. There was a rule for which plates you used, which clothes you wore, how you sat, what shoes you wore, how to clean your house, whether to use a mop or a broom. Every year I learnt a new thing you weren't allowed to do. You weren't to eat Mars bars, Bounty bars, Kit Kat, candy floss, hot dogs, cherry bitters, apple pie, cream crackers, toast, bread and peanut butter, crisps. Not to eat anything except white things with a sticker. White cakes, white biscuits, white *matzos*, white herring, white fishballs.

At Passover there were so many rules that sometimes we just went and stayed with grandma and let her keep them all for us. And that was fun, because until Mary, Uncle Michael lived there too.

Sometimes after school he would say to Grandma,

'Laura's coming with me to pick up the almond pyramids,' and we would sneak off together and stop at the Primrose Tea Shop and look at the cakes in the window: chocolate dominoes, white ones with layers of flake and layers of cream, meringues like round bottoms with white centres, chocolate ducks with flake wings.

'Which one do you want?' he said.

'No! It's not allowed!'

'But if it was, which would you like?'

'The duck.'

and he would go in and wait in front of the glass counter and point at the glass duck and hand over some money and they would ring it up and put it in a paper bag and he would slip out and put the paper bag in my hand and say,

'Secret. Don't tell Grandma Rosa. Just between you and me.'

'Oh, Uncle Michael!'

and it was Perfect, to have a secret with a grown-up, to do something wicked, and most of all, to eat the chocolate duck.

'Don't you ever want to get married?' I asked him one day as we stood on bricks in the back garden.

'I don't want to leave mum alone,' he said to me. It seemed to be a problem we would all have, at some time or other.

'If you married me, you could stay at home and she wouldn't be lonely.' He leaned forward to peck me on the cheek and fell off the bricks.

'I wish it was that easy,' he said.

He brought Mary to the first seder. She had white hands like a nun's, see-through blue eyes and a floaty accent I had never heard before. When we met, she said,

'Oh so this is Laura Cherry that I've heard so much about,' in such a nice way, I felt like a grown-up.

I noticed my mother sat very stiffly when she spoke to Mary, as if her elbows were stuck to her dress. Grandma wore an apron, which she never usually wore, as if to show Mary how hard Jewish grandmothers had to work. Everything she laid down on the table she would comment on, as if Mary had never eaten before.

'These are fishballs. I expect you've never had those before,' she said

'These are called matzo the bread of affliction. It's what we eat this time of year' , and so on.

Every time, Mary would smile and show neat white teeth, and say,

'Oh yes,' 'I know' 'How interesting', or something else marvellously polite.

We started when it was dark outside and I could see my pigtails reflected in the window. I stood on the chair and said the four questions in English and cousin Lucia stood on the chair and sang them in Hebrew. Lucia's hair was blonde and hung loose, but mine was black and in bunches so tight it made my head go white.

ma nish tana haleila hazeh
mikol haleilot

why on this night is the food thin and white, and why do the children stay up late and eat marzipan and play in public?

why on this night do all the family sit like Russian dolls round the table, all miniatures of each other, but the little ones with their hair controlled and pink dresses?

because for forty years we were in the desert

nothing but flour and water and no yeast

the sand was hot, baking and we had no hats and the veils were too thin

we wept salt tears so much we made pools with our tears

our hands were broken and blistered from building the pyramids for centuries and our backs ached

the women carried babies and bundles of clothes and rolled the dough in water

They were Aunt Sonia and Uncle Ezra, cousin Lucia who was clever and sister Hannah who was born to be married, father called Jacob, Uncle Michael with the secret chocolate duck and mother who was always polite

we were slaves and we wept salt tears into our boiled eggs

we built houses with bricks made of apples and almonds and they tasted the best the tears tasted no good at all

After the four questions are the four children, everything in fours like Scottish dancing

the wise child, the wicked child, the simple child, the one who does not know how to ask

all the children are boys

the wicked one isn't wicked at all, doesn't make bad smells or hide beetroot in his blazer pockets

none of the children in our family are boys

maybe if Michael tries he could have a boy but he certainly won't if he stays at home with grandma

then there were the plagues, dreadful ones, blood and boils, locusts, lice with hard backs, fleas that jump all over you, frogs and spiders, blunderbuses and bats with black rustling wings, cows howling like wolves, all these things with drops of wine drop drop drop one for each plague and we chanted them until the dogs foamed at the mouth and all the warts burst Mary too but she didn't seem to mind

later we opened the door and Elijah slipped by me with invisible sandals and bent over the table and dipped his chin in the wine glass so the
wine sparkled on his beard and he licked it with his tongue, his long
tongue in his long beard, and the wind in his deep shoulders made me
shudder as his white toga blew out again through the open door into the
blind black night

and by then I was tired and wanted to climb under the table for the
songs about goats and watch people's shoes and look at the bits of food
and what people did with their knees

After that, Mary left and I went to bed. I heard everyone shouting at
each other, and grandma shouting the name 'Mary! Mary!' as if she
couldn't believe anyone could have such a name, and Michael shouting
and banging the door and grandma running after him and scuffling noises in the front garden, and mum shouting,

'Be quiet. Laura's upstairs.'

I lay in bed, wide awake, trembling, with the light on. I was afraid to
turn off the light. Mother crept into my room.

'It's alright darling. Everything's alright. You don't have to cry.'

'What's happened to Uncle Michael?'

'He's getting married Laura darling.'

'To that nice Mary?'

'Yes.'

'Then why isn't everyone happy?'

'Grandma isn't very happy. But Michael's happy and that's what mat-
ters. Mary's a lovely girl.'

'If she's lovely why doesn't grandma like her?'

'Her family go to church instead of to synagogue. Grandma's worried
about Michael's children, whether they would go to church or synagogue.'

'But Michael hasn't got any children,'

'Not yet, but when he does have children maybe they will be confused.'

I didn't know what 'confused' meant, and couldn't imagine children
who didn't exist feeling it anyway. It all seemed so strange, when Mary
was twinkly, like a fairy godmother, and had nice teeth and white hands.
Maybe Mary had not been a slave in Egypt and that was the problem.

When Hannah crept into bed, I was still wide awake.

'What's happened to grandma?' I said.

'I would never do awful things like that to grandma,' Hannah said,
climbing into bed.

'Like what?' I asked. But I was asleep before I heard the answer.

In the morning, Michael wasn't there. We had breakfast together in silence. Grandma's lips were pinched together, as if she had lost all her teeth in the night. She was still wearing yesterday's apron, as if she hadn't slept or changed her clothes at all. The table was covered with matzo crumbs. It was like having breakfast with ghosts.

'Where's Michael?' I said to Hannah. But she hissed at me, and pinched me so hard under the table I stopped talking and didn't dare to speak again until breakfast was over.

Only when I went out into the garden, and saw our bricks there, did I start to cry.

*   *   *

This time we had to share our rules and rebellions with one partner. I ended up with Donald.

'Do you want to share your story today?' he said. I realised he was grinning at me, reminding me about yesterday.

'Yes, I don't mind,' I said, although I did. 'It was really my uncle's rebellion I was thinking about, when he married out—a gentile.'

'What, are you Moslem or something?'

'No, no - my parents are Jewish.'

'What, both of them?'

I thought these were very stupid questions for a poet.

'Yes. Both of them.'

He was silent, contemplating this.

'That's very interesting,' he said, 'I'd like to write about that. Do you speak Hebrew?'

'No. I was born in Southgate. Why should I speak Hebrew?'

'I thought you people did.'

I noticed all the other partners seemed terribly pleased and impressed with each other. They were all nodding and smiling and some of them were touching.

'What about your story?' I asked him.

'I ran away from home when I was sixteen to be a poet. That was my rebellion.'

'Where did you go?'

'I went to stay in a shed.'

'A shed?'

'Bernie had one at the end of his garden. I took my sleeping bag and some matches and sandwich spread sandwiches and sneaked off at night after bed. Other people did it, Bernard Shaw he had a shed at the back of his garden, and that other poet on Walden Pond. But it was no good, I hated it. Something kept crawling over me, and I got cold and started wheezing and coughing and put my hand in a can of worms Bernie kept for fishing and everything was a nightmare. So I ran home and couldn't get into the house and sat on the doorstep eating sandwich spread sandwiches until dad found me the next morning.'

'How awful.'

'But I had made my point.'

'What was your point?'

He swallowed so the bump in his neck slid up and down.

'I don't have to do what they tell me all the time. I can do things for myself.'

Donald looked as if everything he did alone might make him wheeze. We sat for a while, for the last bit of his two minutes, until Donald said, 'Maybe those others had central heating in their sheds.'

At the end of the session, Leo wanted a summary from each of us about the rule that we had been following, and whether we were happy with it and wanted to change it.

RULES PEOPLE ADMITTED TO

Gloria's rule: I must prove that women can be strong on their own.

Isobel's rule: I must learn not to judge myself

Donald's rule: I must do things for myself

Leo's rule: I must always learn from others.

Daphne's rule: I must learn to let go of things

My rule: I must try and work out the rules, then follow them

I pretended to copy the rules into my diary, but really I wrote the secret rules, that people didn't say, that I could tell from what they were wearing and what they did during meditations.

SECRET RULES THAT PEOPLE DIDN'T ADMIT TO

Gloria's secret rule: I must make everyone feel sorry for me, because my husband left me

Isobel's secret rule: I must make everyone think I'm sexy

Donald's secret rule: I must be mysterious, so no-one discovers I'm frightened

Leo's secret rule: I must hide the fact that I fancy everybody

Daphne's secret rule: I must learn to want the things I don't really want, and not want the things I do really want

My secret rule: I must appear to be an ordinary person, even though I'm slightly mad

I couldn't face lunch again at the Genitals table. I wanted to be on my own, and to think. There were two letters for me, one from Geoffrey and one that had been delivered by hand. It was written in an exciting spidery writing and addressed to Miss Laura Cherry. I put them into my pocket to find a secret place to open them, where I would not be overlooked by Donald or Daphne or Leo.

All the streets smelt of chocolate. The shop windows were filled with chocolate beetles and cockroaches, and cloth witches with large noses on broomsticks. The streets looked scrubbed, as if they had been hoovered that morning. There must be other places where people take their dogs, unwrap their sweets, eat their hamburgers, drop their bus tickets, set down their shopping bags, push prams; but not the streets. They do none of those things in the streets of Pacino.

Not five minutes from the Centre, the road suddenly spilled out into open space and then I understood this was Pacino's heart. Pacino Square, Pacino Lake, Pacino everything. A passenger boat had pulled in from the lake and streams of children in summer dresses were climbing up wet steps into the square. A drinking fountain was sparking in the middle of the square, and a little boy was being pulled away from it sobbing, silver drips on the end of his chin. The smell of white sausage and onion drifted over from a kiosk painted in blue and yellow stripes; and in the next door kiosk, the smell of baking ice cream cones. A mother in a white dress was transferring chocolate ice cream from a little boy's face onto her dress, but only I could see it there. It was the first dirty thing I had seen in Pacino.

There was a long low wall along the lake. Rows of gulls flew in and perched there, then took off again with their noses in the air. Yes yes I would sit on the wall with a white sausage hot dog dripping with onions and read my letters.

The first was from Geoffrey.

Laura dearest

Just to tell you I am thinking about you and missing you. Of course I want you to have a wonderful time but not so wonderful that you don't come back to me! I know your grandma drives you nuts, but you didn't need to go away for so long. I know one week isn't really very long, but it is to me.

The job with the false teeth starts on Monday. I know people laugh, but making false teeth is a very skilled and important job. How would people feel with a tooth that made their mouth the wrong shape or made their jaw hurt when they chewed? How would it look with holes and sticking out parts? You see, it seems trivial, but that's because we take it all for granted and we can do that because there are people like me helping out. So you don't need to feel embarrassed when people ask, just explain to them how important the job is. Every day I thank ha'Shem to have such a good and important job. Anyway, the most important thing is that I'll be earning at last so we can save up to buy a little house somewhere. It will be so nice to have our own place, can you imagine? I'm sure you will love having your own kitchen, I know you say you don't care about that but I'm sure when you have your own kitchen you'll like it and start to enjoy cooking in it. I've been thinking, and thought you might like it if we bought a house near your mother so she could help you in the first years. New wives often say their mothers help a lot, because it can be lonely, suddenly being married and when the husband is at work all day. So I've started looking around Southgate and called up estate agents and your mum and dad are very pleased we may live nearby.

I hope you'll be alright in that place where you're going. Normally I would have put my foot down about you going off for a week like that, but I know you need a holiday and it's bad luck my new job starts just now. Otherwise we could have had a holiday together and you needn't have gone to that place at all.

lots of love
Geoffo

The second was from Sean, the boy on the train with the silver cross.

Dear Lura,
Maybe you remembr me, the boy on the train, you remember we shared a carriage. I was very pleased to share a carriage and then sorry but I did happen to see where you were staying in Pacino. I hope you don't mind that maybe we could meet again as I would be very pleased. I am with the Ramblers at the hostel at the moment, and on Thursday afternoon we are not climbing. That is, maybe if you're free we could meet on Thursday. Of course if you can't I will understand, but if you can , perhaps you could let me know if this is OK.

Yours sincerely,
Sean Kelly

Ramblers group
Pacinoberg Jugendherberge

I couldn't quite remember his face. All I remembered was my feeling about his face. And the sound of his zip. And his whistle, piping like a pixie into the cool streams of air.

I got back in time for the afternoon meditation. This time, Leo told us to meditate on the 'rebellion' story of the morning, and think about what it meant for us today. I closed my eyes, and I imagined Mary and Michael, Geoffrey and grandma in the apron that she wore only for Mary. I had them all clearly in place, Mary with her white hands and tinkly voice, grandma standing on her toes in the front garden to grab Michael by the collar. Then grandma opening the wine cabinet, to toast my engagement to Geoffrey, Hannah saying 'Of course, we all marry young.' I was lucky. I had met Geoffrey so I was inside the honeycomb. But what if I had not met Geoffrey. What if I had met Sean instead. Sean kept sliding over the picture of Geoffrey like a partial eclipse. First there was Geoffrey and I was lucky; then there was Sean and I was unlucky. Lucky unlucky like a slideshow.

I had always thought you just chose someone from the Jewish youth club or during the prayers for the dead when the young people stood outside on the synagogue steps; or Jewish weddings or Hebrew dancing classes or on holiday in Israel; or like me, at a bar-mitzvah. Then you fell in love. All my parents' friends were like that; they had all found suitable people, and their children had found suitable people, and they were all in suitable pairs. Not to be a suitable pair was unthinkable. Why would you be unsuitable, when it was so much more difficult? If you didn't meet your husband that way, how would you meet him? People I read about had met in telephone boxes or on station platforms or in cinema queues, but I couldn't possibly meet people that way. I knew that filmstars and the parents of schoolfriends did things that way: but that was one of the special badges of our people, and it was comfortable inside. People were pleased with everything you did right; you could do things right from very early on. At four you could sing the Passover questions in Hebrew and everyone would murmur and clap and you would feel like a filmstar. Then you were a star every time you did well in school tests, and all your parents' bridge partners would be pleased for you. There were more chances with becoming pretty and cutting your hair, and new boyfriends and getting engaged and weddings and then it all started again. Why would you not want to be a star all those times, with everyone cheering your every step?

So for Michael not to want those things, and not to have met Mary at the youth club, seemed to be a crazy kind of will, a crazy kind of courage. He must have tried very hard to meet her, standing outside pubs or on station platforms for hours, even days.

I couldn't work out where it had come from: he seemed to love us all, he laughed and shouted and ate honey cake as much as anyone when we had parties. So why did he decide the family was no fun and break all the rules and talk to people he hadn't been introduced to?

He could have met her like I met Sean; on a train. He could have. Or like I met Leo. I hate Leo but if I liked him then I'd have met him on a holiday not in Israel. There are lots of places to go which aren't Israel, and you could meet people in any of them. You could bump into them, like I bumped into Sean; then by accident keep meeting them, and before you know it you're in love. It's not because you hate the family or want to break the rules or don't like Friday nights; it's nothing like that at all. In fact, you might still love the family just as much. In fact, leaving them might never have occurred to you. You might not want to be a rebel at all. But suddenly you look, and because you were on holiday in Benidorm instead of Israel you find you're in love with the wrong person and your whole life changes.

I am lucky I fell in love with Geoffrey. If I had fallen in love with Sean by mistake I would have had to be a rebel, and I'm not. I don't have the strength.

CHAPTER 5

Tuesday night

I phoned the hospital but grandma was asleep. They said she was stable. Stable is not any better but not any worse. She hadn't left her bed all day, because she had tubes and drips in her. I rushed back to my room, just in case she visited again.

Donald was sitting outside my door.

'What are you doing?' I said,

'What are YOU doing?'

'What do you mean? I'm not doing anything. I'm trying to get into my room without falling over you.'

'Isn't that a shame? Wouldn't you rather read my poems?'

I didn't think about laughing at him until later, when I went over the conversation again in my mind.

'No I wouldn't. I'm busy.'

'Busy. You said you weren't doing anything.'

'I'm writing my diary.'

'Writing diaries is a substitute for living,' he recited.

'Who says?'

'I do. Come on little girl. You're much too frightened. You think men are only after sex.'

'No I don't. It never occurred to me.'

'Well it should occur to you,' he said.

I was getting confused and he was getting in my way, sitting against the door. So I kicked him. He jumped up, dusting down his jacket.

'OK, OK, I get the point. Just thought you may be into poetry,'

and shambled off down the corridor.

When I got into my room, I turned on all the lights and locked the door. Then I sat on the bed to think.

I thought of the night before I caught the train to Switzerland. We were fighting about the Pacino holiday.

'Why you want to go like this to some school in Switzerland? What for that they can't teach you here? What kind of engagement you have that you go on holiday like this maybe meet other boys?'

'It's not that kind of holiday grandma, you're just old-fashioned.

Geoffrey and I don't have to do every single thing together.'

'Every single thing not, I agree. But from time to time, yes. But you in Switzerland, he in London, it's not so good for meeting from time to time. Not so good at all.'

'We will be fine. Geoffrey is working all summer. I won't have a chance like this again after I start working for Uncle Ezra and after we're married.'

'I tell you, you won't have a chance again like this to send your engagement into a dustbin.

But I thought she was stupid and old-fashioned and didn't understand how much Geoffrey and I needed each other.

By now it was midnight, and I hoped she was sleeping well. But she came, very quietly, without opening the door, and sat on the bed beside me. She was elegantly dressed in a coat with a long swatch of tiger-coloured fur from her chin to her toes.

'You're so elegant!' I gasped.

'Not so, you shouldn't say so,' she laughed. But I could see she was pleased, and her paleness grew slightly cherry along her chiselled cheek. She must have walked, because her shoes were split at the toe and the heels were worn down. Her stockings wrinkled above them, round the ankles.

'What do you think, I'm going to a matchmaker.'

'Are you sure?'

'Oh yes, I've decided. I am too tired to find a husband for myself. I don't know where to meet husbands and I'm not at all interested in having to dress up and be specially pretty and hope that the men who notice are suitable.'

'But you're so beautiful. You will easily meet men.'

'No, no. You see, it will save a lot of time and embarrassment. You can have a hundred friends and people still ask 'und so?', but just one husband and they stop asking. So you see, it will be quieter and not so many questions.'

It was June 5th 1946, and Rosa had been in Britain six months.

*   *   *

On Thursday, after passing the sign every day for a week, Rosa copied the notice down from the Whitechapel newsagent.

Mrs Fischer. Discret matchmaker for edeler Menschen. Special new arrivals. Europeans. Only 10/6 to make happy couple..

This was one week's salary at Marjorie's Guesthouse. But one week of Marjorie's salary well-spent could free her from Marjorie forever. This was incentive enough.

But there were more incentives. She could see the guests narrow their eyes when she spoke to them, and see them whisper as she shuffled out of the room in a nylon apron with their bacon rinds.

'She's a German, isn't she?'

German, German, German she heard buzzing round the breakfast room.

'I am Polish, Polski,' she told them at last. 'Polski, you understand?'

Mrs. Fischer would understand. Her edeler Menschen would understand too. She would not even need to explain, because it would be the same for them.

I need my own people, do you see?

All them foreigners find their own people, they stick together. That young girl, you'll have trouble, she won't stay, you mark my words.

On Friday, Rosa Klein bartered her boots for 10/6. The boots had walked over with her from the Litvak winters. They had two layers, lamb's wool inside and soft leather outside. They knew more of Rosa's story than anyone or anything else in London. The pawnbroker put his hand into the warm soles and wore them like gloves. But 10/6 was all he could offer.

On Saturday, the Sabbath, Rosa took the day off from Marjorie's guesthouse, and lost 1/6 of her wage. Mrs. Fischer lived in an apartment block in Whitechapel with a clanging iron gate that could chop you to pieces as soon as look at you. Outside her door was a piece of card:

Mrs Fischer. Discret matchmaker for edeler Menschen.
10/6 per introduction.

Oh yes, Mrs. Fischer. 10/6 for one introduction? This is rough business. Surely, for 10/6 could Rosa not expect an album of nice pictures to choose from, a file of names and credentials - hair and eye colour, height, occupation, salary, family background? One introduction, for a young woman who had never gambled before even so much as a zloty? Maybe, you would say, that's life? One chance is all you need. But one choice, that's another thing, that's a cruel roulette.

Mrs. Fischer showed Rosa into the sitting room. The room smelled of mothballs and dust. There were brown photos in silver frames on the mantelpiece, and yes, these faces were very similar indeed. Their brown dresses and velvet collars, curls and silk ribbons, were quite the same.

They sat at a table in the middle of the room. It was a cheap table that folded away when visitors had gone, and certainly would not be the table for dinner guests or Friday nights. Not a table for honoured guests.

'10/6 please Miss Klein. I like to get the business out of the way first.'

Four half crowns and a sixpence came out hot from Rosa's pocket.

'You are very pretty,' she said, 'quite beautiful, and all the men who meet you will want to marry you. So we will have no problem. For you I have many men and you only must choose.'

'Well tell me,' Rosa said.

The furniture was covered in green embroidered flowers. Even the walls seemed to be covered in green embroidered flowers. Mrs Fischer spread her papers on the table, and flicked through them with a long fingernail. She must have grown it long for the purpose.

'How religious are you, Miss Klein? Is it important to you to have a husband from a religious family.'

'No, no. Anything will do.'

'We have a young man, Mr. Karminsky. He came to see me himself. Nice young man.' Her fingernail scraped on the table like a claw.

'I like the name. It's a good name.'

'He lives in the City.'

'Which city?'

'Near Paddington. He lives with his mother just now.'

'So, good. How old is he?'

'He is—' she ruffled through her papers, 'not quite forty.'

'Not quite?'

'Well, maybe forty, forty one, forty two.'

'I won't be able to cook like his mother. I'm sure he wants that. Is he— does he have independent means?

'In the catering business.'

'Catering. Maybe. Do you have a younger man?'

'A young man, a Hungarian, nice, Mr. Medgyes.'

'Medgyes, yes. How you say it?'

'His name is a cherry in English.'

'He will maybe change to a cherry.'

'I don't know my dear. You would have to ask him about that.'

'I would feel better with such a name that they understand. What else do you know about him?'

Mrs. Fischer underlined her notes with her fingernail.

'He was born on August 17th 1920.'

'It is the year I was born. We are the same year together.'

'A young man from Budapest. Arrived——'

'When?'

'After the war. Six months ago.'

'Family?'

'Alone.'

Of course.

'How does he live?'

'A good business, a gentleman's tailor. He makes for gentlemen.'

'Yes, this is a good business. He will be good with his hands.'

'You will choose. *Etzbah elohim,* the finger of God will help you choose wisely.'

Mr. Karminsky who lives with his mother , who is forty and who is in catering: Mr. Medgyes who is young and Hungarian and makes suits for gentlemen.

'The young man.'

'Mr. Medgyes. He will leave you a message, my dear.'

Rosa needed to leave quickly, before the room choked her.

'If the business is done I must go now.'

'But where will he leave you a message?'

'I live in the guesthouse. Marjorie Danks, China Street, EC2.'

As she pulled the door closed behind her, she heard Mrs Fischer say, 'Oh, and he's almost blind.'

Rosa and Gabor met for Sunday lunch at Blooms. He was not blind. He could see perfectly well through his pebble glasses, and she was an elm-like Russian princess in a coat of wild tigery fur, with wide-chiselled cheeks and black rainwater eyes. He was a delicate, small-shouldered man in the suit he had made himself, cut right in under his arms so he was tiny and dapper today like a tap-dancer. Already he was proud to be sitting beside her, and already she was wondering where his head would finish when he stood up - would it be at her chin, or at her shoulder, or at her elbow? Would it look, as they walked side by side, as if she might swallow him up?

His cheek was round still, like a boy's, and there was something kind about the way his lips lay one above the other, just from time to time unsealing a speck of white front tooth. He enjoyed the salt beef and enjoyed Rosa's coat, and enjoyed the men in the restaurant watching them over their wives' shoulders. His eyes behind their lenses spun round and round the room like little bright beads.

'Well, I tell you straight away, I am not rich yet but I will be.'

What I mean is, 10/6 is my one shot. You see, if it's not you, please God could I find a woman for myself when I spend from 8.0 to 8.0 each day making suits for men who eat too much, and living in the spare room 101 Whitechapel Road with a bed so small your dog would get cramp.

'My family,' he said, and swept his hands across the table, wiping it out,'it will be you.'

'For me, too,'

'Budapest,' he said.

'Vigry.'

He nodded. Then he said,

'Where?'

'Fifty kilometres from Vilna, across the border.'

'A field,' he said.

They understood each other exactly.

'Where I live they all think I am German. You know, this is not nice. In this country, we are all the same, you see. We are all foreigners.'

'A foreigner? A foreigner?' he rocked back and forwards in his chair. 'They are the foreigners.'

It was quite true. Rosa had never thought of that. It depended on who was looking at who.

'But we are in their country.'

The future husband stopped rocking. 'Und so?'

'And so they can't say your name. It is so foreign, they will not even be able to speak it, you see.'

What I mean is, if your name is mine we will be forever foreign.

'Is no problem. I don't say their name, they don't say mine. You see,' he touched his heart, 'I am a fair man.'

But Rosa pulled the name like a tooth, slowly, and planted in its place the one that fitted in, the one that did its job, the name that made life easier. Cherry, they were, like the fruit.

When they planned the wedding Rosa thought about Mr. Karminsky, who she had never met and who lived with his mother and who she might perhaps have loved. She had known a Karminsky who played the piano like a demon, with long white fingers and wildcat whiskers. She would like to have seen him now, grown tall and maybe grown a red beard with gold wisps.

Maybe now he had a team of cooks and waiters who helped him to cater, serving soup in white bowls with a towel over his arm.

But she would never know, as she walked up the aisle to meet her dainty shortsighted tap-dancer, if Karminsky was really the one. Not that Gabor Medgyes was not gentle and fleshy and funny, a solid good man in a good occupation; OK not a single living relative but doesn't such a man make good friends? Mr. Karminsky, where there is a mother, maybe also there are six sisters, two uncles, seven cousins, who knows? a whole family maybe he has, one with a flat in Baker Street, another who can make dresses and another who can drive a car.

But then maybe such a man would not cling to his new family as

Gabor might to Rosa. Mrs. Fischer, the one choice was one too few.

Marjorie was not surprised. She never expected Rosa to stay long, even though she had been so good to her when she had nothing, and only asked one day's salary in return for board and lodging and only made her work six days a week, and gave her two evenings off, and talked English to her so she would learn to speak properly. Oh yes, other people would not have been so kind what with an accent like that, after all these foreign accents sound all the same. No that was a good start she gave her, and the work not too dirty and not too much bending and carrying. But she understood it was not ungrateful of Rosa to get married, after all it was her own life she had to get on with.

At the garden gate she bent down and picked Rosa a handful of lilies-of-the-valley.

'Something white, for the wedding,' she said.

That was kind of her, she did not charge for the lilies even though they left a bare spot in the flower bed.

Mr. Sussman the tailor led Rosa up the aisle. Everyone under the canopy except Rosa had suits made by Sussman and Medgyes, 101 Whitechapel Road. If only their labels had been hanging out, for all to see.

Under the milk of her veil, she could see Gabor's face, pride lifted off his cheeks like a vapour.

The wedding party went back to number 101 for kiddush wine, also to measure up visitors as they arrived. There seemed to be no point where the shop ended and the house began. There were sheets of pinned suit and half-cut cloth everywhere, and Rosa was afraid to sit in case there were needles hidden in the chair. Mr Sussman lost his wife in the first blitz on London, and it seemed that he had not done any washing up since.

So she perched on the arm of Gabor's chair with a wine glass in her hand.

'Already she is your right hand,' Mr. Sussman said.

'Please God not my left hand. Already I have two left hands,' Gabor quipped.

But he was a man playing truant on a summer's day, his shower of lilies at his hand.

I am glad he is so proud, and, for me, well now I have a place to belong and a people who understand me even a little and I could have done better but I could have done worse.

All afternoon, clients were coming and going to have their suits measured, and Mr Sussman would rush to the cupboard to unearth another

wineglass, blowing off the dust and giving it a quick wipe with his hankerchief. They all teased Gabor and made him blink behind his glasses.
But he glowed from his first summer, his first taste of holiday, he was
never outside Rosa's touch, the smell of her lilies - his finger on her
hand, or his knee against hers, or his cheek in her lilies.

A man shaped like a fishball with one grey whisker and one black one
was fitted up at the back of the shop. With a carrot on his head you could
put him on a plate. Mr. Gobelman measured him in his shirtsleeves under
his arms, and he was talking all the time, the client. Mr. Gobelman nodded and grunted with pins in his mouth, while the man lifted one arm,
then the other.

'...and I need her moans like a hole in the head,' he was saying, 'what
do I do? I listen all day, I'm a good son, I don't worry her, strange girls,
you know, I don't do any of that: I shop for her, even I live with her, what
more can you want of a son? Don't you think, Mr. Sussman?'

Mr. Sussman grunted, climbing into the man's left armpit.

'I say she should be glad I don't bring a wife to fight with her in the
kitchen, she should be so glad to have the kitchen to herself. What could
a woman want more than to make soup for a son who eats, don't you
think Mr. Sussman?'

Gabor smiled a sideways half-smile.

'This is a man who has lived too long in east London,' he whispered to
Rosa.

'I hope you don't believe him,' Rosa said.

'I believe him like I believe you are ugly,' Gabor said, and turned his
lips to whatever part of Rosa was nearest him. It was her neck, and in
kissing that, he took in too the long smooth bowl under her chin.

When the client had gone, Mr. Sussman came back, runnning his hand
through the piece of hair left to him.

'Oy what a *meshuga*, will he never stop the talking, what a trial for the
poor mother! No wonder no woman will have him. What woman would
have him but a mother? Only a mother doesn't notice when a man is like
a monkey.'

'Who is he?' she asked.

'Mr. Karminsky, lives with the mother, problem boy, tries one business
after another, now he makes salt bccf sandwiches and he thinks with this
you can live. Who likes so much salt beef?'

Gabor took off his glasses to wipe them clean.

'No mother, no problem,' he said.

'Let me wipe them clean,' Rosa said.

She held his eyes in her hands and felt the weight of the lenses as he
watched her through his haze, wiped them gently with her own hanker-

chief that smelt faintly of primrose, and placed them carefully on his nose. It was the first time she touched him.

Etzbah elohim: : may the finger of God continue to save me.

They lived round the corner from number 101, so Gabor could walk on the days the 43 bus was late. Their furniture was other people's bits and pieces, Marjorie's ironing board, Mr. Gobelman's double bed which he said he would never need again, the butcher's kitchen table with knife marks down it. All day Gabor was out cutting suits in the dark front room of 101, ruining his eyes. Every year he needed thicker glasses. Rosa spent the day picking up fruit at the Whitechapel Market and smelling it. Some of the fruit she had never smelt before. The oranges made her sneeze, and the lemons made her eyes water. She pretended the fruit was too soft or too hard, and walked on to the next stall. In the afternoons for one hour she sat in the public library and read at the no smoking table. Her favourite was the *Shorter Oxford English Dictionary.* Each day she read ten new words, starting with A. She learnt *Aardvark, Aaron's beard* (a name), *abaca* and *abaciscus* on the first day, but even with the dictionary explanation she couldn't really understand them, and there didn't seem to be any opportunities to use them. So the next day she started volume 2 and learnt *marl, marlite* (a variety of marl), *marmalade* and *marmoset.* These seemed more useful words, because she knew for a fact that marmalade really existed because Mr. Gobelman had a pot with the word written on it. Anyway, with words written in front of her she had hope again, even if she couldn't understand them; and she could talk quietly into books and they quietly back to her. They were the best conversations of the day.

Gabor was a kind man but marriage had only changed him by making him a little poorer.

'Before I marry you I have just enough. Now I have just too little. You know what is the difference between just too little and just enough? The difference is your wife is happy your wife is not happy.'

And it was true, Rosa was not happy, with a quiet white-hot not-happiness that she never spoke, and it filled her with a fury that Gabor could see it. The idea was that Gabor should not see it, so she could work out what to do about it without him interfering.

'You such a lady, such a princess. You come from a village, middle of a field, but you such a lady,' he would say. Half of him was proud to see her in their brown room with her limbs like spilt milk and her cheeks like an empress; half of him was afraid of her, with her mind that opened and shut like a trap. He never knew what she had caught, what was stirring. He just knew she moved on all the time, and he didn't and couldn't.

And him? He from the big city but learnt nothing there. She never understood, that city he came from had such class, such style, but didn't give him any of it. Was the city so greedy to give him none of it?

One day Rosa said to him, 'It's a boy, I feel that it's a boy.'

He touched her stomach where it began to rise.

'A boy Cherry?' he said, 'what kind of thing is that, a boy Cherry?'

'An English boy. A Jewish boy. He will be both,' she said. 'He will be our pride and joy. He will be a doctor or lawyer.'

'My poor son, already his mother gives him university place and he still has no teeth,' Gabor said.

'And we'll call him Jacob.'

'Jacob? After the kosher butcher?'

'No, no. Jacob after the father of Joseph and Benjamin.'

'And the *bris*, Gabor! You would only look at the room to weep.I would never want to invite even a hole in the head into our room, never mind to invite the rabbi.'

It was true. Everything in the room had grown together into a brown glue. The bed had become the carpet, the carpet had become the sink with brown streaks down the porcelain, and the porcelain had become the gas ring with its ancient crusts and cracks.

'No, no, is true. Rabbi likes nice furniture,' he said.

'Gabor, your Mr Gobelman, you work harder and harder, he becomes richer and richer, you live in one room. Is there something wrong? Do you maybe notice something?'

'What should I notice? I work well, he is pleased,' said Gabor.

'What should you notice? You should notice you are stupid and Mr. Gobelman is clever.'

'So what to do if God ha'Shem made us this way?'

Rosa pulled herself up on her heels so she was tall enough to see the round patch on the top of Gabor's head.

'Start our own business. I will do the accounts. I know how to. I learnt before, in Vilna. I will deal with customers. I can talk to them. I can speak like any of them.'

She was moving on. Gabor's glasses grew steamy in the rush.

'Don't be in such a hurry,' he said.

'Don't be so slow,' she said.

*　　　*　　　*

After the engagement party, she talked about grandpa.

'He, a sweet man, but he couldn't pull himself out of a ditch. To pull him out the ditch I used all my sweat.'

'You built up grandpa's business, you made him proud again.'

'No, no, he was never proud,' she said, closing her eyes, rocking back and forwards. 'He was never proud. But you, for you it will be fine. Let this fiance, let him do the sweat. You keep your hands nice.'

'What do you mean? You mean Geoffrey does all the work? No no that's not what I want.'

'Yes, yes, you say so now. But for you it will be an easier life. Thank God for you it will be easier.'

'No, no grandma. It's not like that at all any more.'

But she was hushing me, like a child with nightmares.

'I wish you well, ha'Shem, may He give you mazel.' she said.

I closed my eyes while she blessed me. I gave in. She had carved milestone with her own hands. Milestones, tombstones.

When I opened my eyes, she had gone. I began to shiver, though the summer night was warm. The light was acidy, so I wrapped myself in a blanket and crept out to the corridor to collect one of the honey scented candles. In the darkness I bumped into Leo, also wrapped in a blanket, also creeping down the corridor.

'You again!' he said.

'It's you! You're the one that's here again. Why are you here every night?'

'It does strange things to a person, the night,' he said. 'All the revelations I ever had were at night, about this time, whatever time it is.'

'I know what you mean,' I said.

'Once it made me give up the world, you know, and go into purdah, the male kind. And another time it made me do the opposite. You never know!' and he winked, a rude undressing wink. 'You should try it.'

It was like meeting an animal in the dark. His blanket was beginning to slip, and the tops of his shoulders began to appear. They were so white they looked almost silver, and so bony you could hang washing on them. Seeing his skin and bones like that made me tremble. I felt a sudden urge to see if he was silver everywhere, to rip his blanket off and see what happened. The idea made me tremble so loudly my teeth began clattering together like a rattle.

'Sorry, little girl, maybe I'm being presumptious. Maybe you are trying it,' and he hitched his blanket back up round his neck and moved down the corridor like an Apache.

Dear Geoffrey,

Yes I understand all that about your job being important. Grandma of course agrees. She said she built up grandpa's business with her own sweat, but with you I won't need to do that. She thinks I will stay at home and enjoy the kitchen. while you work and earn money. You two, you agree on everything. I think you must meet in secret and decide what to say about things.

I think all those years, she just lived with Grandpa because they were married and being married was a thing you had to do. Maybe they didn't expect to love people in those days.

I don't think any of her dreams were there at all. I don't know where they were. Even when she was young it seems that all her dreams were finished.

Dear Sean,

Of course I remember you. I do have a boyfriend whose name is Geoffrey, but even so I would like to see you again. There are some things I would like to tell you. A lot of things have happened since I saw you on the train. Here where I am there is no-one really I can talk to. Actually, the people make me quite miserable.

There is an ice cream place in the square that bakes their own cones. It has a stripey roof. Let's meet there on Thursday, at 2.0pm.

Laura Cherry

Grandma, all those years, where were you really?

CHAPTER SIX

Wednesday

In the morning I found a note pushed under the door. It was a poem from Donald.

> *why does she commune with the moon*
> *that can give her only a god's light*
> *when on the streets, in neighbouring rooms*
> *are men with thighs of steel*
> *who can give her flesh's joys*
>
> *because it is not the moon she sees*
> *not its light or its god-face*
> *but herself: everywhere she looks*
> *just herself writ large*
> *and us poor mortals grow small*
> *and disappear*

Donald will never be famous. I scribbled a note back to him. *'Your language is old-fashioned. No-one writes 'writ large' any more. I don't know what you mean about all that thighs stuff. Laura '*

Without stopping to think about it, I pushed the note under his door. To be truthful, I was tired from my strange night, and a little mad.

Leo didn't look at all as if he had had a late night. He was lighting the stick of incense this morning when I arrived in the gym and chose a cushion. But me, I felt yellow from my night, and my eyes stuck together with sleep.

Leo talked to us in the first session about change and healing. He said that we were often the cause of our own illnesses and we had the power to heal ourselves through change. I'm sure grandma didn't cause her own heart attack. The thought of it is terrible. She shouted at grandpa and Michael and she was rude about Mary and whenever I mentioned her childhood mother hissed at me to be quiet. But none of those things would give you a heart attack. I thought it was about eating butter.

Then we had to share our aches and pains with a partner. I was with Gloria. She hadn't taken off her ankle bangles since Sunday.

'After my husband left me I got all these strange stomach cramps and rashes. Then I realised it was because I hadn't acknowledged my anger and had bottled it all up.'

'What did you do?'

I expected Gloria to tell me what she did, but instead she began screaming and beating the cushion. She did this until the cushion was bunched up like a cauliflower. When she stopped, she sighed and gasped and swept back her fringe which was sticking to her head.

'That felt good!' she said.

She was still panting from her scream, so it gave me time to think about my illnesses. I didn't think I ever really had illnesses, apart from sometimes feeling sick: before exams, before school dances, before family parties, before gym lessons, after eating too much peanut butter, after getting engaged to Geoffrey. But none of those counted because I wasn't actually sick, and I only fainted once.

'I caught veruccas at the local swimming pool,' I said because that was the only illness I had where I needed medicine.

'Interesting,' Gloria said. 'Tell me more.'

There wasn't much more to say, really.

'It cleared up with methylated spirits.'

'What about the swimming pool?'

'It had chlorine in it.'

Gloria looked at me as if I was very sick.

'I mean did you go back to the swimming pool?'

'I don't really like them very much. I hate getting that smelly water in my eyes.'

'Do you know about your own birth experience? Did you ever ask your mother?'

'No, ' I said, 'I never did.'

'You may have some primal memory that makes you afraid of water.'

I didn't dare ask her what a primal memory was, but I was sure I hadn't had one.

When we finished sharing we had a meditation, and I was glad of it. But every time I closed my eyes I was back in the cave with Geoffrey lighting a fire, Rosa and Gabor there in strange thin clothes, the smoke building up and I was beginning to choke. When I opened my eyes I would see Leo, and would remember him with silver skin and no clothes on, and close my eyes again quickly. It was giving me a stomach ache.

The Wednesday theme was rituals and ceremonies. Leo put questions up all round the wall. We had to find a question we liked and scribble down our feelings about it while noises were playing in the background. Leo told us this was the music plants made when you stroked them.

Stay here and think about christenings. Do they mark for you the beginning of life?

Stay here and think about confirmation. Did you feel membership of a spiritual community?

Stay here and think about graduation. Did you feel initiated into wisdom and learning?

Stay here and think about your wedding. Was it a confirmation and validation of love?

Was there a moment or event that for you marked the end of childhood?

Was there a moment or event for you that marked the beginning of freedom?

I noticed Gloria stopping by the radiator where the wedding questions were. Donald hung about around the graduation question. Isobel and Leo sat together by the 'beginning of freedom' question, where all the soft cushions were. Daphne and I were together at the end of childhood. She was drawing pictures, I noticed, sketches of big rocks, wild flowers and hairy ponies. I tried not to look, but noticed they were really quite good.

Rituals and ceremonies

Samson Henry was mysterious in three ways. Firstly, he was almost Teenage. When I was only just twelve, he was already turning Teen. Secondly, he was a boy, which was a rare thing to be as none of my friends were boys at all. Thirdly, his name was Samson, which made me gasp. Tina herself didn't seem at all aware that she was living with a Mystery. She had inherited his Desparate Dan duvet, and hated it. She said boys had all the luck because no-one expected them to be human. Samson wasn't expected to make tea for Mrs. Henry's bridge parties, to speak, or to eat with a knife and fork.

When his bar-mitvah invitation arrived, he became even more Mysterious. It was on a white card with a frilled edge and tracing paper lining, and the letters were gold and bumpy when you stroked them.

On the Saturday I wore Saturday clothes: black patent leather shoes with long white socks. I could see myself in the toes of my shoes, like a round button at the end of a tunnel. I was the last girl in the class to be wearing patent leather shoes with rubber soles. But Mother wouldn't understand why this was stunting my growth.

'You don't want to grow up too soon,' she said.

'I do,' I said.

So I trailed to synagogue, kicking my toes to make them less shiny, Mother tutting and hurrying me along. In the women's gallery the only thing to do until the service began, was to look at the women and tut about their clothes. Mrs. Henry was wearing Brighton rock pink, and she was kissing everyone as she squeezed along the rows to the front of the gallery where she could hang over Samson. Tina arrived after Mrs. Henry. She flung the door open, so the hats nearly fell off in the excitement. She was wearing a red leather skirt and stripey red and white tights. None of Tina's friends wore socks and she only spoke to me in public places like schools and synagogues.

'That girl is wild!' Mother said, sending Tina a cold lipsticky smile which Tina returned.

'God Tina, you look fabulous!' I breathed.

'Mum hates the outfit, but I don't care,' Tina whispered back.

Then she threw her ponytail in the air and walked off to sit in the front row where the boys could see her.

From our seats we could see the shiny tops of heads below us where the men sat, and the embroidery on caps, and the white silky arcs on shoulders. If you were in the front row and were lucky, you could hang over from the waist and catch some glances, some eyes looking up searching the rows, before the women would hiss and tst tst, and pull you back into your seat.

Samson was standing on the *bimah*. Another boy was with him, clutching his book up against his chest as if he had stomach ache. The wide white striped shawl draped gorgeously over his shoulders and the fringes quivered in rows of gold plaits. I watched the rabbi bending over him, and his father beside him with the black prayer book with gold edges tucked under his arm. The three of them stood in a row, the older men all hairy and crumpled, the other boy smooth and rosy with his hair glistening like a shield.

First Samson read. He looked puffed and buttery with his cap skewed on one side and his voice sticky and broken. Mrs Henry nearly fell over the balcony in her joy.

Then the other boy stood up in front of the golden scrolls. From the balcony, you could see the kerby grip in his cap working itself out of his hair. He was pink and reedy like a recorder, with his mouth at the end puffing out the stops.

I could never be so brave as to look out at all the men like he did, and then look down so the red spread in from the edges of his ears to the tip of his nose. And then, although you were so red, I could never imagine being able to sing like that, like a pipe puffing, puffing its last breaths.

'Who's that?' I whispered to Mother.

'The Pelter boy,' she said.

'Who?'

'Geoffrey Pelter, poor Ena's boy.'

'Why's she poor?'

The lady behind us begain saying 'tsk tsk' to quiet us, so Mother didn't reply.

It was Samson's turn to sing, the scroll rolled out on the lectern and the two men on either side of him like bookends. All the pink faces where the men sat pointed at him like rows of baby chickens in a nest.

'Don't make such a show of yourself,' Mother hissed.

'What do you mean?'

'Falling over the balcony like that.'

'Mrs. Henry is.' I hissed back.

'Well, Mrs. Henry!' Mother said rolling her eyes with disgust. Tina in the next row crossed her right leg over her left knee and her leather skirt moved up an inch. Mother looked at her down her nose.

'That family,' she sizzed in my ear, 'you wouldn't want to look like them.'

'I would,' I replied.

Then the rabbi began his sermon, how the time had come for Samson and Geoffrey to take their places in the community and become men, how the honours of the family would now fall on their shoulders, how the traditions of study and worship lay now in their hands to continue and what a great and heavy responsibility that was. Tina sat on her hands and swung her legs. I think she was even chewing. But no-one was telling her to continue the honours of her family, so she didn't need to worry. She could chew as much gum as she liked. When everyone was kissing and saying how good Samson and Geoffrey were, she rolled up her eyes and looked bored and swung her red shoe with her toes so it slipped off her heel.

Afterwards, people pressed towards the honey cake in the synagogue hall, kissing on the way and spreading the room with powder. The men swooped down clutching velvet bags, and Father was there advising people about their pensions. Samson and Geoffrey stood by the table like teddies, being pinched and kissed.

'You are brave,' I said to Geoffrey, when I got near.

'Oh, it's easy!' Geoffrey said, with one hand in the honey cake dish.

'I could never do it.'

'Girls don't do it anyway,' Geoffrey said.

Then he looked at my black patent shoes.

'Not girls like you, anyway.'

'What do you mean?' but an aunt began to wrap him up in her coat so I never heard the answer.

I looked at my shoes and thought about the heavy responsibilities and great traditions and being a man. Near my shoes I could see Tina's that she could slip off and dangle with her toes.

Girls don't do it anyway, it was true. Girls like me, they sit upstairs in patent shoes and none of the pink faces turn to me like baby chickens. I stood in the corner and watched Tina being looked at. It took a lot of time, being looked at. Tina spent all her time being looked at. You had to be either daring, like Tina, or not care at all about other people, like Tina's mother who wore pink when she shouldn't. Mother hissed about both of them, and put her nose in the air and set her lipstick in a pout when she saw them.

It's not that I wanted to be looked at, like they were. It's that I wanted to do something, like Samson did, and that Geoffrey, standing on the stage like a filmstar, being a man, all the men listening and the women falling over the balcony to hear better. They were milling around Samson now saying to him, 'well done', 'like a rabbi' 'like a man' and he was bobbing up and down, kissing and shaking hands and aunts were pinching his cheeks. There was something about that I liked. There's something about that I wanted.

So I decided to fast for Yom Kippur because that was something I could do that I knew how to. What you did, you just stopped eating. You didn't even have to wear special clothes.

Yom Kippur, the day of fasting and atonement, came three months after Samson's bar mitzvah and the day I met Geoffrey. First I had a shoe fight with Mother.

'Why can't I wear high heels?'

'You're just a little girl', Mother said.

'Tina wears them and she's only twelve.'

'Well, Tina, that family will wear anything.'

The next fight was the breakfast fight.

'Eat your porridge, it's good for the bowels.'

'I'm fasting.'

'Well, just eat your porridge and then you can fast.'

'That's cheating.'

'It's not cheating if it makes you ill.'

'It doesn't make me ill.'

There were too many people for the synagogue, so they had hired the cinema to fit us all in. All the women sat upstairs in the box circle, the £2 seats, and the men sat downstairs in the stalls where there had been all-in wrestling a week ago. They looked miles away, like the little people at the end of a telescope, like gold and white pieces in a kaleidoscope whirling round and round in tiny patterns.

Mrs. Greenberg was there as usual. She had saved two places for us, up by the Fire Exit. She and mother kissed and bumped hats, then she kissed me and squeezed my cheek and said,

'Aren't you growing up?!'

Mrs. Greenberg's house was next to the synagogue and was full of sponge cake. She never ran out of sponge cake.

'If you are hungry, you just say to me,' she said.

'I'm fasting this year, Mrs. Greenberg.'

'What, you fasting? She's fasting?' she said to me, and then to my mother. Mrs. Greenberg never spoke to one person at a time. Mother shrugged and rolled her eyes,

'She thinks she is, we'll see if it lasts,' she said.

They didn't deserve for me to sit beside them. It was no good, if they weren't going to be impressed. I wanted to sit next to Tina, so she would tell Samson and that Geoffrey I was fasting, how good I was, and how I could do things they could do.

'I want to sit with Tina,'

'Stop fussing.'

'I'm not.'

They walked in together, Tina and Mrs. Henry, and everyone drew in their breath. Mrs. Henry looked like a liquorice allsort.

Every part of her was black and white stripes, and her dress was like a liquorice tube that you could uncurl. Tina looked as if she had raided a smarties factory. She had smartie-coloured bangles all the way up her arm, which clanged together when she walked, and her hair was plaited with thousands of matching tiny beads.

'That family,' Mother snorted, 'what will they do next to make a spectacle of themselves?'

I didn't care. I asked Mrs. Greenberg if she would let me squeeze through a minute, and she flattened herself against the seat and said,

'You do what you need to dear,'

and I did, I joined up with Mrs. Henry and Tina and followed them to their seats as if it was an accident. Tina didn't really notice until I was sitting next to her.

'I like your hair. How did you do it?' I said.

'Had it done on the beach in Ibiza.'

'Ibiza!'

'Yea.'

Mother began craning over the other heads to see me and poked at the empty seat next to her with her fingernails and pointed her lipstick into a spike, but I ignored her.

The service began and it was slow. The book was thick and we had to get through it, or they had to get through it, the men.

It didn't matter at all what we did, we just looked from the box circle every now and again to see how they were doing and what page they were on but still no-one was quite sure and they'd say, -18, no 24, no we've started again, no we're doing an additional bit, this bit isn't in at all, oh no we've started again again doesn't Mrs. Henry look dreadful doesn't Tina look grown up are you at the big school yet- oh it's page 80 I recognise that, that bit's here, oh it's here as well, and again here, so which bit is it?

Tina and I fidgeted and whispered messages.

'I'm fasting this year.'

'I've brought a tube of cherry bitters.'

'No, not in here?'

'Yes, I have. Look.'

They were in her culotte pockets, wrapped in a hankerchief. They smelt so much of cherries I could almost taste them.

'I'm not going to.'

'What, not even one?'

'I'm fasting.'

Tina looked at me as if I was mad. Mother looked at me as if I was selling my body on the street corner. I felt miserable, so I read about things I should be repenting.

sinning in public and private

immorality

wronging a neighbour,

insincere confession,

contempt for parents and teachers (Mother scowled at me and said, 'you see?!')

a session of vice,

exercising power,

foolish speech,

impure lips,

Evil Inclination,

brazenness,

throwing off Your yoke,

'I like Evil Inclination best,' Tina whispered. 'Which one do you like?'

'I like, 'throwing off Your yoke,'

'It doesn't mean egg kind of yoke. '

'I know,' I hissed.

Then all the women in the row in front turned round and shushed me as the chazzan down below stood with his mouth a little pink ring inside his beard and cried into the open ark:

mi boker

ad erev

May our cry arrive from morning
and may our praise find favour by evening

and I strained over the balcony to see if I could see Samson. I thought I saw him several times, in the front row looking like a blue velvet spot, by the Fire Escape clutching his book under his shawl with all the tassels hanging down, squeezing past the men in the third row holding his cap on his head, but they couldn't have been him because he was in all those places at once, and when I looked again, none of them were quite him, though one of them had his buttery cheeks, and another had his pink mouth and another had his big square shoulders.

'What's so interesting?' Tina sissed.

'I was just looking.'

So the morning went by and we fell out the Box Circle to breathe some fresh air. A huddle of boys collected around Tina, to pick at the beads in her hair. Mother and Father came and pinned me in between them. We had a short Lunch fight, but Father was on my side.

'Let her, it's a girl's prerogative to fast at twelve. If she feels well, why not?'

'Because she won't admit if she doesn't feel well. I know her.'

They fought over my head, and I stood pinned between them in my socks, scouring the hall for Samson. Mrs. Henry breezed by in a puff of jasmine perfume and blew Father a kiss.

'That woman!' Mother scowled, 'I don't know why you have anything to do with that family.'

Both Father and I said, 'yes' at the same time.

Samson was in the bead-picking group of boys with Geoffrey. Both of them were blushing.

'Happy New Year,' I said.

'It's not meant to be happy,' Samson said with a grown-up kind of laugh, and flounced off shaking his fringe in the air.

'I'm hungry,' Geoffrey said, and his ears went red.

When the afternoon service began, I still hadn't eaten or drunk anything since brushing my teeth. The day was going on for ever and ever, and everyone was making it difficult - Mother with her porridge, Mrs. Greenberg with her sponge cake, Tina with her cherry bitters. Fasting was meant to be a spiritual and holy thing that you did because it was traditional and full of honours, and you took your place in the community and everything like that. But they were making it a string of fights over porridge and sponge cake. They spoilt everything.

I went back to my seat next to Tina. Everyone was yawning and talking to their neighbours and looking at their watches. Tina looked as if she was sucking something. She didn't evenglance at me when I sat down.

Then we all had to stand up. Everyone stood up, shuffling, smoothing their skirts and culottes and shawls and leather liquorice tubes, and looking for *'the congregation stands'* in the book, finding *'the congregation stands'* on page 37, and 49, and 55, and 112, and 147, so it didn't help.

We stood, and the men rumbled like a train in the tunnel, and then we stood some more and the men rumbled some more, and we rocked and rocked, saying sorry for evil-thinking and guilt-offering and vice and yokes, and I rocked some more and said to Tina,

'I'm rocking,'

'Course you are,' and I began to say,

'No, really- '

and that was the last thing I heard, because the dome and the specks of shawls and hats began to break into a pepperpot of black spots and the women's gallery began to sway like a ship on a slow wave and the whole ceiling began to roll and heave and grow black and I lifted my arms to bring down the pillars with the rolled ram's horns and the dome with the painted babies, and the rows and rows of tiny men with pink faces and caps like coloured beads the whole golden casket tumbling open and pulling the roof into steaming rubble around me black spots cold arrows hailstones crashing around my feet crashing so fast the rocks broke into dust and I down with it down down with it and the ground rushing up to meet me.

When I opened my eyes I was at the bottom of a pothole. There was a circle of heads looking down at me from an enormous height, gabbling in a strange human babble. It was another planet and I let them wash round me, their fingers prodding down the pothole and echoing up the walls of the cave. The roof had fallen away, it was further than it had been and the ground was nearer, the jigsaw of coloured beads, the rumbling train, they were two shades nearer.

'She's awake,' I heard,

and then someone reached down the pothole, a long metallic arm, a noisy jointed arm that shifted and rolled and caught the light in strips of strobe red and pink and green that made my stomach roll, and suddenly I was hooked, clipped under my shoulders and heaved up the miles and miles, out of the echo chamber and the upside-down mouths and round peanut eyes

and the world flipped back again.

'You fainted.'

'She's fine.'

'Sit her down, here - '

'She should eat -'

'I'm fasting' -

and then the knees and new shoes disappeared again.

When I woke up, I was on Mrs. Greenberg's sofa, and Tina was kicking her legs under the table, eating sponge cake.

'Thank goodness you're awake. I was getting bored,' she said.

'Did Mrs. Greenberg invite you too?'

'I said I felt faint too,'

'What, really?!'

'I've never had a friend who fainted before.'

Mrs. Greenberg and Mother ran in from the kitchen.

'Now will you stop this fasting business?' Mother said.

Tina had got through a lot of the sponge cake, and there were crumbs all round her mouth.

'What's the time?'

'Ten to seven.'

'When does the fast finish?'

Mrs. Greenberg put on her reading glasses and pulled out the order of service.

'6.58 God be willing,' she said.

We sat in a circle with our stopwatches, Tina pecking at the cake crumbs, Mother tutting and clicking her teeth and pacing up and down with Mrs. Greenberg, tapping her watch at me and scowling at Tina whose fault it all was.

Then at 6.58 Mrs. Greenberg brought me a bowl of noodle soup from the kitchen and I ate it slowly, each spoonful steaming and slippery, while Mother watched. When I finished, they went into the kitchen for some more.

'Well what a story!' Tina said.

'I wanted to be grown-up.'

'You still wear those shoes.'

'Mum won't let me wear high heels. It's not fair.'

'D'you want a cherry bitter?'

'Yea.'

We sat round the table, sucking our cherry bitters so our mouths went sticky with cherry lipstick.

'I like 'session of vice' best,' Tina said.

I rolled the cherry bitter round and round on my tongue. 'Will you tell Samson and that Geoffrey?'

'That you fainted or that you fasted?'

'Both.'

'Yea.'

'Can I try on your shoes?'

'Yea,' Tina said.

*　　*　　*

Donald said graduation was the biggest con for him. They were launched in ermine gowns with scrolls and mortar boards and five years later half of them are still unemployed.

Gloria said the wedding ceremony was the biggest con. She discovered a year later that her husband had another lover all the time. After another year he left her for a third woman.

Isobel went on about virginity, how she had thought losing it would mark a great change, a great rite of passage, but it hadn't at all.

Leo said that he planned to join a Buddhist monastery in Nepal. They suggested that before the ritual, he spend a week away from the monastery, to think about it. He went to Kathmandu and sat by the river, watching people cremate their fathers and wash their saris. A beautiful woman was soaping herself under her sari, unwrapping it skilfully and holding it out like a screen. The sight gave him such pleasure, he decided he was not cut out for the monastery.

Daphne asked me about my story.

'It's a lovely story, Laura. It says a lot about you.'

'What does it say about me?'

'Well, it says what opportunities you give yourself, what risks you take.'

'I don't really take risks,' I said.

'I think you do,' she said. 'You're taking one now.'

I nearly said,'Oh no,' but the way she looked at me made me say, 'Yes, maybe.'

I was two people, I always had been: a pre-wedding and a post-wedding person. The first person was immature and bossed about by relatives, the prey of bad spotty poets and lonely train carriages. The post-wedding person was clever and wise and mature, terribly confident and good at everything, always making the right decisions and saying, 'my husband and I.'

But when I closed my eyes, the post-wedding person wasn't me at all. It was somebody quite different. I tried and tried, but whenever I imagined the post-wedding person, the face changed. It was Hannah's face, or Mary's, or Daphne's, but never mine.

Daphne touched my shoulder.

'You listen to your own voices,' she said, 'and remember how brave you are.'

I thought that in the afternoon I might move round to the 'beginning of freedom' part of the room with Isobel and Leo.

At lunchtime I was at the 'Throat' table.

The throat shakra relates to the sense of hearing and the colour blue.

It relates to the qualities of creativity, communication, self-expression and sound.

I thought this was much better than Monday's genitals, but still not as good as 'heart'. This time, I was sitting with Daphne and Gloria. Gloria spent the whole meal telling us about how important communication was, and how much it helped her recover from her husband. Daphne and I just nodded and smiled and said yes but didn't manage to say a single word.

I wanted another glimpse of Pacino square. When I got through the high iron railings, I almost ran through the chocolate-flavoured streets. It was such a release to be free of the prayerbells and searching eyes and dreadful poems and candlelit corridors. To be free of my own pictures that I never thought about out in the open air where I could breathe the primroses and cowbells coming in from the hills and breeze coming in from the lake. I carried grandma on my shoulders into the open cobbles and it was all still there. The drinking fountain, the icecream kiosk and the hot dog stall, the low stone wall with the snooty gulls, the steamy lake with a mist coming down over its outer edge and the passenger boat piping towards the other shore.

Today I bought an icecream, chocolate fudge and strawberry sorbet. The strawberry had real tiny fruit bits in it. I sat on the wall and felt my mouth grow clowny with chocolate and strawberry and I didn't care at all. In the breeze and bustle there were new lovely sounds taking off with the gulls. It was a flute spiralling up, puffs of flute, and then some string sounds balletdancing, falling off the gull's wings.

The musicians were further along the pier wall. The guitarist was sitting with an orange leg up on the wall, the other hanging down like a teddy's in a soft boot with red laces. His head was hairless under a multicoloured smoking cap, an egg. He was grinning, grinning, one gold tooth catching the light, his guitar like a swatch of silk over his knee. The violinist and flautist were huddled round him in a kind of icecream tryptych, two vanillas and a neopolitan..

I liked watching them. Their eyes moved between them as if they were attached to each other by a thread, up and down on an invisible surf of sound. Sometimes I liked closing my eyes and just listening. They were threading, winding round each other, spreading like confetti. When one pulled the cord a little tighter, the others would trapeze and spiral on the thread; when one climbed the others would fall away to give free passage; when one would lose heart the others would rally underneath and scoop up the sound. The whole square was infected. The sound was making the boat sirens ruder, the ice creams messier, the summer dresses pinker.

I wanted to go back for the meditation but I didn't want to leave, not for a day or two. But I did leave, slowly, straggling in front of the musicians, one foot walking backwards and one forwards. Then I leaned forward and threw the change from my icecream cone into the open violin case. The guitarist turned his head and winked.

I don't know why, I felt like dancing all the way back to the school.

My notes from the morning session had been tidied up and left on a cushion under 'the beginning of freedom'. I was in time, just, for the third meditation lesson with Leo.

Monday had been the image of the candle. I found this one sent me to sleep.

Tuesday was a key word, a mantra which we had to repeat and repeat in our mind, emptying it of everything else.

I couldn't empty my mind of everything else. In fact, it became even more cluttered than usual, trying so hard to empty it.

Today Leo asked if any of us had any questions about meditation. I said I was no good at meditating. He explained that it took a lot of practice, a lifetime: I should keep trying, and just let things happen without worrying about them or judging myself.

He said, 'there's no right or wrong.'

I said, 'but you explained that it was right to clear the mind.'

'Just do what you can,' he said. He seemed slightly irritated and I felt like a dunce. I wonder whether everyone else in the group could clear their mind.

Today he told us about meditating with a riddle. The riddle was impossible to solve, and by thinking about it we could learn to live with uncertainty and not-knowing. I thought I might be good at this one. The riddle was:

Show me your face before your mother and father were born.

In fact, I wasn't good at this one either.

I could not imagine my mother and father not being born.

Even less my grandmother.

She was always born.

I was always born. Somewhere, even if I didn't know it.

Even if I wasn't there, then someone else was.

The group were sitting around me in a circle on red cushions. Leo was sitting at the head of the circle, his knees knotted below him like strips of rubber. His face looked terribly smooth under his beard, his eyelashes panned out on his cheek like a baby's. I began to meditate on how different he looked then, to his way with Isobel, when his face was often smug and lustful rather than self-contained and quiet. It was true, he was more in repose than the others around the circle. Isobel was shuffling from knee to knee, Donald was screwing up his fists so his knuckles stuck out like four white eggs, Daphne had fallen asleep again and her head was beginning to roll.

So there must be something in this path of faith that Leo talks about. He is definitely more at peace than any of us around the room. Geoffrey believes in being Jewish, but he could never meditate on uncertainty. He can't tolerate uncertainty, even for a moment. Either there is an answer, which you can prove and measure, or it's all rubbish.

I meditated on the riddle, but other muddles came into my mind instead.

It was my wedding I could see. I was walking down the aisle but something was wrong. Firstly, I was there alone. My father wasn't there to give me away, nor was Geoffrey there at the end of the aisle. I was walking the slow bride's walk, but the synagogue was in darkness. There were just lines of tall candles instead of people. Then I saw that my gown was black, my train was black, like a nun's.

I opened my eyes but the image didn't go away, nor the terrible heavy feeling. I cannot imagine myself at my wedding. I cannot imagine myself at my wedding.

When I think about a future with Geoffrey I go backwards instead, to when we were thirteen and first met, to when we were eighteen and danced close at the disco like two wooden dolls. I can't imagine being older with him, only younger, so young that I am little again and back in socks.

So I went to the Yin: Yang room. One half of the room had masculine things in it, like reindeer antlers and pictures of Krishna with a blue face. The other half of the room was feminine. It had giant beanbags that squashed into your shape, and a big round soapstone that you could stroke and hug. The telephone was in this bit of the room.

When I was sure it was all clear, I phoned Geoffrey.

'Oh Laura, I was just going to phone you, do you know, at that very moment. I knew we were thinking the same way. You see, it shows we're just made for each other, because just then I was by the phone to phone you. I've got a surprise for you, I can't wait to tell you.'

'A good one, is it a good surprise.'

'I'm coming to Pacino, I'll be in Pacino on Saturday. What do you think!'

'Oh, Geoffrey— but your job, your job at the clinic with Mr. Pick, all those dentures?'

'When I arrived at Mr. Pick's clinic, it was all locked up. The caretaker came to the door after a lot of knocking and shouting and said Mr. Pick was on holiday all through August. I said that couldn't be right, I was meant to be starting the job today and he had confirmed it in writing so he would have to come home from holiday wherever he was. I was really upset and the man was being really stupid when I thought about getting the letter out. '

'Yes, and–?'

'It said 9/8/89, that's it August 9th. But the caretaker said no, that meant September 8th, because Mr. Pick was American and put the dates the other way round. I never heard anything so stupid and ignorant. The caretaker was so rude, he slammed the door in my face. It was the last straw. I have to leave the country. I wanted to come immediately and rescue you from that place. I've already checked out flights to Zurich and I could fly in on Saturday morning arriving 10.08 and catch a train to Pacino station leaving Zurich 11.40 and arriving at your place 2.18, I just happen to have the details here by the phone. What do you think? I know it's a bit last minute but I thought what a good idea, what a perfect thing to do and I was glad Mr. Pick had made that stupid mistake. Isn't that great, Laura, we can have a holiday together after all.'

'Yes,' I said, but I was surprised that my stomach said, 'no.' It shot out the word as if I had kicked it.

'So you'll meet me at Pacino station at 2.18 on Saturday?'

I don't want to miss the meditation class. I'm just learning how to do it.

'Yes,' I said, and put the phone down.

Then I sat in one of the beanbags and it bunched up around me.

I could hear Daphne saying,

'You want him to come because you don't want him to come.' And I could hear myself say, 'no, no'. Then I could see Daphne looking at me, with a half-smile on her face and a grey tendril curling down, until I began saying, 'yes, yes. You're right. I want him to come because I don't want him to come.'

CHAPTER SEVEN

Wednesday Night

I wondered if grandma would come to see me tonight. I had questions
to ask. Why did she go to the matchmaker, when she had cat eyes and
tiger coloured hair and a coat with a long fur bolt from collar to toe?
Why did she choose a cold marriage when she could have chosen a love
match from any number of admirers? What had she left behind that
made her so cold? She was taking me backward, into her inside skins, and
one question led to another, one story to another.

When she came, she was like a cobweb scratched onto glass. I could
see through into her veins. I had never seen her like this. Her dress was
worn thin like another skin, and her shoes had burst at the toe. There
was a haze of cold around her, as if a whole snowscape had wrapped
around her and made her white. She began shuddering, clutching her
arms around herself in her thin jacket.

'I arrived, but I don't know where to go,' she said, but she didn't seem
to be talking to me, or to anyone at all. 'I don't know where to go,' she
was muttering, again and again under her breath.

'You can stay here,' I said.

She looked at me as if I was the one who was half invisible. When her
sleeves fell back her wrists and arms were thin as ribbons.

'What has happened?' I cried.

'What will happen next?' she cried.

She had just arrived in the streets of Vilna, now in the independent
state of Lithuania, fifty miles from the Polish border. For two years it
was a brief safe haven from Nazi occupation. It was February 1940 and
she was nineteen.

*   *   *

A man appeared from the sledgehammer sky and lifted her onto the sled
so tightly there were blue bruise rings round her armpits. He dropped
her at the city edge and said,

'Find the shoemakers' street, and tell no-one who I am.'

'I don't know who you are,' she said.

She was too tired to see where he left, just that he disappeared back
into the sky and the cobbles heaved in and out like turtle backs. The shop

fronts and the iron railings of churches with gargoyles and cobbles slipped, slid underfoot. The church was falling but it was her, she was falling; and the city moved slowly trapped in its frost.

Does Lunke the stonemason live here? We knew him from Vigry he married my friend, my Lola , somewhere is their house and it is safe.

His was a street of craftsmen; he had always told her that. His doorway would bear a plate:

A.L. Lescynsky Stonemason: all stone carvings, memorial and celebration.

A woman in a black dress and black scarf opened the door. She stood in the doorway and looked at Rosa. She watched her begin to form a greeting, and begin to open her hands to embrace hers; she stepped back into the doorway as Rosa began to move forward on bruised feet to reach her, and as she made the steps there towards the warm well of a home, she felt her nose suddenly pinned, flattened against the back of the door.

Rosa stood on the doorstep for a moment, too surprised to move. Then the old lady opened a window above and shouted,

'Get back to your own people. We don't want you here.'

'Is Lunke there? He is my friend,' she shouted back.

'He doesn't want you here. Get back to your own people. You're not welcome.'

Do you know the shoemakers' street? Does anyone here make shoes? Does anyone know the stonemason?

'Come inside here, don't talk such nonsense.'

She heard it in her ear, as if a bee was sitting there. It buzzed around her ear.

'It's curfew. You mad walking in the streets?'

It was an old man with braces and a missing tooth, and his lips were blue from the cold as he stepped out of a doorway and pulled her in by the edge of her dress.

'How long we have to go looking for you?'

None of it made sense, but it didn't make sense for so long and so far back that maybe after all it did.

'Are you Lunke?' she said, as he pushed her indoors.

I am alone suddenly behind a wooden screen with a basin and a jug of ice-cold water. I feel my own mouth shaping the water's sounds and it is me, sending out gasps, gasping like the centre of the earth sending out steam The water is a spray of stars, the dust hisses off me. Everything I have washes off in lumps of mud and grit, insects with metallic backs and hairy claws, monsters that crawled out of icy ponds and dug their teeth into my flesh, I can feel them falling and cracking at my feet. The poison from purple mushrooms seeps out of me like treacle.

And now things appeared, soundlessly, over the top of the screen. At first she held them and opened them out and questioned them as if she was an animal that had never dressed, didn't know quite what to do, to drape them over limbs, to feel the cotton and linen and silk against sore skin. She thawed slowly like the lake and under the surface there was life threshing its silver tail. In the ice where everything was stripped back every colour stood out like a drop of blood on white skin.

Everything stood out in the frost: the cotton slip,carefully hemmed in tiny hemstitch to the height of a teenage girl, a pair of enormous bloomers in shiny silk that she hitched up over her other pair, a heavy wool serge jacket with a large bosom and a silk lining that had been hand-stitched in, a matching skirt that dropped to below her ankles, that she rolled over three times at the waist. She stepped into the loins of a large woman whose flesh she could feel warm in the linings of her clothes, and clasped her twice over in to her waist and breast. Finally, the boots. She had never seen boots so perfect. When she slid her hand into them, they felt like the warm haunches of a lamb. They had an aureole of fur around the ankle, and tiny laces that smelt of soft leather. Her feet were in twin palaces. They had closely moulded another foot, the dent of the bone at the big toe was there and nestled around her like a lapdog's tongue.

So she stood behind the screen, recreated from top to toe, playing the lady with the large bloomers, the teenage girl with the tiny slip, her toes spreading in their warm hides.

'Miss, come out,'she heard, gently.

So she came out, into the room of Abe Tabaschsky and his son whom she was to love, Jacob Tabaschsky.

The table was set for three, white tablecloth, candlesticks and they were waiting for her, sitting on either side of the empty place, their caps on their heads. It must be Friday. For so long, there had been no days or nights, only light and dark.

'Say the bracha for the candles, it will make us happy,' said the son.

Blessed are You Lord our God King of the Universe who makes us holy through doing His commands and commands us to light the Sabbath candles.

It was a kindness that they made her say the words. You make us holy through doing His commands.

Then she sat in the chair and folded her hands, and noticed that the older man was wearing an apron with the waist tied high up almost under his arms and that he and the younger man disappeared in and out of the room, whispering and clattering outside and re-appearing with basted chicken and soup tureens with square dumplings. She noticed that the younger man had a beard like the whorls of a walnut tree, and he sunk inside it.

'You wonder where are our women, two men, incompetents in the kitchen,' the older man said, scooping the soup into her plate. 'Well, we too, we wonder where are our women. My daughter, she has gone to marry in the other country, and my wife she has gone to help her have baby.'

'The other country is your side of the border,' the younger man said, not looking up, looking into his soup spoon.

'And you, we wonder where are your men that you should come alone?'

'I was not alone when I started.'

'Shush father,' the younger man shot out, 'she needn't say.'

'My son, he is not a great talker.'

They scraped spoons for a while, silently picking through the lumps of loosed chicken and bubbles of grease breaking the surface of the soup.

'It would be polite if we introduced ourselves,' said the young man. 'Father forgets the courtesies. I am Jacob Tabachsky and he is my father Abe.'

'I know your name, the Tabaschkys.'

'We are Tabaschsky the scribes, we make the sacred books for all this place, all around every yshivah and synagogue has a scroll made from us. Now father here, his eyes are not so good, we are building up the bookdealing business you know, so he can do less of the close work. Not good for the eyes, you know. '

Yes yes Rosa too in her home in Vigry had books bought from the Tabaschskys. Her father Julius came many times to Vilna to buy books, and carried them safely on the sledge wrapped in shawls, unfolded them on the table like baby kittens. They remembered him too; they remembered how loud was his laugh and how regular his custom and how strong his winter coat, lined with fur.

'A good man, your father, a good man.'

'I left him in Vigry and have not been able to send a message.'

'He is well,' Jacob said, quickly.

'Tomorrow we will send message you are well, with parcels, tea and sugar. We will send, he has ways,' Abe said, winking towards Jacob. He waved his hand, and sprayed soup across the table.

In the morning Abe Tabaschsky talked to Rosa severely.

'They told me to find the shoemaker's street.,' she had said.

'There is no shoemakers' street. You will stay here. You will not think of leaving us until it is safe. It is a terrible thing, a terrible thing, but those that can must stick together and those that can help must help and those that cannot help must shut up. When we finish Shabbath Jacob will show you to go for de-lousing, and you will feel more clean.'

He talked so fast he was out of breath by the end of his sentences.

Rosa went into their kitchen, uninvited, and did what she should do while they went to Shabbath prayer, not sure where to find bowls and spoons, or whether to use the cabbage and carrots and pans of chicken necks thrown onto the cupboard floor. The warm ghosts of the women had slipped out of this kitchen leaving their pans and vegetables half done for the Shabbath meal. A pan lay on the stove and she touched it, sniffed it, it had a strong sweet smell and it looked a thick slimy black, not tasty at all. She wiped it with her forefinger and recoiled - ugh - a preparation of crushed nuts and gum, Jacob's ink concoction. Not tasty at all.

While the men were gone she explored the house. There was a half smiling lady in a silver frame on the mantelpiece, with wide cheeks and eyes that stretched across them in black strips. Then she was there again, on the arm of a young and dashing Abe Tabaschsky, on the street in their wedding suits. She found a knitted bear in the sofa crack, curling irons and amber hair clips in the drawers, and sewn red hearts on the corner of the girl's petticoats. The daughter who had married and had a baby must have been half a child herself. She could have passed the bear straight on from one childhood to the next in the same breath.

Then Rosa explored the room that was the eating room in the evening, the girl's bedroom at night, the bookdealers' library by day. A book was laid out on the table, that Father Tabaschky had been reading to himself.

Rabbi Yochanan the Sandalmaker used to say: Every assembly for the sake of Heaven will bear fruit.

She pondered it, in its spidery script. The sandalmaker, Yochanan made sandals by day and prayed for his people by night.

She liked the sound of Yochanan the Sandalmaker, but he was a stern master, uncompromising, and if you are not fruitful, well then, you are fruitless.

And one that is not for the sake of Heaven will prove fruitless.
How like a rabbi.

The place where Jacob disappeared during the day she had never seen, and she drew back the heavy velvet curtain that divided it from the rest of the room. It felt like a sacred place, and instinctively she stepped backwards. Two desks were pushed up under the windows with the shutters flapping against the edge of the sills. A half finished parchment was rolled out under two ink-wells, and the strokes of the pen wound into the grain of the paper like the trail of a spider. The goose feather pen lay on its side, and the well of ink beside it ready for refilling. Rows of tiny lines were laid across the parchment like hairs, preparing the nib's route over the rest of the page.

In the afternoon, Jacob walked with her through the city streets. Away from his father, he talked quite a bit, and bossed quite as much as Abe did. He showed her the market where she could buy fruit, the kosher butcher, the small apartment where the men met to pray and the children to study, the teachers' room and the Jewish school.

'I am staying a while?'

'Maybe you will stay a while. If you stay, these are the places you should know.'

He paced through the streets in a fast troubled way, looking out edgily, steering her gently without looking at her, just glancing off the corner of her chin or the edge of her shoulder with his eye. She was a beautiful woman he was half ashamed, half proud to be with. From leaving the door to returning, he had cast over her the sense of the taboo, the secret, the hidden. Without even having looked at him, Rosa felt afraid of what she might reveal if she were to do so.

So the first day passed, and it was Sunday, and on Monday Jacob took her to the de-lousing centre and waited outside for her to finish. On Tuesday he prepared a package of tea and chestnuts and coffee, for her to send home to Vigry with a letter.

Dearest Father, dearest Mother,

All I can say is baruch hashem I am safe and I pray that you are too. I want to speak to you only of the things I have to thank hashem for, I have found a wonderful family who are caring for me and I cannot say already how much they have done and how thankful I will always be.

I hope , father, that you still read aloud to yourself with the lights on late at night. What are you reading? I hope, mother, you are lighting the fire and stopping your fingers growing blue. It's so cold now, I worry you are warm enough. I hope you have enough chickens and purple vodka to go down your throat like fire. You must be nice to each other: you said yourself we can't expect others to like us if we don't like each other.

I am lucky, I have plenty to eat here, and in fact I am even getting quite fat. The house is warm, they have a woodburning stove and sitting on the tiles is the warmest place to be.

Mother, you would be pleased, I am learning the Pirke Avot because Jacob, the son reads them to me in the evenings when he has finished work. He read to me:

You should leave your home and go about the world and actively promote peace in the community, as it says: 'Seek peace, and pursue it.'

That was Simeon ben Eleazor. So you see, even the wise men say it is sometimes a good thing to leave home. If you think you can, why don't you come here too as soon as you can? It is safe here, Jacob says it is one of the safest places to be now, because the Russians have a pact with the Nazis and they will stay away from here. Please come.

Here is a secret for you, and then I will quickly seal the letter and send it. I like Jacob, he is quiet and a bit secretive but when he talks it is quite wise and sometimes funny. He is gingery, you know that kind of browny red that we like, Mother? When he stands up straight, he is really tall, much taller than any of the boys in Vigry. He looks like a Russian prince. I wish you could meet him.

I don't know if this letter will reach you safely, but I wish that it does and I will imagine that it has and carry on writing to you and writing and writing until I know you are well,

With my love
your Rosa.

It was another secret, to let Jacob help her wrap and post the present, not knowing that he had been talked about in the letter.

So one day became two, two days became a week, a week became a month. She did not go, and they did not ask her either to go or to stay. Just they expected her to be there like a daughter, like a sister. She spread her borrowed clothes on the sofa in the sitting room which was also the front hall, where the door opened straight onto the open street and where clients came from early in the morning when she was still rolling the blankets away.

Every afternoon, Abe Tabaschky ran out of breath and put himself to bed in the darkened back room. Jacob worked behind the velvet curtain, and she heard him moaning and sighing and praying, his nib scratching the parchment. For hours she sat the other side of the curtain and laid the books from the shop open on her knee, dusting them, reading them, writing the prices in the ledger, dusting them, reading them.

'Your eyes will go, reading in the dark,' she said, when he appeared from behind the curtain, his eyes narrow and red from squinting.

'I need to work like this,' he said.

He would bite his lip, and sometimes his tongue would peak out and suck strands of beard.

'Don't wait for me while I work,' he said. 'I can't have any distraction, knowing you are sitting there.'

'Let me help you, then.'

'Maybe it would be a good thing for you and for us too if you take orders and keep the ledgers. Maybe this is your talent, to read the books and to organise the men.'

'Then teach me.'

He sat beside her, and laid out the ledgers and the accounts, moving the lamp across the table so they could both lean into its light and see more narrowly.

'Now look at this, see. We have a sliding scale of fees. It's good business, sometimes to be kind, sometimes to be tough. The business is to know which is which, and when is when. We do *tefillin, mezuzot, ketuba, get,* and *sefer torah,* you know this: but you need to know, how much is each worth? The *yshiva* , they send their boys for the tefillin here, they collect it here with their own hands. You put the tefillin into the very hands of the boy, and tell him he must sign the receipt here. Now this receipt, it guarantees the thing was perfect when he took it away, perfect, that's my job and I make sure of that. Now if they come back and say this is blotted, this is smudged, here it's torn, there it's torn, you know, you can be sure, it was them that did it, you have the guarantee signed.

Now, for *mezuzo*t, the family will send a boy, sometimes too young, they should be in school, their braces hanging round their knees. I put the house of God into his hands and hope God will keep him without dropping my house of God in the ditch on the way home. Now for the *sefer Torah* only five holy men is enough, you will receive the rabbi and his friend, his teacher and his student and the father of his student and they will be proud to carry it and bandage it.

The favourite for me is the *ketubah*. I do them with birds and flowers, fruit and fish, I do them in gold and in colours and sometimes the whole family comes to collect, the happy groom and father of the groom and the mother of the groom, all come to collect. This you will like, the happy occasions. The divorces, they're not so pretty, but we do good business with those.'

Rosa learnt her lessons well. As the weeks went by, it was she who greeted the rabbis, their students and teachers, the bridegrooms with their parents, the bar-mitzvah boys with their fathers. She inscribed the ledger with their orders and took the deposits they left rolled up in paper cones, while Jacob and Abe worked at their desks, bending under the lamps with their goose feathers and their noses almost rubbing the parchment and the heavy curtain making their corner dusty and sacred.

One night Rosa was woken by the front door opening and closing. It must have been 4.0 in the morning, and the windows were iced on the inside, it was so cold. There was someone in the room, bending over, a crackling noise while he pulled off boots. She gasped, just a split second.

'It's nothing,' he said. Jacob's voice, his few words.

That was all. He padded across the room in his socks to the room she had never entered with the iron bed. This happened the next night too, and the next and again the next; until she couldn't sleep until she had heard him push the door open and let in a crack of the frozen street, claw off his boots on the doorstep and leave them steaming in the darkness by the door. During the day Jacob's forehead would drop down onto the book he was inscribing, and stay there for an hour, with his hand twitching on the desk in his sleep.

'You are out all night, and sleep during the day when you should work.'

'By day I work only for money,' he said.

'And what do you do at night?'

'You know what I do?' he said, 'you know how well I know the forests between here and Vigry? We delivered books, father and I, from my childhood. We travelled there in carriages and sledges and trains, I know every ditch and village and friendly house and home with a mezuza and home with a prayer book. I printed them on my mind and now each memory is the life of a man or the life of a woman. You know what people do to get here, how they hide in ditches, hang onto trains, steal sledges, walk through snow up to their chins? Of course you know, because you did it.'

'I did it,' Rosa said.

'But you know what information is? How information is life? Will you give it now to save a life?'

'You do,' she said.

'Yes, I do.'

After a month, Abe Tabaschky invited Rosa into the back room. She was curious, not a little suspicious.

'Come,' he said, 'I want to show.'

It was Mrs. Tabascky's wardrobe. They both stared at the lines of coats and shoes in silence.

'She was a *balabooste*' Abe said. 'She would want the clothes are worn by an elegant lady. She is too far to wear them, but you, you can do that instead. She will be pleased.'

'I don't want to take her clothes. No, I couldn't possibly.'

'What you couldn't possibly? You want they are useless here? Good clothes, why waste? You want you go naked, catch death of cold? Death you can get other ways, why this way? Are you crazy not to take it? Take it, take it, what good is it to her, are her arms so long she can get dresses from out the cupboard and be in Poland? Touch them, you think they bite?'

Rosa touched them as she might have touched Mrs. Tabaschky, had she come quietly into the room. Respectfully, with a sense of her privacy, touched each one, the dresses for Sabbaths and for bar-mitzvahs and for sitting quietly on the tiles of the woodburning stove sewing hearts onto petticoats.

'The coat, I'll just borrow the coat until she returns.'

It was the coat Rosa saw on Moscow sledges in picturebooks and in her dreams, with tigery fur draped from neck to toe, draping lush and full over her shoulders and lined deeply with another soft pelt of fur.

'We did very well, we did very well,' Abe sighed.

So Rosa's life was a strange yes and no. Yes she had untold blessings - boots that hugged her like a lamb, and each day it mattered that she thought clearly and worked quickly and passed books from hand to hand, holding sacred texts in her arms as no woman ever had. Each day Jacob read to her from his favourite books, and they would discuss it, the sayings of the fathers, the laws of Maimonedes. the tracts of Mishna, and she felt her landscape unfolding. But no, no because there was no word from home. Day after day, there was still no word. And for Jacob and Abe it was the same. Day after day, no word for them from Mrs. Tabascky and Julia on the other side.

One day, as she was walking with Jacob, she met the stonemason from Vigry in the street.

'Lunke! Lunke!'

'Rosa Klein.'

'I have longed to find you. You are well? Are you well? Is Lola well? Are you living here, did you come here safely? I have thought of you and thought of Lola so often.'

'Lola speaks of you too.'

'How is she? How is Lola? I would love to see her. Can I come, can I come now to see her? If I come with you, will she be there?'

'Lola isn't there.'

'She isn't?'

'We are moving away.'

But it was Lunke, moving away from Rosa as fast as she moved towards him, following him over the street as he walked like a crab half towards and half away.

'Where are you moving to?'

'You can't come there.'

'Lola said to visit her,'

'She made a mistake.'

'No!'

'Lola can't see you. She doesn't want to see you. Lola and I, both of us. It is better to say I never saw you.'

'What do you mean?'

'I never saw you. I knew you but I am forgetting you,' and he turned away so his back was the wall, the back of his head, the edge of his ears, the hair on the top of his neck, everyman's head, any face, moving away from her, moving fast away from her. She watched the woman in the coat screaming,

'You can't walk away, you can't!'

and gradually, as Jacob led her away, recognised herself, with horror recognised she had stepped out of herself and gone briefly mad.

'Lola was my friend, I loved her,' she sobbed. 'Lunke was our friend, I always loved them.'

'He's a gentile.'

'I never minded. I forgave them.'

'You were wrong to forgive them. They are not your friends.'

'You are wrong, you are wrong, you don't understand anything,' she screamed, and beat him with her fists so he held her arms, and she butted him with her head, and he let her do it, butt him until she was too tired to carry on, and he let her droop in his arms, and all the time, said not a word, just let her break to pieces in his arms and gradually feel him like a fort around her build her back together.

From that day Rosa felt loss in a different way. She learnt not only that people were lost from your five senses: not only that you couldn't any longer see them, or touch their hand or smell their clothes or taste their cheek when you kissed them or listen to them laugh or snore or read poetry. That some people you had to lose too from your heart: you had to cast them out, so you didn't pine for them, or turn over memories of them, or catch your breath when you saw the same footstep or the same coil of hair or the same lisp or the same dimple in someone else. You had to send them out of your heart. Lola and Lunke were the first ones.

She learnt too that Jacob was a sandalmaker by day, a healer by night.

Six months after she arrived in Vilna, Rosa and Jacob had an evening alone together. Father Tabaschky was staying with the school teacher in the next village. It was the only time. They were very proper, the same as they were every other night. She lit candles, as if it was Friday night.

'Why candles, Rosa. It's not Friday.'

'I thought they would be nice,' she said.

She could hear he was not swallowing comfortably. She thought maybe she had made the noodles too thick.

'The candles are too nice,' he said, at last. 'They make you look too beautiful.'

Then she found it difficult to swallow too. Maybe she had made the soup too hot.

'It's difficult to live like this, with you so close every day like a sister. But not a sister, I don't feel as if you are a sister.'

He had been staring at his soup, but then he looked up and she had to look at him too, and both their faces were red, and both of them were shivering.

'You are not my sister. In my heart you are already my wife.'

She gave a cry. She couldn't help it. She thought maybe this would be a beginning, but he had travelled already to the end.

'In a normal world I would court you, and take you on my arm into the streets, buy you amber earrings and invite you to our Friday meals, let all the family say 'and what a beautiful girl, when is the happy day?', and tease them with not replying, travel to your village, sit at table with your mother and father and wear the cap with the gold thread while your father says the prayers, travel to you in winter on the sledge holding the ring in my glove, and ask to marry you, and toast the engagement with the Friday wine, toast it with your people, toast it with mine, Julia and mother baking bread for your father, your father and mine sitting on the bench together with a vodka while we watch for the women's backs to turn in the kitchen and kiss and touch each others' lips and eyes. In a normal world I would show you slowly and in a thousand ways how graceful, gentle, brave and wise I think you are, how I feel your beauty before I see it, how I feel your beauty when my eyes are closed. But I can't do it that way. I have to do it rudely without knowing your parents and never visiting your village, I have no liberty to tease my family because they care not about marrying now, their minds are set on living from one day to the next, I have to do it rashly and go from our first kiss to our last in one night.'

'The wine has made you drunk,' she said quietly.

'No, the wine has made my head clear so I can speak, and the speaking makes my soul clear and not full of deception as it was.'

He would have said more, but if she didn't kiss him at that moment she would have died of thirst. His face was a watermelon held out to her, and she drank it as if it was the first watermelon in God's creation. She was shaking, bursting with its bright red droplets.

They were out of breath as if they had swum too far and the whole room changed, the whole room became the place where they began. His chest and the ginger hairs of his forearm and her cheek and the tip of his finger and his tongue all pulled into the black centre the place where they drowned drowned lifted up to the warm lick of the lake where the stars span and melted like diamonds on her skin. She lay across his arms and he spread her like a temple on his bed and rolled her into the centre where the sheets bunched and the iron bedhead bowed towards her as she inscribed his body with hers and he inscribed hers with his.

When she woke with him in that strange dark room with the wooden shutters flapping, flowers had bloomed in the night wherever his hand had touched, and his warm body had become a forest where she had laid her footprints and plucked the leaves.

'You know this is God's marriage,' he said, 'and I will have no other.'

'Nor me,' she said, but he put his finger on her lips.

'But you, ' he whispered, 'you must give yourself a chance.'

'What do you mean?' she said.

'One day soon you will leave and find yourself a proper life.'

'This one, this one,' she said, taking his fingers into her mouth and kissing them.

'Not this one. Believe me, a proper life is one with a future.'

'With you.'

'Wherever you go, you are written in me, and I am written in you.'

So she was safe, and curled against him like a warm bird.

In the morning she wrote to Father and Mother.

Dearest Father, dearest Mother

I want you to know that even in this dangerous and cruel world something wonderful has happened. I am engaged to Jacob, the boy I told you about who has been so kind. I know him very well, it is not like he's a stranger. I have been living in his family house for six months. He has good work, he is a scribe and everybody in the whole region comes to the house to buy from him. He is a great success. Father, you must know him. He remembers you coming to the house to buy books and I remember you bringing them home.

His father Abraham Tabaschky is like you, always giving me advice, and he does the cooking with an apron tied up round his armpits. He is too tired now to do very much work, and he sleeps every afternoon and runs out of breath: but he and Jacob work together and gradually he is passing on to me all the business side of their work.

I know you would be so happy. Jacob would love to meet you but we know it is difficult to travel: all the same we are all still hoping you will arrive soon in Vilna. Jacob could arrange it if you just say.

You didn't answer my last letters. I hope and pray you will be able to answer this one.

Yours, now very happy, engaged
to be Rosa Tabaschky

'Why should we not marry now, why not today, when we could do it today, when the rabbi would be only too pleased to have something nice to do?' she said the next morning. And again, the next day, and the day after that, and again the one after that.

'Because this is not the world for our unborn child.'

'Because a fiancee cares for her own life, but a wife cares for the life of her husband. A fiancee is free to leave, but a wife is not.'

All of them were riddles she hated and she chose not to understand. She pretended it was just a long engagement, but Jacob's delays, his fierceness frightened her.

'Now,' he said, one day, as the days of 1941 grew longer towards the
summer equinox and the silence from Vigry grew heavier and louder
each day.

'We have been in the eye of a needle, a window of peace,' he said, 'and
it is closing. See this light, each day I see it dimmer. Now if you could
find a way to let the light in again, would you not take it? I have a chance
for you.'

'I don't want a chance if it's not with you.'

'Your chance is mine: with us, it's the same. Not two mice in a trap: one
only.'

'You mean, first I leave, then I help you to leave?'

'That's the way it would be, if you are brave enough.'

'You go first, I'll stay.'

'That's not how it works, Rosa. This time it has to work differently.
You have papers to enter Switzerland, you have a place to go. There is a
Jewish homeland in the east where you can wait until the time is right.
It's name is Borobidjan, and you will be waiting for passage to
Switzerland. When all this is over they will receive you, the Abelhofers
of Switzerland.'

'Why should they receive me?'

'They had a daughter, your age, exactly your age. Maya Abelhofer. Say
her name.'

'Maya Abelhofer. Ach, it's strange.'

'You say it well. Here your father has saved you, in teaching you perfect German.'

'Why should I say her name?'

'She would be twenty one this year, like you. She is a Swiss gentile, you
are not. This is the only difference between you and her, but this difference is very important. So important, you must change into her.'

'Where is the real Maya Abelhofer?'

'Already it is too late for her.'

He handed her the papers, warm from his hand, wrapped in torn
brown paper, wrapped again and again so she had to spread the sheets
over the arms of the chair. In the middle, sitting like a human heart, was
Maya Abelhofer's passport. Rosa turned the pages, so Maya's face fell
out, speckled from her journey, browning, her eyes close together and
dark, her cheeks a gentle pale line down to the pointed edge of her chin,
her dark hair coiled tightly round her head and ears.

'It could be you, could it not?'

'How did she die?'

'She is beautiful, isn't she?'

'How did you get this?'

'She would have given it freely, if she could.'

'What happened to her?'

They both stared at the face until it seemed the softly closed lips moved and the skin began to breathe.

'She drowned. It was a natural death, it had nothing to do with war.'

'There is nowhere to drown in Switzerland. I don't believe.'

'There are lakes.'

'I won't be Maya Abelhofer. Give this back to her.'

Jacob gripped her suddenly, roughly.

'Don't you understand. Rosa Klein has only days left. Maya Abelhofer has a lifetime.'

It was the next day, the train.

'I picked mushrooms,' Father Tabashcky said, putting a brown paper bag into her hand. This would have been hard work. A carriage ride to the forest, bending over at the roots of trees, turning over the leaves. It would have hurt his back, it would have used his breath.

'No, no, you must eat them,' she said, 'they are your work.'

'Here, for safekeeping then. Send them back when you're finished with them' and he winked.

Jacob made her pack a suitcase of Julia and Mrs. Tabachsky's clothes. He stood over her, and waited for her to do it. Then they walked to the station silently, he looking ahead awkwardly, furtively, just like the very first time they walked through the Vilna streets. The station was packed, people with battered suitcases and long coats, chains of children holding on to each other, laden like packhorses with satchels and scarves. No-one was speaking: the children weren't howling or crying or talking. Everything was frozen, apart from the train itself. The train was snorting, steaming, a monster, a troll. Shoulders and backs were walls, children were welded to parents like steel, the ground was an obstacle course of bundles and suitcases with metal corners.

Jacob folded Rosa into his coat, and she let him, and they stayed there while the crowds pressed around them, and she put her case down for a moment, then remembered and picked it up again.

'When will you meet me?'

'The minute I can.'

'When? Tomorrow catch the train to Moscow? I'll wait for you, I'll stay in the station until you come.'

'No, don't do that. When you get to Borobidjan, remember who you are. You are Maya, and she will write me a message.'

'You say you'll come when you can but you don't say when.'

He could make no time with his tongue, he could not make his tongue lie. Even now she did not believe that he would stay behind, and that he meant to send her out of Lithuania without him. His silence was like stubborness, it made her hate him.

'You won't come! You won't come! You never meant to come!' she shouted, beating his large coat with her fists so the frost fell off in lumps.

'In this thing alone you have no brains,' he said

'I see what you do with brains,'she spat at him,'I have a heart. Marry me! Mary me now on the station! Here, before I go, marry me!'

He gripped her shoulder until it hurt.

'Listen to me. My father will die soon, of this I am sure. He will not need a bullet or a knife. He will need only his heart. Do you understand me? He cannot move and I cannot leave him.

You want to drink my poison? Do you want to? What I give you is the gift of life. It is the greatest thing I can give you from my love. Now catch that damn train! If you love me, go!'

She was afraid of his fury. She wondered at the fierceness he would be as a husband. But the crowd was prising them apart and lifting them away. He pushed Rosa in front of him. And his height and fury made people give way and propelled her forward like a claw affixed to his arm. The crowd threw her onto the steps of the train like a sack. He stayed below on the platform, and it was hard to forgive him for staying on the platform and hard not to forgive him. He was jostled and shoved, blotted out by elbows and children handed through open windows. Shoving passengers pressed her against the window till her nose became a snout, she hung on with her nails, tried to wave goodbye but was carried away from the window in the press of bodies as the train began to move. It fumed and shook itself like a dragon, throwing them in a heap against the carriage doors: and they were pulling away from the station's jaw and the silent children, out through the steaming tunnel somewhere east into the muzzled forests of Siberia. In the black well of forest, figures sprang against the trains' haunches. She heard the thud of flesh against metal, and eyes catching her for a split second before they fell back into the night.

An old lady with a headscarf opened a carriage door and pulled her in by the edge of my coat.

'Come, sit inside', she said.

At first glance there was no room left in the carriage. The old lady's family seemed already to be occupying it in layers, child heaped upon parent heaped upon satchels, knitted dolls and piles of boots tied together by the laces. She lifted a child onto her knees, howling, her plaits bolt upright in her head.

Rosa could not sit. She could feel the bodies clutch the windows and drop back, banging against the carriage metal, thudding back into the ditches. Three guards in the corridor were sharing a bottle of vodka. Their singing was getting louder and louder.

'They're harmless,' the old lady said, reading Rosa's mind. 'They're too drunk to be dangerous.'

The old lady, supervising the door, slid it shut and tapped her head as if to say, 'They are mad. The men are mad.'

The train was moving in a tunnel of freezing darkness and there seemed never to be landscape, only the laughter of the guards in the corridor drinking vodka and playing cards, the long rattled breathing of the old woman snoring in the corner of the carriage, the chundering of her grown-up sons in their sleep. And Rosa sat upright looking out through the window at her own image, a ghostly negative in the glass.

What a way to leave. What a messy stupid way to leave. All through the journey, the rattling, the snoring, the chundering, the vodka-drinking, Jacob repeated through her as if they had turned inside out and it was she left behind and him on the train. The landscape crumbled as they passed it, broke off and hurtled out into the blackness so she wanted to stop the trees and barns flash by, shout 'Let me keep that,' before they passed and crumbled and were lost.

In the morning, Rosa opened the bag of mushrooms and passed them round the carriage. At the bottom was a lozenge of paper, folded and folded so it was the size of a thumbnail. She felt it inside the bag, let her nail slide under the folds to count how many there were, careful they should not tear. Then she excused herself. In the stinking toilet, she unfolded the paper and read it in the light of the grimy window.

Memorise me. I am your name and your address.

Maya Abelhofer
Phonixstrasse 90
Pacino
Switzerland

You will find me 3 hours from Zurich when you are ready.

Then she tore up the paper into small pieces and ate it, piece by piece.

The next day the German army occupied Vilna. That day or the next day the locals went on a spree of destruction against their Jewish neighbours. Was that the Tabaschkys? was Lunke there? or Lola?

I can't quite make out any of the faces, all the detail is lost. I don't know if it was some nightmare, or something I read, or just the terrible stories that travellers invent. I waited for him. I wrote to him from Moscow, and Borobidjan, and then the places on the way to Switzerland, the boats on the Baltic, the trains through the Alps, and when the war ended I thought maybe I would hear and wrote to him from London, to every Jewish agency and relief agency and family tracing agency. I sent my letters every day into the empty space of the train. I didn't give up in case just one of these reached him and in case he too hadn't given up and was waiting somewhere.

Then one day a letter came from Australia.

4th June 1946

'I knew Jacob Tabaschky. We were in Belsen together. I cannot tell you about this place, but maybe you know. Jacob was a strong man and they gave him to work. He never finished to have courage. His courage helped to others. We had many talks; he knew books by his heart and he would speak them to us. He thought he would see to the end but unfortunately not. He was taken with typhus July 1944. He did speak of you and had hope you would meet again. So I know of you and wish you long life.

His father was blessed to see no more of this place. He died of his heart the day the Germans come, in his own house.

You are lucky to know these good people. They were both blessed, and to have no regrets for your life,

Yours

Ryszard Arkaschky

June 4th 1946. The next day, Rosa Klein visited the matchmaker.

*   *   *

Rosa is looking for Maya Abelhofer in Pacino.

Her other self.

The one who was safe when she was in the mouse-trap.

The one who was in the mouse-trap when she was safe.

Maybe sometimes it's me, I am Maya Abelhofer. Maybe that's who she sees when she looks at me strangely.

I will sleepwalk all night.

I will carry her story, back and forwards, all night.

I found a long corridor to sleepwalk in, the one that ran all round the chalet past the bedrooms, and that opened at the back onto the balcony that smelt of the wind coming black off the back of the rock, round and round, round and round to let Jacob sink into my heels, hang in rags around me.

'You like the night too, then,' I heard, almost in my ear.

'Oh God you made me jump. Don't do that, don't frighten me like that.'

'Well you do like the night, don't you.' It was Donald, the edges of his ears silhouetted by the candle. 'It's a perfect night out there, warm and starlit. I'm going to sleep outside on the balcony. Want to come?'

I thought I did. I thought, I need some help to sleep, I need some help to not think. I had learnt from Leo that I was too suspicious and too closed and I knew it made me lonely.

So I said, 'Yes, yes I will. I'll get a blanket,' and I pretended I didn't see Donald's teeth grinning in the yellow lamplight.

Grandma was free for one moment. I will be free for one moment, not free to be with Donald but free not to be with him. If I want to sleep on a balcony under the stars I can.

I walked in my bare feet to my room to scoop out a blanket. It felt faintly romantic, pulling blankets around in the dark, only it was unfortunate that I didn't feel at all romantic about Donald. I only wanted to be there, because it might help me to sleep, to take my mind off the dreams I had about grandma.

'You're half-way round the other side of the balcony,' Donald hissed.

'What does it matter? I'm here to sleep, not to talk to you.'

'I thought the idea was to keep me company.'

'I never said that. The idea was to sleep under the stars. That's what you suggested.'

Everybody here was so annoying.

'Well since it was my idea you could be more friendly. You, you're so up tight, you know that. I've watched you and you don't give away a thing. What's up, what is it you're hiding?'

'If you don't shut up, I'll go back to my room.'

To my surprise, Donald went quiet, and I rolled onto my back, and pulled the blanket up to my chin. The stars sucked round and round, some of them sharp as crystals, others milky pimples, and I felt better to know they were there and it had been their sky too and still was. I was thinking about this, when I heard Donald's drone bringing me back to the balcony.

'You didn't like my poem.'

'No,' I said, because I wanted to go on thinking about the stars and what they had seen.

'How do you know about writing?'

'I write diaries. I always have done, ever since I was nine.'

I could see his head craning round over the blanket to look at me.

'Just writing about yourself is very limiting, you know. It's not really an artistic process at all.'

'I don't just write about myself. I write about people I meet and what I think about them, and what they say and do.'

'I bet you haven't written about me in your diary.'

'I have, actually.'

Now Donald pulled himself up onto his elbow and blocked out the stars.

'Have you really! Have you actually written about me in your diary?'

'Yes, but you wouldn't like it, what I've said.'

He dropped back under the blanket, and the moon popped out again.

'Well I wrote about you, in my poem.'

'I know, but I didn't know what you were talking about.'

'Why don't you lie here naked? You'll feel better. It's great. The air is really warm.'

Oh no. Donald is trying to do something by himself again. I didn't even want to look, to see what had appeared above Donald's blanket, the fuzzy pinkness in the dark.

'I don't want to. I feel safer like this.'

'Safer? What's unsafe? Don't you trust me?'

'No.' There, it was out. Easy as pie. Straight from my pre-life-enhanced life style.

'Come off it. Do you think I'll rape you or something?'

'I thought the whole idea was to lie here and watch the stars quietly.'

He went quiet and I was relieved. I had done that well. I listened to his wheezing beside me, and tried not to look at his unwelcome thighs thrown to the night air.

As the night rolled over my skin I began to feel quite forgiving. Maybe Donald had the best intentions after all. I would never have thought about sleeping on the balcony, had he not suggested it. Maybe, as long as my nature is so closed, I will never have a night like Rosa did on the iron bed. Maybe he has helped me to be less closed.

I was thinking about that, and wondering what other things I could stop resisting, and even whether I might throw off my clothes too , when a dreadful throat-wrenching roar split the night peace. Though we had been silent before, we both froze. It took me a while to work out what had happened: that it was a couple exploding with pleasure, somewhere else on the balcony.

I didn't know what to think. Leo had talked so much about feeling safe with each other so we could relate as whole people, not just as men and women: and we had all just met for the first time, and were practising this. I was feeling shocked, when Donald let out a dreadful guffaw.

'I don't think it's very funny,' I said.

'Come on, little girl. This isn't a monastery. What do you expect? People are on holiday.'

I remembered how, in the session on belonging I had felt miserable, and in the session on dealing with illnesses I had felt sick, and now practising feeling safe I felt really unsafe. Maybe I had joined the advanced enlightenment course by mistake.

I didn't sleep too well, and lay awake for hours, wondering what Donald would do next, whether the other two on the roof would discover us, what they would do next, who they were and what would happen at sunrise when we all woke up and discovered each other. All of this did distract me from thinking about Jacob and Rosa, but it didn't help me sleep.

In the morning, when the light came up over the balcony and geraniums, there was only a crumpled sheet left the other end of the balcony.

CHAPTER EIGHT

Thursday

Until now the nights and days felt separate. But since I shared that night on the balcony with all those people, the nights have become less secret. It is strange what you show to people you don't trust, and what you don't show to people you do trust.

When Leo said our opening circle was about 'making peace' I couldn't understand. I had an image of Rosa's war and Jacob's peace and couldn't think how we could make these in Pacino. Leo's language made no sense. We had to find a partner we hadn't yet worked with, that is, someone we didn't like very much. We had to share 'the top of our mind'. My mind had no top at all. Everything about my mind was at the end of a tunnel. But Isobel found the top of her mind easily.

'I never want to leave here,' she said, 'I feel completely fulfilled here and I dread the end of the course.'

She was wearing a shirt tied round her neck with shoestrings, and you could see the knobs of her shoulders with all the bones standing out.

'All the things I want in life are here and I just dread what might happen after Sunday.'

I wasn't allowed to say, 'why?' but even so, I said,

'Why?'

'Because I feel feminine and delicious, that's how he makes me feel, and I feel strong, like really strong, I could just get on now and do things because well, this man really loves me, that's what I feel, he's all loving and sensuous and it's like a religious experience with him. So I don't want the week ever to finish in case then we have to say things and make commitments, now it can just go, you know, I know I will see him every day and every night and it's no effort, we don't have to do any special thing to be together, and that's so good, you know, mostly I have to worry they may go away, and it's so great not to worry because there's nowhere for him to go.'

She talked into space, her eyes were looking out as they did towards the kitchen on the sausage day. Sometimes she picked up her hair and dropped it, sometimes she hitched up her shirt, but she never looked in my direction. I felt like the wall.

I didn't know what to say. I thought I knew who this person was who made her feel so great and I had a good idea where she had been with him last night and what he would do at the end of the week and where it would all go. I would never forgive him for laughing at me, for wearing no clothes in the corridor, for spoiling the balcony and the stars. Although he called me little girl whenever he could, I was grown-up enough to know he would hurt me if he could, and not to let him.

But Isobel, for all her snootiness towards me, didn't know all that. Though I didn't care about her at all, I found I was listening. I was thinking, 'oh my God, she's manic, she's a bit mad,' when she suddenly looked at me, with her hair in her mouth, and said,

'What do you think? Do you think I'm mad?'

'Oh no, ' I said. 'But you must be in love a lot.'

She looked at me as if it suddenly mattered what I said.

'But do you think it's mad to be so much in love?'

'It's not mad. But it's dangerous. You get lost, loving someone too much. You end up with nothing left for yourself. If they walk away, you end up just a shell.' It just popped out. Rosa said it, I didn't. She looked at me, amazed.

'You know then?' she said.

Then Leo rang the little prayer bell to change over. I noticed he wouldn't look at us at all. I thought that was strange, as I usually saw him every morning looking at Isobel's shorts.

When it was my turn I suddenly felt too tired to make something up.

'My grandmother visits me at night,' I said.

'What, past the night porter?'

'Yes.'

'God, I thought this place got locked up at night.'

'She doesn't come past the night porter, I don't think. I don't think she uses doors at all.'

'What does she use?'

'I think about her and she appears.'

Isobel nodded and said,

'I know what you mean.'

I never expected Isobel to say that.

'What does she do?'

In these sessions you weren't meant to ask questions or stop the other person talking. But I liked her questions and I was glad she asked them. It even made me like Isobel a bit.

'She tells me about her life. She doesn't tell me. You know what I mean, she actually takes me there. You know what, my dad's name is Jacob and she would always say, 'Jacob your father,' as if there was another one, and on Friday nights she would pray in Hebrew then she would say, 'blessings to Jacob your father'. But all along there was another Jacob, and all along she was thinking about him.'

We both sat in silence. Isobel had dropped her hair and T-shirt and was staring at me and I didn't mind at all. I thought I might cry and I hated the idea of crying and Leo thinking it was something to do with his peace session.

'Who was he?' Isobel asked at last.

'Someone she loved,' I said. It was the other sacred word. I had let the word escape. 'I'm sorry,' I said to Rosa.

'I'm sorry,' I said to Isobel, 'I can't say any more.'

'Did your grandfather know?'

'No, but when she was with my grandfather she thought about Jacob all the time. I know it.'

'How do you know?'

'She teased him and snapped at him and sometimes they made each other cry.'

'I don't know, that's just how people are with each other.' Isobel said.

Isobel was real after all. Without Leo, she was a real person.

Then Leo rang the bell.

'Don't tell Leo. I don't want him to know,' I said quickly.

She threw me a look of real horror.

'Why should I tell Leo?' she said, so intensely, I thought maybe I had got everything wrong.

The theme for today was journey. I could still feel the rhythm of the train and see the landscape broken off through the black windows. Leo was saying that our rites of passage, our rituals, were stations on the journey. Rosa inside Jacob's coat: that was a station. Saying goodbye to Geoffrey, mum and grandma at Victoria Station, that was a station.

We had to draw our life like a journey, with mountains, streams, deserts, forests. We could use paints, crayons or clay, or we could cut out masks.

*　　　*　　　*

My journey

My first important journey was to the boy's school when I was thirteen. The girl's choir were joining the boy's choir for Elgar's *Dream of Gerontius* with the youth orchestras of north London. All the girls in the class were suddenly terribly interested in Elgar, though we had never heard of him before. I wanted to go too.

'I'm going to sing with the boy's choir,' I said to mum.

'But you're not in the choir,' she said,

'You can't sing for toffee,' said Hannah.

So I went to Miss Doubleday the music teacher.

'I want to join the choir,' I said.

I had never really thought about it before, because only the girls with glasses who were good at maths were in the school choir. Until that moment, it wasn't at all something you did if you wanted to be admired by older girls in stockings.

'Sing me something,' Miss Doubleday said.

I sang the seduction song from Carmen which I had practised in front of the mirror, combing out my hair to look like a gypsy and singing la la la instead of the words.

'You have a very nice texture to your voice,' she said. 'Let's try a few oral tests.'

She played a few sounds on the piano and I had to go la-la-la to them, then I had to go ta-te-te ta-te-te at different speeds.

'I think your voice has matured very nicely, Laura. You are lucky. You also have a good musical ear.'

'I have a good musical ear,' I said at dinner that night.

'That's a laugh,' Hannah guffawed, and some potato spurted out of her.

'Then how come you only hear what you want to?' dad said.

'Oh shut up, that's got nothing to do with it,' I spat.

'Now don't start squabbling,' mother said, which we did, just because we had peas in our mouths.

So I went to the first rehearsal of the *Dream of Gerontius*. It told the story of a man being judged at his death, and meeting a whole crowd of mean dancing demons, and ending up finally in heaven. At the rehearsals, we had to practise smiling and making notes in our stomachs and further down and also making high notes in our foreheads. We had to shout aaaa to the opposite wall, opening our mouths and making our stomachs go hard. At first we giggled and blushed, but then Miss Doubleday would reach for the piano and our noises would lift up onto a bed of bunchy dark brown chords.

After a month we were ready to rehearse with the boys. Lots of the girls came to school with their elder sister's high-heeled shoes in plastic bags. Before the boys arrived in our school hall, they were all in the toilets hitching up their skirts and changing their shoes. Some of them fell over on the way to their seats.

The boys were all wearing their blazers and school ties. I thought we would be sitting next to the boys, but they all sat separately at the back, so you would have to crane your neck round to see them. Miss Doubleday began the voice exercises and the boys giggled at the back as much as we did. In fact, Miss Doubleday had to shout at them to get them to behave.

We began the *Kyrie Eleison* with Miss Doubleday on the piano and the girls came in with papery voices and floated off into little puffs of ash. Then the boys' voices rolled in and I was knocked through the back of my neck into a beanstalk world with giants rolling boulders round the edges of the world. I could feel them thumping behind me with their giant feet, and the benches were purring like cats. The sound through the floor grew trees up through my heels and washed my stomach dark like a plum.

'Now boys, you need to watch the beat, not each other!' Miss Doubleday shouted. I could feel the dinosaurs snorting behind me, and the giants with troll black hair thundering through the mountains like yetis. But when I turned round to have a quick look, I was shocked to see the row of boys still there, some of them spotty and with dandruff on their blazers.

The next rehearsal was in the boys' school. It smelt differently to our school, and I kept tripping over muddy trainers and football shorts. The choir master was called Mr. Harris. He was shorter than some of the boys, and from the back you couldn't tell which was the teacher. He turned a Tesco crate upside down on the floor and stood on it. Some of the girls in the front row giggled.

The choir teacher began some exercises with us, and every time he said, 'diaphragm', all the girls in the row where I was sitting collapsed laughing. 'What does he mean?' I whispered. Tina, sitting next to me, said 'Don't be an idiot,' so I never knew. At first I thought he was a very short teacher, but the more we sang with him, the taller he grew. His hair also grew longer and began flying about. When we sang the angels his face began mincing like an angel, and when we sang demons his face became all spikey and mean. There was a boy, Horris or Borris, he didn't like and kept shouting at, 'Borris (or Horris) look at ME, not at the wall!' We all got scared, and looked at him a lot and were glad he didn't know our names. But by the time we reached the final movement, 'Praise to the Holiness', we were all singing for our lives and rolling back the gates of heaven and great hot clouds of glory were leaping down and turning me over on a spit, and we were leaping through hoops of fire with the devils following with red tongues and yellow eyes.

Oh I loved Mr. Harris because of his Tesco box and baton and the way his hair flew over his face and the way he threw it off his eyes with the back of his baton, and the way he jumped on the Tesco box and pointed his toes.

We wore black and white for the concert and I sang angels from the pit of my stomach and devils sprang from my head and heels and Mr. Harris and I went higher and higher on the gold chariot with the horses kicking and foaming on the edge of his baton. At the end, he nodded, he nodded at me, and mouthed,

'Well done, very well done,'

while behind him all the little people stuck in seats clapped and cheered.

At Christmas time Mr. Harris sent me a note in a blue envelope. It was on the boys' school headed paper.

'To the Elgar veterans: We are having a Christmas carol party and would like to welcome the girls to sing with us.'

The note was addressed to Miss Cherry and had his signature on it. I looked at the signature under the lamp and under a magnifying glass and it looked like real ink, not a copy.

The fact that he talked about the 'veterans' and 'the girls' was a bit strange, but maybe teachers had to do things like that when they wrote to schoolgirls, in case they were taken to court. I folded it up, and read it every hour in between lessons. Then Tina said,

'Are you doing the carol thing?'

'What?'

'Did you get that letter from the teacher guy with the little legs?'

I didn't answer because the letter was my special secret.

I wanted to go to the party, but Tina didn't because she said the grammar school boys were no good and she'd found some better ones at the football club.

We practised first with Miss Doubleday, and she gave us a songsheet with all the words. They had titles like, 'Little Jesus meek and mild', and 'Jesu joy of man desiring'. Even ones that began quite promising, like 'Once in royal David's city' ended up with words about Jesus being laid in a crib. The words were so bad, I had to fold them up and hide them in the lining of my maths book in case Mother or Father found them, or even worse, grandma Rosa. But I liked the tunes so much, and I liked the feeling of making Os and OOs with my mouth, and I loved the thought of Mr. Harris pointing his stick at me so much, that it was all worth the secrecy. I had to practice the tunes at the bus-stop or between my teeth in case Hannah recognised them. And when we had carol practice, I had to pretend it was extra rounders.

'It's a funny time of year for rounders isn't it dear?' Mother said.

'We're doing it indoors, in the gym,' I said.

She looked a little surprised, but as Mother didn't know much about rounders she didn't ask any more questions.

Then one day, we had to take a letter home to our mothers. Tina and I steamed it open in the sixth form kitchen. It said,

We are writing to let you know that your daughter has been invited to take

part in a Christmas carol party at the Lord Lupton Boys School on Friday
December 11th at 5.0pm. after school. A school bus will escort the girls from the
girls playground to the boys school hall at 4.30pm. We would be grateful if you
could collect your daughter at the main entrance of the boy's school at 7.30pm.

'They'd never let me if they knew it was Christmas carols, all that
Jesus stuff,' I said.

'Well, we could type it out again and change it. We'll do it tonight on
Samson's typewriter.'

'Samson's got a typewriter?'

'Yea.'

I was impressed.

But it was a small tinny typewriter that punched holes through the
paper, and though we cut the logo of the school paper and stuck it at the
top, and forged Miss Doubleday's signature, then photocopied it for 5p at
the local library, it still looked unconvincing. So we tried the original letter, but painted out the words 'Christmas carol party' and typed in 'geog-
raphy field trip'. The number of letters filled the space almost exactly.

So I went to the party. The school hall was decorated with a giant
Christmas tree covered with hundreds of fairy lights, and there were
streamers and balloons slung between the wood panels and over the football trophies and paintings of headmasters, and the boards with the
names of head boys had been decorated with reindeer antlers. The
school dinner ladies had made hot mince pies and custard, and hot grape
juice with slices of oranges floating inside.

Then the carols and Mr. Harris was wearing white shoes so you could
see him point them and point his stick and point his chin when he pout-
ed, and I sang about Jesus with my mouth full of cheesy sounds virgins
and babies and the strange churchy smell it made in my mouth while the
lights glinted in the school windows and as the light came down the
school prefects lit candles round the room and Mr. Harris's teeth went
blue in the light.

Polly's mother took me home, and I was pink with the excitement and
the taste of custard and purple grape juice.

Mother said, 'Was it a nice field trip?' and I said,

'Oh yes, so so.'

She leaned forward and pulled a green streamer out of my hair.

'Don't tell grandma Rosa about it,' she said.

*   *   *

Donald stopped me on my way to lunch.

'It was good on the balcony, don't you think?'

'Yes, I thought so. But there were too many people.'

'Oh you! You never like anything.'

'I do.'

'You didn't like my poem, though I wrote it for you. You didn't even understand it. What I said was, you only think about yourself. It's true, you do. You never even think about me.'

'I told you what I thought. I thought there were some changes you could make.' I tried to push past him. He was like a mosquito, he picked at you.

'Look, I rewrote it. I did what you suggested,' and he pulled a folded piece of paper from his pocket. 'Will you read it now?'

I wanted to say, 'No, go away,' but I said, 'yes, if you give it to me I will some time.'

'No, will you look at it now?'

He got so near I could smell his breath and wondered whether he had washed after his night on the balcony.

'I'll read the first line,' I said, and opened the paper. It had been folded and folded into tiny squares like one of those party game puzzles.

I know you're out there baby
but you just pretend
you're not here at all and no-one sees you

you've no notion baby
just who's watching you
just who knows you're there when you are sleeping

'You can sing it to the tune of 'Mr Tambourine Man', he said. 'Shall I sing it?'

'No thanks. This poem isn't like the other one at all.'

'No, it's a new one. I scrapped the other one.'

'You said you revised it.'

'Well I did. I did what you said and used modern words.'

'But why do you have to copy someone else's tune? It's no good if you have to sing 'Mr. Tambourine Man' at the same time.'

'Isn't it?' He looked genuinely crushed. I was surprised.

'I don't know. You're the poet, not me,' I said.

He was irritating and I was hungry and didn't want to end up on some awful genitals or armpit table. I pushed him away and went on to the dining room.

I was with Isobel and Daphne, and it was the table for the 'the crown of the head or the Third Eye'.

This is the Ajna chakra, representing intuition, far-seeing, vision and tran-scendence.

To see is to know.

To know is to command.

'I don't like the bit about commanding,' Isobel said.

'It doesn't mean bossing each other around.'

'No, I think it means commanding oneself, directing oneself in the best possible way.' This was Daphne.

'I've no idea how to do that,' Isobel said. 'I wouldn't know where to begin.'

Daphne laughed in a kind way.

'Well I think we've all begun, somehow or another. Otherwise we wouldn't be here.'

'That's not why I'm here,' Isobel mused. 'I'm here because my father sent me.'

We went silent for a moment, so you could hear the fried onions and potatoes crackling. Daphne put her hand on Isobel's, but Isobel moved it away quickly and went on turning over the onions with her fork.

I had to get to the ice cream kiosk for Sean at 2.0. so I missed out the pudding course which was awful smelly-sock cheese. Isobel raised her eyebrows and said,

'Busy?' and I said 'yes', because I didn't mind being mysterious.

I wished myself different in the mirror. I wished my eyes were longer and my bones brighter like Rosa's. I studied myself, as if the roundness would go away, and the shine on my cheeks would grow matt like an adult's. I tried my long sun dress but it made me look like Ophelia, as if I was drowning in sea-weeds. Then I tried my jeans and tied the ends of my shirt in a knot at the waist, but then my shoulders looked like a bull-dog's, and my jeans made terrible wrinkles when I moved. I practiced wearing my T-shirt like Isobel did, with part of it falling off the shoulder, but it just looked as if it didn't fit, not sexy and casual like Isobel's. Finally, in despair I finished with the jeans and the giant man's shirt of Geoffrey's that I loved, because I disappeared inside it, and the collar stood up round my neck like a ruff, and the sleeves puffed at the shoulder like a cowboy.

Now on my way to the ice cream kiosk I had to build Sean's picture again in my mind. When I thought about him spikes came up under my skin. I remembered the milkiness of his face as if I had blown its tiny hairs; and I remembered the crush of blue marbles in his face with the mountains spinning behind him. His face filled the whole window, and the mountains were like toys.

There was no-one by the ice-cream kiosk when I arrived. The baking cones made my nose tingle, and I stood in its scent and waited. A man in a long coat walked by dragging his left leg behind him: and a schoolboy sucking a stick of rock. Both times, I thought it was Sean until they came close, and both times I had a terrible lurch of panic to think that I had misremembered him so badly. But in the end, he appeared and slid into my memory like a knife into soft butter, with bright freckles and a fringe like a blue flag, and a blue-white smile and handshake.

'Oh good to see you, and here is the Swiss handshake, you know. It's the way they do it.'

I chose a tutti frutti and he chose a rum and raisin, and we sat on the fountain edge letting the cream run down our wrists.

'Now how is the holiday going here?' he asked. He ate the ice cream as if they were kisses, large kisses with his mouth and tongue and all his blue-white teeth.

'Oh it's good, it's going fine. In a Centre, a school chalet up the lane there.'

'I wouldn't like that at all as a holiday, sure. Being near a school gives me the heebee-jeebees. I was never a one for school.'

'What about yours?'

'Och I love it, the mountains. Nothing better. Nothing better than the air up there, and not too many blisters now. But the crowd, well they're a rum lot. Dead serious, you know, they take it all awful serious.'

The streets were being hoovered with orange engines and scrubbing brushes.

'Sure I should take one home!' Sean said.

We watched while the brush sucked up paper bags and ice cream cones from the gutters and sprayed the cobbles so their backs shone like wax.

'Well we'd better watch ourselves, you know, in case we dirty the road.'

We laughed and spilt icecream and watched the brush zizzing round the square. The musicians from yesterday had taken up their positions further along the wall. The violinist was sitting on a box and tuning up, looking cross-eyed down his strings. The guitarist was unzipping the guitar case: it peeled off like a duvet. They set up their instruments snug into their bodies - against the lip, over the knee, on the shoulder, and their eyes were all making that cobweb I remember from yesterday, and then the flautist bobbed her head and they all began.

The sounds separated themselves from the tinselly sound of the teapot roundabout in the square. The guitarist was grinning, like he did yesterday and his yellow teddy bear boots padded in and out with the beat.

'Well sure, that's a good sound!' Sean said.

'I like watching them. They all play together so tightly, they're all so close.'

'Now if that's not the Tullochgorum reel!' he said. 'They're doing a grand job with the reel,' and he began whistling to their tune.

We listened the length of our ice-cream cones, then Sean bounced up onto his feet.

'Well, but Laura, I have a plan for you, and that's to show you a mountain, now it's not too much of a walk for a strong one like yourself. What do you say to that, to a walk of sorts?'

'Yes. I'd love it. But we have meditation in the Centre at 4.0.'

'Well now, we have meditation on the mountain any time you like, day or night, you just say the time Laura and there it is. Now we'll go, will we?'

Yes and we went, we took the steep lane up from the lake that wove up between chalets, with balconies hung with baskets of geraniums, and wooden shutters with leaf shape slits, until the lane trickled into a path the width of two feet. At first we had fields like a soft green skin with rock breaking out like the shoulders of bulls, higher and higher until the skin fell off and there was a jigsaw of scree under our shoes. Then I felt the ground rollercoaster under me, and a great cutting away of rock so the mountain plummetted from my right heel for hundreds of feet to a table of grass below me, and we looked down over the heads of cows and beyond that the birthday lights of Pacino with the lake like a silver tray in the middle, and tiny stripes pulling across it.

I breathed fast and let each breath lift me another foot another rock, and each breath had the sharp edge of the ice cream air in it. I followed the hair on the edge of Sean's collar, it moved up in waves like a slow boat, and I followed it, letting the rocks and air race in, and letting the height shrink me. Every so often, and only then, Sean looked round, and said,

'Now, are you alright? You OK there?'

and I panted,

'Yes yes I'm fine'

and we went like this until the lake was a pinpoint and the path was imprinted with sheep hooves and the mountain rounded at last to a rocky knob. Sean threw open his arms and the wind beefed out his armpits and wrapped him like a parachute.

'You see Laura! You see how it is up here. Now here's a place for singing, don't you think!'

Yes yes I spun round, round and round because the world panned out on all sides and I could see the globe in all its roundness, and some of its peaks an old white and some a bone white, and some which fell away like a god's shawl, and in some of its thighs and arms were shining pools and in others were old ice like dirty lace. Only a bird would ever know this, only a bird and us.

'Now Laura, do you need a meditation class now?'

'No no, I don't, it's true.'

'Now as for me, there's nothing else at all I need, only a good companion to see it all with.'

'Not in your walking group?'

'Och no, they're a strange lot you know. They're some for sure a little strange in the head.'

'Some in my group are a little strange in the head too!' and we both laughed the rude laugh you have when you're mean about people, and the birds on the rock took fright and leapt off the mountain into nothing.

'Now sure, there's God's own world up here.'

'You talk about God a lot,' I said. 'You believe in Him?'

'Now if He's there, sure I hope he forgives my blasphemy calling Him up every now and then.'

Then he turned to me, and his eyes were small slits against the sun.

'Now, seriously now, I'm a Catholic and no getting away from that. Job for life. Are you a Catholic?' he said, suddenly.

'No, no. I'm Jewish.'

'Now that's interesting. Now that's another job for life for sure!'

And we both laughed again, and the laugh went dead into the wind and picked up the sound of cows playing their bells in the distance.

We sat with our knees bunched up to our chins and let the wind blow through us.

'Now what was it you were to say to me, you said in your note, now. There were some things you thought to say.'

'I'm not sure whether you will think I'm very strange if I tell you.'

'Sure I will. I think you're very strange already.'

'Do you believe in people being in two places at once, in a hospital bed sick and at the same time somewhere else quite different?'

'Sure, in your head there's all sorts and I believe in them all.'

'You do? Well I have dreams like that, of my grandmother being in my room young and quite different, but I know she is really in a hopsital bed. I dream of that every night, but so clearly it's more real than when I'm awake.'

'Well sure you're getting a good sleep then. Now it wouldn't work so good if you were sleeping with some snoring old goat like I am.'

'Are you?'

'Youth hostels, you can't be choosy about who you sleep with, you know.' And he winked, in a way that made my skin unwrap. 'Now serious though, you say this about your nan visiting, well aren't you the lucky one to see her so clear. There can't be many has that.'

'Do you think so?'

'Oh for sure. Now if you were some dunhead in the family would she choose you now? Or if you'd go saying it's rubbish, then would she go telling you her stories? Sure not. Now it's for a reason, it's all for a reason.'

'Do you think it is all for a reason?'

He stopped and pointed his chin in a thought.

'Well no, for sure some of the things, they're pretty difficult to find a reason, I'd be hard pressed to find one. But other things are pretty easy. The things I like are pretty easy, that's the long and the short of it. Well, but maybe it's because I'm not bright enough, you know.'

'Oh no, you don't think that. You don't believe you're not too bright. Some of the things you say are the best things I've heard.'

He looked pleased, his mouth twitched a fraction.

'Sure that's nice,' he said. 'You're alright yourself.'

And my heart leapt off the rock on the back of a gull.

We walked back down the path until it widened again and flattened and dressed itself and we were back on the paddy grasslands and then the dust-track and the road with its baking armour.

'Now for sure, I know nothing about you, but I hope it's something with your song you're doing when you go home again,' he said, as we dropped back down into Pacino.

'No, it's the law. I'm going to train as a legal executive in my uncle Ezra's company.'

'Sure no? Not the law for you? Well I never, and goodness me I never thought to be up a mountain with an executive.'

'It's not an executive.'

'With a lawyer then.'

'No, it isn't a lawyer either.'

'Well sounds like it's the lawyer type you'll be.'

'I'm not the law type.'

'Well Laura that seems a worry to me, you don't want to go working in any uncle's law company if you're not the law type.'

'You're right,' I said, 'but I don't know what else I should do.'

'Now I don't believe that. You think again. You go back up that mountain and look at the view there and think again. Now never mind those meditations in that school place, you need to be out there and look round and round at the view and see what's there. Now I don't want to be bumping into you in ten years and you say, 'Oh Sean you were right and the law was the big mistake I made.' Now I don't know, I don't know what pushes you or who pushes you or any of that, about your parents and uncles and aunts and maybe all they expect of you. But if you're not the type then don't you go fitting yourself in where it's no good and getting out of shape. Now and don't you listen to me either if I'm saying it all wrong.'

'You're not saying it all wrong. I like it. I want you to say some more.'

'One week a year I get up a mountain and fifty one weeks a year, you know, I'm in an office without a window.'

'That must be terrible for you, when you love to be up mountains so much.'

'Well listen, I did it wrong then and it's more difficult, like, once you've started the mistake. So what I think is, don't start the mistake at all in the first place. Now, as for you, now there's a joy in you and you don't want to go killing it off for no reason. You're not doing some kind of penance.'

'Nor are you,'

and we both laughed, but I felt more like crying than laughing.

A cuckoo clock struck seven above a shoe shop, and the cuckoo came out and did a dance on a wooden tree and all the clock wheels went round and round.

'That there cuckoo's got an Irish jig on him,' he said, and began clicking a tune with his tongue.

We walked back to the Centre, and at the doorway the hot smell from his shirtsleeves made my skin spikey, and I had laughed so much I was hoarse.

Then Sean put a hand in his pocket and brought out a packet wrapped in gold paper.

'A wee gift for you, compensation prize for going to school in the holidays.'

I unwrapped it and inside was a chocolate cockroach with folded wings and a ridged chocolate head.

'Och it's strange I know but the shop was full of them, and I thought well better you didn't miss out. Just close your eyes and think of me when you eat it!'

I put it in my pocket, because I wouldn't eat it for a while.

'I had a great walk, Laura, thank you. It was good you came, and without special shoes and all.'

'Me too, I loved it. I will never forget the mountain, and I'll never forget the things you said to me.'

'Now that's good, it did us both good.' Sean said. 'Now I'll be down by the lake Friday night at 7.0 if you ever cared to join me.'

I stood on the doorstep of the Centre until he had disappeared down the high street and between the chocolate shops and tea shops with pink curtains. The door was open to the Centre and I walked straight through it, straight through where the corridors smelt sweet of ashy incense with strips of light under the doorways, and up to the flat balcony, and stood on the balcony as a breeze began to shake the geranium heads and they burned electric red in the slow evening light.

I looked out over the balcony to the blue head of rock with a rib down it, and then began with the cockroach. First I broke off its wing leaving toothmarks on its back, and the chocolate where my tongue had been went dark and melty, and then I bit that off too and the back with its ridges went crumbly and I licked the crumbs so the second wing began to melt onto my tongue, and only the head was left, so I licked that until it was smooth and wet and it collapsed onto my tongue in a moist black heap.

CHAPTER NINE

Thursday Night

It was nearly time for the evening meal. When I went back to my room, Donald was there.

'You missed the meditation,' he said.

'I was busy,'

'You were never busy before for the meditation,' he said, 'you never missed one before.'

'Well this time I did. I had something else to do.'

He put his hands in his pockets, the way he often did. The pockets had stretched halfway down his trousers.

'Come rowing with me,' he said.

'What?'

'They have these rowing boats painted red and you can rent them for the afternoon.'

'There are all the big passenger boats on the lake. We'd get squashed.'

'No, no not this bit of the lake. It's quiet and nice, especially for people rowing. I saw it, I had a good look. I thought that would be really nice, just to be on a boat floating and we could take sandwiches and lemonade, I would row, you could read my poems, I would bring some for you to read. I saw the rowing boats and this lake, and I thought I would like that, I thought maybe you would come with.'

I almost said,'yes' by mistake, out of a kind of habit of saying 'yes', also because it did sound a good idea to be on a red boat on the lake with sandwiches, but not with Donald.

'I might,' I said instead, 'but I'm quite busy.'

'Well tomorrow after the session, go on, say yes, I've already got the lemonade. I bought it this afternoon.'

I began to make a face for the word, 'maybe' when grandma Rosa appeared by my side, and I gasped.

'Oh, but it's so early!' I cried.

'We could have lunch here first. Will you come?' Donald went on.

'No, it's almost too late,' Rosa said, 'and you must come now or not at all. Will you come?' She was out of breath, she must have run up the stairs and down the corridor, but so lightly that no-one heard or saw. A thin dress lay flat across her girl's chest and her hair was loose in red-brown tangles on her shoulders.

'Yes, yes of course I will,' I said, but she was already turning.

'You'll come on the lake with me?'

'Follow me then, you promise?'

'Yes, yes, I promise.'

I saw Donald's jaw dropping open but I was too busy to work out why.

'I'll bring the lemonade and my poems,then' he said.

But grandma Rosa was sprinting down the corridor with her hair flapping on her shoulders. I ran after her, leaving Donald staring after me with his mouth open.

It was September 2nd 1939, the night Germany occupied Poland. Rosa was in her home village in the north eastern corner of Poland, three weeks after her nineteenth birthday.

*   *   *

Marek was pacing up and down by the door.

'Why do girls take so long?' he was saying.

Father was pacing up and down too, picking up bread rolls laid in a row on the cloth and turning them over as if he had never seen them before.

Luba was packing curling irons.

'Mother, how many dresses will I need?'

'One a day for a week,' Marek shouted from the door.

'What nonsense. She should pack warm boots,' father said.

'What good are boots if she has no clean dress?' mother snapped.

Rosa was tying up her red tangles round her head in bands.

'You look ugly,' Luba said.

'Now girls, now is no time to quarrel.'

'Why does Luba have to be pretty all the time?' Rosa spat.

Rosa stood in her father's library while Luba finished packing. She ran her finger along the spines, the leathery ones, the papery ones, the ones with gold letters, the ones with marbled covers like the patterns in iced pools. She sealed them into her head, anointed them with her finger. The books hadn't changed today, nothing about them was disturbed. Long may it be so, baruch hashem.

Marek was getting impatient and kicking the logs about in the fireplace.

'I'm going alone,' he shouted.

Father held Rosa's shoulders.

'Be nice to your sister. She is the younger one, she can't be as wise as you.'

'She wouldn't want to be,' Rosa said.

'You must take care of yourself, don't neglect yourself even now,' mother said, adjusting Rosa's coat collar.

'You are the one that must take care,' Rosa replied.

'No no, the Germans have no business with old women like me.'

'I mean you and father. You should be nice to each other.'

'What do they want with so many bread rolls?' Father was saying to himself, squeezing the rolls one by one along the cloth.

Marek was now standing outside the door and cold air was blowing into the kitchen. Father put his arm round Marek's shoulder,

'Look after my girls. In one month I expect to see you all back, in one month I want to hear all the stories.'

'You will Mr Klein professor,' Marek said, stamping his feet, 'we'll all be back.'

'There's always room at the table,' said mother.

Luba and Rosa at last were ready and on the doorstep with their warmest coats and boots and stockings and bags with combs and clips and more stockings and boots. On the doorstep they hugged in silence one by one for each parting. No-one knew why they should be crying when it was only a week, a month they would be parting. Mother would continue to bake, to pluck chickens, to sprinkle poppy seeds on dough. Father would continue to read through his new spectacles, holding them down on the page like a magnifying glass, and scholars would continue to stream into the front room to read his books and annoy mother while she was cooking. Just a few Friday nights would pass with their chairs empty, but it would all go on as usual, with the candles and the embroidered cloth for the bread and the noodles. and then they would be back. In the first war it was like that. This one would be just the same. And yet they were all crying, and could not say why, and the more they hugged the more Rosa could not stop the hot streams wetting her father's shirt as she laid her head against it.

It had to be Marek who walked away first, because none of the others could have done it. They began to walk on the road, the everyday road, to the skating picnic forest, Father and Mother standing against the door's lintel, mother stooping to stop a chicken walking through the door.

They had learnt how to find mushrooms, from Sunday afternoon picnics. You look around the tree roots, turn the grass over with your foot and the tiny button ones are hidden there with purple fins on the underside. The flats opened out into pink marsh with pools which ice over after October. Usually men were there dropping fishing lines down through the ice. No-one today, with the air on the cusp of winter: and they walked in a line, not speaking, Marek at the front, Luba just behind him. She had left a swatch of thick brown hair over her shoulder, the way Marek liked it.

In front of Rosa Luba tripped over a treetrunk and went down heavily onto the toes of the tree. Marek pulled her up, scooping her under the
shoulders. He brushed her down with his hand.

'You must take care because I am your warden now,' he said.

'Why do you have to be so helpless?' Rosa snarled to Luba through her
teeth. 'It's not the time to start flirting.'

There had always been spirits in these forests, Lola and Rosa had
talked of them during picnics, when Marek was splashing in the freezing lake and Elias was sitting on tree trunks with his nose in a book.
They were there now, ushering the group in to the long spikey shadows
and the black empty branches, the cracking pools with wolves footprints
frozen in the ice. Marek grew taller in the forest, jumping up to touch the
branches, and cracking open ponds with his fingers so they could watch
the threshing of a trapped tiddler. They walked on mulches of leaves
and crisp frost and patchworks of fallen branches. At times, Marek
walked at Luba's side, touching her arm to steer her forward.

'You walk faster than your sister,'

'Only when you push me. She is much stronger.'

'You need more looking after.'

'I hope I am not a burden.'

'Not a burden at all.'

At midday they stopped and opened their sacks. It was a monk's meal,
of bread and water, and raw eggs which they drank down neat like
vodka.

'It's not the forty years in the desert,' Marek said.

'It'll be worse than that if we finish our provisions too soon.' Rosa
said. Marek was eating as if his bag would refill like manna.

'Well I'm hungry,' he said, 'while we've got it we might as well eat it.'

Rosa worried about his philosophy, but admired his will.

Their first stop was Mirka Wilk's trout farm. She was feeding the tiddler trouts in the tank. They were the size of worms, wriggling as she
broke the water with their feed. She carried on for a while, with her back
to the trio, moving from tank to tank, bending over them and moving the
water with the end of her fingers. The tanks were graded, one for each
size trout: they grew silver and caught the light with pink edges. They
floated to the top, their mouths gasping, pecking at the water to catch the
seed.

'They are happy to eat and swim,' Mirka said,'that's all they want in
life.'

The tiddlers wrote question marks all over the water. They were hardly born, yet for a moment Rosa envied them. For a moment, being the
width of a hair seemed safer and travelling round a tank seemed a bet-

ter journey and eating seed seemed more comfortable than her journey; and the furthest from grown and silver with gills and fins, the safer, the furthest from grown-up the better.

Mirka picked out a fully-grown trout for their dinner, held it tightly round the gills to stop it threshing, and slit it from head to tail so its orange eggs spilt out. They ate it braised over the fire.

'Are there only three of you?' Mirka said,'I was expecting six.'

'The three Radescevsky boys are following behind, maybe an hour behind us,' Marek said.

'An hour is late,' Mirka said, 'they should be careful in the dark. They should not make light.'

'No, no they won't make light,' Marek said.

Luba, Mirka and Rosa slept in the kitchen by the stove. The stones were still warm from the fire she had made, but they were bumpy and knobbed and they spent the night shuffling on their coats to find a smooth patch. Marek slept in the back room which was cold as ice. In her sleep Rosa heard the other three arriving and going out to sleep under the trout tanks in the barn.

'What do you want most?' Luba asked Rosa as they were falling asleep.

'I want all this to be over, so we can all be together again. Then I want to go to the university and become an elegant lady of learning and marry a rich man and live in the city. What about you?'

'I want to go back to Vigry and marry Marek.'

'Oh no, Luba, not Marek.'

'Yes, why not? What's wrong with him?'

'Because he - oh Luba, how can you trust him? He slaughters chickens.'

'That's just stupid. There's nothing wrong with slaughtering chickens. Someone has to do it. That doesn't make him a bad person.'

'Anyway, who says Marek wants to marry you?'

'Oh he does, he told me so.'

'Oh no, Luba, he didn't!'

'Yes, he said I'm the prettiest girl in the village and the one he wants to marry most.'

'It's not the same.'

'Not the same as what?'

'Well, wanting to do something and doing something are different things.'

'You're such a know-all. How do you get to be such a know-all?'

'Oh Luba, just be careful, you have to be careful.'

'Why should I be careful?' she said, and curled up on her coat, smiling like a cat. She was seventeen and it wouldn't be fair for Rosa to spoil things.

It seemed they had only just begun to dream, when Mirka was shaking them awake.

'Best go,' she was saying, 'the other boys are on their way already.'

Marek was waiting at the door, blowing on his hands. Snow had fallen in the night, and the boys' footprints were clear as a fishing line right up to Mirka's door.

It snowed steadily all day, peppering over tree trunks and baby mushrooms. As dusk fell, a papery layer of snow was laid over the forest floor. Every footstep sucked down to their ankles and pulled up splat leaving holes of black water. It was tiring, working every foot out of its mould. Rosa could feel the water slapping between her toes inside her boots.

'I'm tired,' whispered Luba.

'Of course you are. If you weren't tired, you wouldn't be normal,' Rosa said.

'How can you walk and talk at the same time?' Marek said to Rosa, as she caught up with him. She laughed, and the sound surprised her.

'Well you do too, you walk and breathe at the same time.'

'I have to, but I have to think too.'

'Well we all do.'

'You just follow me, hoping I know the way.'

'You do know the way don't you?'

'I don't know.'

Marek walked on, his hands great swollen paws in their gloves, his feet crunching into the ground. And Luba behind Rosa, her jaw hard with cold, watching Marek like a mantra.

They found the house the second night too, though Rosa was beginning to doubt it. Three boys from the village had arrived there before them, and already were sitting round the farmer's kitchen table, scooping stew out of a tin drum with handfuls of home-baked bread, too tired to talk.

The boys exchanged stories, clinking vodka with Don Barek the farmer, the vodka moving round between them like a silver fish. They drank until their words became bleary and began falling off the bone like the chicken's flesh. Marek sang a song weaving around his vodka glass, drinking out of Luba's eyes for a memory of the words. She mouthed the words for him, he plucked them out from her lips like plum stones.

'This war, we'll fight them in the forests,' he caroused.

'In the forests!'

'From the ditches!'

'It's the resistance that wears them down, the invisible resistance!'

'I don't think so,' Don Barek said, more used to the heat of the home-made vodka, with more brawn for it to soak into, more cold sober around the pitted table.

'You, just a stay at home!' roared Marek,

'It's our luck that he is,' Rosa said, 'otherwise he would not be here to receive us as he has done.'

Marek retched, right down from the knob of his throat.

'Bah! Staying at home does no-one any bloody good.'

'You young toughs, you think it's just a game,' Don Barek shouted, scraping back his chair to get a distance from them.

'You fancy yourself playing soldiers in the ditches, but really you're limping from one safe house to another, just parasites, putting us all in danger.'

Marek took another piece of stew and grinned.

'Oh Don Barek none of us mean what we say today. I'd be in a home with a little wife making me stews if I could, if I had one. But I haven't.'

Then he leaned over and breathed at the girls, fit to set them alight, first at Rosa, then at Luba, as if to say, 'Which of you will have me? I'll take either of you.' Luba stroked her long brown plait and blushed.

'Do you mind him drinking?' Rosa asked Luba when they were alone that night.

'It's what men do,' she said.

'You think you can change him. But you can't.'

'You don't understand. You're too sensible about everything. You don't see him like I do.'

'I hope I never do,' Rosa thought, remembering the way his words lost their edges and grew purple with the smell of liquor.

They fell asleep in the straw with the chickens walking over their faces, and the men still heehawing around the table.

It was their turn to move on first, in advance of the three village boys. It was lucky, because at dawn they were laid out in front of the stove on their backs like three grounded whales, their mouths open.

'The woodcarver Jerzy will wait for you.,' the farmer said. 'There you are at the border, his barn Poland, his chimney Russia. Take care. The guide will meet you there, and the last part you go by sled with 'official' papers', and he tapped the side of his nose. Marek's eyes were red, and there were rope marks like railway tracks on his face, where he had fallen asleep on the mat face down. They filled their rucksacks with turnips from the farmer's larder, and set off.

It was a grey day at dawn when the light showed. The snow and sky were locked together like a mousetrap. The snow was powdering like flour, and there was no sun, it was painted out grey

grey day they walked and grey blocked the shifting of the sun around the sky and the winding in and out of the shadows

white mushrooms sheltered in families under the cracking leaves

the snow powdered on powder powder

wolves printed claws in the frozen pools and howled among the birch cathedrals

birches on tiptoe in the corridors

they walked in a chain with Marek at the front holding Luba by two fingers

the snow powdered on pow pow

they walked scattered like peppercorns finding their own routes through the sunken ditches

they walked like Siamese triplets into each other's footprints

the snow punched in pow pow

they walked in silence, biting the inside of their cheeks for warmth

they walked in whispers, Marek whispering to Luba, 'yes, yes, you are strong enough, another few minutes, another few minutes and we'll be there,'

they walked with Rosa at the front and Marek at the back

snow pow pow powdered and pounded on

they walked with Luba at the front and Marek behind her

they used Rosa's eyes to find the way, then Marek's, then Luba's

they listened for the howl of a wolf, the thresh of a trout, the creak of a stork, the crack of a gun, the trail of a chimney

the snow pounded pounded on pow pow

their senses were broken teeth rows of broken teeth

and the snow pounded powdered wild wilder

white whorls long white tunnels

white winding mad coils coiling coiling sucking them in

head hands first into a wild dervish pounding demon dance

Inside Rosa was cursing

my shoes my eyes my heart my muscles my smallness

we are lost we are lost we are spun around and juggled

and blinded

It built up speed, flattened out like the skin of a drum, beating outwards, bowling out against them, spinning them round, stringing them out through the forest.

a house, a roof, a fire, the eye of the needle, the eye of the wind, a place to be still

came up on them in the spin of the snow in the wind

They all three felt it together and moved together in a line towards the place of being saved, and the person there in the threshold, another person with eyes and a nose and a face stood there watching stood still as stone but they knew she was real by the moving of the eyes and the falling of the hair under the scarf and the jumping of the hair in her breath.

As they came nearer, she stayed planted there, without moving. Her eyes and theirs focused, and narrowed. They were all human, she in the threshold newly warm from the fire inside, and they the three of them drowned into transparent ghosts of themselves, washed in and out and in by the storm.

She watched them and took in the story of them, learnt it by heart and learnt what to do. She swivelled round, like a doll on a stick. They saw the strings of her shawl spiking down her neck. She moved faster than they did, by a footstep. As they moved nearer, she moved into the door, opened it, slid behind it, and as they came into its shadow, it closed clack matt against the wall.

Marek went up to the door and hit it with his fists. They heard the bolts drawn. Rosa called through the cracks in the shutters,

'We don't want anything, we don't even want food, we only want shelter,' and the shutters flattened from inside clack. The snow moulded around the house and the house sealed itself in and sealed itself out while they watched.

Hidden in the open barn, stumbling over frozen chicken droppings, they shored up with their rucksacks and blankets, huddled together like baby chickens, they tried to sleep.

'Will I die of cold?' Luba said.

'No, no,' Rosa said, but she didn't know for sure.

After less than an hour, Rosa heard Marek moving, rustling, stamping.

'What are you doing?' she said.

'It's dangerous for us to sleep. We will die of cold. Even in the pitch darkness it's better we keep moving. We can hold on in a chain, we can feel each other walk. I'll lead.'

He reached a hand out to her, and she felt it brush her neck and then flatten over her shoulder.

'We will lead each other, like this.'

Before she could resist, his hand levered her round and into his arm, and his mouth reached out from the ink and pressed against hers so fast it made her gag.

'We can keep each other warm this way,'

'No,'

'Why not? Why shouldn't we? It's so cold.'

'I don't believe you,'

'Why not, I'm a man, it's not a crime. Come on, Rosa, no-one cares now. We've got nothing to lose.'

and he began to fight her against the wall of the barn, bruising her arm with his grip, his mouth landing on her neck and ear as she twisted hers out of his reach.

'Get off me. Luba trusts you even if I don't.'

'I didn't ask her to,'

'You did. You flirted with her.'

'What if I did.'

'Now is not a good time to break her heart. Now we have other things to think about. Get off me.'

'You're cold, Rosa, no-one will want you like that. Why are you so proud, who are you waiting for?'

Where was his hand? Where was he touching, what was he touching? How mad was he?

Nothing in the forest was still: everything was raw, everything kicked and fought.

So she kicked him with a quick pincer kick that made him groan and leap away doubled up and cursing, 'Fuck you, woman,' moving on out of the shadow of the wall into the breaking light cursing. He kept moving, on into the forest, his rucksack sunk in the ditch, going on not looking back humiliated the tears coursing down biting his cheek the inside of his moist hungry mouth thinking, 'how can I go on, how can I go back?, how can the impossible become suddenly more impossible?' the snow so deep, every footstep an effort, when she saw the shadow falling in the snow.

They came at him from both sides, two soldiers in Russian uniforms. One shouted to the other, then they hit the snow at his feet with the butt of their rifles. He froze there, the terror in his face, a split second, then his back, almost lifted under the soldiers' arms, being marched away, crack crack two moves over the edge and they were gone gone irredeemably gone cut out of the scene and just the boots the marching the shoulders scrunched up to his neck cut into her eyes and his rucksack still warm from his pillow leaning against the frozen wall waiting.

Rosa stayed awake until Luba stirred.

'Russian soldiers, we must go,' Rosa whispered. 'Russian soldiers.'

'Russian, that's good. We've crossed the border.'

'Not good, Marek has been taken.'

I did not know she felt so much, I did not know it was the reason to escape and the reason to be young and wear her plait long, I did not know that seventeen is as old as you can be and as deep a volcano as can be. I did not know that was the way she wanted it.

Luba planted herself in front of the house and screamed. All I could do was run, run and fall and stumble away from the scream, away from its wrap, its vice, its heavy khaki arm.

It would not be long. She would not need to be long, waiting for her lover. This is how she wanted it. This is how it was to be seventeen and to love the butcher's boy.

When the man appeared from the sledgehammer sky and lifted Rosa onto the sledge, he could have been friend or enemy, man or wolf, Russian or Jew, she was too tired to know.

She had been lain on the hand of the snow and gutted.

*   *   *

'I had hoped you might travel with us, but they say you are already in Vilna. I'm so glad you are safe. Maybe I will find you there,' grandma Rosa said, as she ran away down the corridor.

I opened my door and the corridor was already empty. In it had been Rosa and someone she saw in me, when she looked at me. Someone she mistook me for. It must be like that, to lose a sister. It must be like that, when everyone has made a mistake, you have, she has, he has, and then you can never get it right again, never ever.

I was thinking about this, when I heard a sound, a noise coming from somewhere, a sound like something between a cat fighting on the roof and a baby left too long in its cot. I stood for a moment, to understand the noise. I moved along the corridor to see what happened to the noise. It grew louder, it grew into a pinpoint near the balcony, on the balcony, it grew into Isobel, her head and arms and knees all wound up together and terrible noises coming out of it all, sometimes as if she was gasping for breath, sometimes low almost like a rattle. I went and sat beside her against the wall.

'Isobel, what's happened?'

She looked up but never stopped the choking noises, the low thunder noises, and I could see the shine on her cheeks and the curling over of her mouth.

'Leo,' she sobbed, 'he dumped me.'

I thought of all those nights, that silver skin he had, those long bones, and the sneaking away before morning, the crumpled sheets on the balcony and what she had told me this morning in our session.

She cried like a tiny girl, the same tears and curling lip and shining cheeks. I rocked her, with my arm around her, crying too I didn't know what for.

CHAPTER TEN

Friday

Leo looked the same as every morning, pink as if he had just been pinched and kissed in bed: and his eyes slid around our shorts and T-shirts as they always did, and his voice was sleepy and hypnotic as every day. I hated him for being the same as any other day. I'm sure he'd said slogans to himself and pasted up angel cards like 'peace' and harmony' and sniffed lavender or something to make sure nothing bothered him. I saw in the first second that Isobel hadn't appeared and was probably on her bed in a heap and somebody should be doing something about it. In the second moment I caught sight of Donald sitting on a cushion and moving his eyebrows around in a strange way. I realised by studying him that the eyebrows were meant to be secret messages sent to me across the room.

We began the opening circle in pairs 'sharing feelings'. Donald was my partner.

'I've been excited about our boat trip ever since you said yes,' he said.

'I didn't say yes.'

'You did. Last night outside your door you said, yes I promise.'

'No, that wasn't to you.'

'Who was it to?'

'Not to you,' I said.

He looked at me out of the side of his head like a fish.

'I don't understand you,' he said, 'sometimes you're the weirdest thing.'

Leo sat in the circle with his hands flat on his knees just watching, not joining in. His red beard was poked in the air, as if he was looking down his nostrils at us. Feeling him there distracted me. I could see his beard and nostrils over Donald's shoulder. Wherever he was, I could sense him with my eyes closed.

'You're not listening,' Donald said.

'No.'

'I said every morning I wait for you to come into the room. I wrote a poem about being in the boat with you.'

Once when I was with Tina at the cinema, a boy pushed a note into her hand as we were leaving. It was about how he had noticed her red-striped stockings and what it made him feel and how he wished they had been alone in the back row, and it sort of rhymed and was a love poem. I thought nothing could be more exciting than to be noticed that way when you weren't even trying. But Tina said, 'I'm not interested in schoolboy fetishes,' and dropped the note into the ash tray. I thought then you had to wear stripey stockings, or purple nails, or crucifix earrings, or brown legs or have a pierced nose to be noticed. But since meeting Geoffrey I knew you could be noticed and be quite normal. What I had never thought about until now was the person who did the noticing. They must all see in a special strong way that makes them write notes and poems and organise boat trips without any signs or messages from the other person. They must be so sure about what they see that they don't care about themselves: whether they will be laughed at or their note torn up. I have had moments like that, when I first noticed Geoffrey with his black and white shawl and pink cheeks: when I first saw Sean's silver cross: when I first heard the musicians in the square. They were strong moments that made me lift off inside. Noticing things in your heart takes you outside of being yourself: they make you better than yourself.

So I said, 'Yes, I will come rowing if I promised.'

I looked around the room. Leo was holding hands with Gloria, Daphne was falling asleep cross-legged in the corner, and Donald was smiling with all his teeth.

'There's something I have to do,' I said, and stood up.

As soon as the door closed behind me I ran upstairs to Isobel's room and knocked on the door.

'It's me, Laura.'

'Go away,' she said.

So I turned the handle and the door opened easily. She was lying in a heap of sheets and the pillows were wet from her hair and tears and sweat, and the room had a horrible stale smell like a sick room.

'I can't go on,' she said into her pillow.

'You can,' I said.

'No, no, you don't know,' she sobbed, 'you don't know how bad I am.'

Her face was bruised and puffy with tears.

'You'll forget him soon, you will,' I said, but I didn't know.

'You don't know what I feel,' she moaned, biting the sheets, 'you don't know what it's like. I can't bear it all. No-one ever wants me, no-one ever stays with me.'

Then she went on saying something, but I couldn't hear, it had gone so low into her and sometimes it knocked out her breath and she was gasping to speak and breathe at the same time.

'He said I was in pieces. I am in pieces. He was right. I thought he believed in me, but he didn't,'

'You weren't in pieces a week ago, before you met him.'

'I was. I was nothing then and I'm nothing now,'

and she was dissolving, as she spoke her edges were going blurry, she was pouring herself away, emptying into the sheets. We had all been turned to water, we had all been made invisible, we had all gone dark. I sat on the edge of the bed and her shaking and low rattling sounds pulled me more and more into the dark, everything I knew began to peel away and I felt the broken boulders rolling out of Isobel throwing us out onto the edge of the world, onto a slab of land.

And then, on this island some words touched me in the throat. They were hazy at first, but then they came to me, clearly,

God of Wrath
look what has become of your child
in a foreign land.
Difficult years
so many countries
I can no longer remember my prayers

sieh was ist mit siener Kindele
in eyner fremnder Land
schlechter Jahre
so vieler Lander
meine Gedienst ist fast vergist

'You don't understand, you think it will all go away, you think you just have to be nice and it will go away,' Isobel said,

but I could feel Rosa's finger on my throat and the words repeated again and again 'I can no longer remember my prayers' and the words were draining away, draining out like the end of a dinner down the pipes and I was catching them as they went, picking them out soggy and faded from my memory.

I stayed with Isobel for a while as she slept. She wheezed and snorted and her nose ran, but she looked more comfortable and after a while I thought there was nothing very much I could do while she slept and it was getting a bit smelly in the bedroom so I might as well go.

I went back to join the group. Now Leo was talking about moments of discovery, moments when we learnt something new and it changed us. He talked about our 'roads to Damascus', and how sometimes great theories and philosophies began in a single moment, like the apple falling off the tree or the bath water rising. Every moment I learnt something new and each time it changed me. It was 1984 and I was fourteen.

My moment of discovery

I was miserable. I had picked 'Indian gods and goddesses' out of the hat for the General Studies project. Everyone else had interesting topics like 'African body decorations' or 'Carnival in the Caribbean'. I'd have liked 'body decorations' because then you could do tattoos or pierced ears. The books didn't seem so bad. They had colour photos of temples, carvings, wall paintings and wall hangings. I was interested how many concubines Krishna had and how Kali's face was bright red and how many arms she had, and how the gods were also elephants and monkeys.

On the shelf was one with a cover I liked the look of. It was called 'Erotic Art in India'. 'Erotic' must have meant 'from the east' but I wasn't quite sure because they hadn't taught us that word. Someone had renewed the book five times in a row, and it was all bent back where someone had marked their favourite pages.

When the book fell open, it sprung up and touched me.

There was a large-hipped lady carved in stone and she was round everywhere, her breasts, her hips were bursting out of the stone and she was opening her sari so everyone could see. Her head was thrown back in ecstacy, and there was a scorpion on her thigh, feeling her, almost juicy.

On the next page there was a stone donkey with a pointed chin and a man inside him, and the donkey had a rude perky smile under his little pointed ears.

Page after page were smiling donkeys, and men with fingers in different women, and women opening their saris and touching themselves and people's bottoms and women sitting on men and smiling blissfully.

My skin came up to touch me.

With each page a piece of me broke out of my uniform .

Krishna with the sweet smell of marigolds explored me with his fingertips, from my ear lobes to the bowl of my neck, the wings of my shoulder to the cracks between my fingers and the mound of my breasts, and I turned in his fingers to the pulp of mango the glaze of the lychee the lip of the lily leaf

stupid white buttons of school blouse buttoned up to the neck
stupid shoes with the round toe and leather straps and clover leaf cuts
stupid navy blue skirt with zip's teeth and tight waist band
stupid belt with elastic stripes and metal teeth like clarinet keys
I am opening up like Alice
waterfalls are making shapes around me and my skin is leaping up to meet them

never again will I wear pigtails
never again will I sleep with a teddy
never again will I let Father pick me up from the youth club
Krishna 's tongue grows and grows and turns me to steam
I will be a gazelle
I will be the leaping salmon
I will be the heart of the lotus flower
never again will I wear sensible shoes
never again will I wear cardigans on Saturdays

I have never felt like this since I had mumps

I don't know how the book got into the school library.

When I went to the bus stop after school that day I noticed new things. I noticed a group of grammar school boys by the school gate, passing a cigarette round the circle inside their blazers. Elephants in Africa would do that, stand in a circle to do their business: I had seen pictures. But I wondered what it would be like opening a sari with one of them, and wearing transparent veils; and I wondered what they would be wearing at the time, whether it would be a loin cloth like the men in the book, and whether they would be on deep cushions with tassels.

Two older girls walked by with legs like noodles and wearing high heels. I watched all the boys spin round, following the legs with their eyes, like cows do when they're waiting for food. I'd like that, for them to look at me that way that makes them drop their cigarette ends onto the pavement. It wasn't really the high heels that made them look at the girls, it was the way they wobbled, as if they were falling off their shoes. I could do that wobble, without the heels. I'm sure I could, if I practised. I tried a bit, in the cloakroom. It helped to hitch up my skirt, at least four inches. Part of the walk, too, meant throwing your head up in the air so you didn't notice the wind round your legs. That was the difficult part, because you never knew if something on the pavement might trip you up.

When I felt I had mastered the technique, I took a deep breath and walked out the door. I walked straight past the boys with my nose in the air, and didn't breathe in case they heard. It felt strange, as if I was on stilts, and I could feel my face crackling with heat. But then, at the end of the lane, I turned round, just quickly to see if any of them were watching. But they weren't. None of them were. They had all gone back to their cigarettes.

Tina was at the bus-stop eating cherry bitters. They gave her a big red lipsticky mouth.

'Tina,' I said,'how do you get boys to look at you?'

'Change the long white socks. I'll do you a deal: you go for stockings, like the real thing, and I'll go for hotpants, like really short. We'll walk past together with our noses in the air like we don't even care about boys. They'll love that, you wait.'

So, for the next walkpast, I borrowed a pair of Hannah's silk stockings and high heel shoes, and took them with me to school in a plastic bag. It was my first time ever with stockings, and my first time with high heels.

I struggled with them. I couldn't imagine how people wore them year in year out with all those dangling parts and cold gaps. I practised walking but it was November and it felt like someone was breathing down my knickers. But, I thought, some girls do this all the time and they look quite natural. You can't tell it's so cold and uncomfortable underneath.

When I appeared from the toilet, one of the older girls said,

'Look if it isn't the sophisticated Laura Cherry in silk stockings!'

Those girls, you could never win. However old you were, they were always even older.

I loved the high heels but I had to be careful not to move in a hurry, in case I left a heel behind. The heels seemed to move slower than the rest of the shoe, it was strange. I walked past very slowly in my high heels, so as not to fall over. The most difficult thing was to pretend you had done it lots of times before and not to look at your feet as if you had never seen them before. We practised in the cloakroom when the prefects had gone, then Tina and I set out for our adventure.

At first when we came out the gate there appeared to be no grammar school boys there at all, and it all would have been a waste of time. Then Tina whispered out the side of her mouth,

'Keep walking. They're by the tennis court.'

They were. There was a cluster huddled there together, and all their heads were facing through the wire mesh towards the tennis court. Tina grabbed my arm so we could walk snootily past, and we did, we walked snootily past, and as we passed their line of blazer backs and the dandruff on the back of their collars we saw through the mesh the sixth form tennis double girls running up and down the tennis court with tiny tennis skirts flapping on their bottoms and their hair bobbing in pony tails and their legs stringing down into rabbit white socks and tennis shoes. The boys were standing there in a line, their noses fitted through the wire diamonds of the fence. They didn't move, even so much as a hair on the back of their blazer, as we walked past.

We marched arm in arm to the bus-stop, with our noses in the air.

'I hate them anyway, the grammar school boys,' Tina said.

'They look alright to me.'

'Naa, they're not real men,' Tina said. 'I like real men.'

We waited at the bus-stop, and I thought about real men and what Tina meant and what real men were like and what the men were like on the walls in India, with loin cloths and rude smiles and their licking tongues.

I was thinking about this, when Tina leant over,

'Have a look at your knees.'

There was a dark pencil line around my knees, and at first I didn't understand it. I had to climb off the carved cushions with tassels and the moment when I unwrapped the boys' blazers in a temple with marigold blossom and candles. Then oh then, oh horror, I saw the silk in wrinkles round my knees, the whole thing sliding down in shiny folds like a snake-skin and my own knees underneath all pink and shorn. I will die: only death could be so lonely.

'Just take them off altogether when we get in the bus,' Tina hissed in my ear, 'no-one will notice.'

'I don't know how to,' I hissed back.

'Don't be daft,' she said. Sometimes Tina was very helpful, and some-times she wasn't helpful at all.

But until the bus came I had to stand in my moulting skin, and Tina stood in front of me so I couldn't be seen from the pavement but I could be seen from the road. And I don't know what the cars would think, or what would happen if grandma had come by in a bus, or Hannah had come by in a car and stopped at the traffic lights and seen her silk stock-ings round my knees. I longed for the bus, I died for the bus, the bus was my carved temple.

Tina sat on the outside so I could fumble around on the inside and pre-tend not to. I fumbled around until everything went snap and the wrin-kles fell round my ankles. It was bliss, the air spread evenly along my legs.

'You're my best friend,' I said to Tina.

'Yea but don't wear stockings again till you know how to wear them,' she said.

I walked home with Hannah's high heels in their plastic bag. Hannah was furious about the stockings.

'You didn't borrow them, you STOLE them,' she said.

'I didn't. I don't want to keep them. I never did.'

'Well they're useless now, you've laddered them.'

'The girls they like wear tennis socks, anyway,' I said, and went to my room to cry.

In my room I thought about boys. Because of them I would have to worry about stupid things like heels and stockings and whether my breasts were big enough or small enough and if my legs were as long as Tina's. And I would have to do this, even though the boys were stupid and spotty and lined up by the playground fence to watch girls in tennis skirts that flapped on their bottoms. I would have to rely on them because in Southgate there weren't any men with marigold blossoms and loincloths who sat cross-legged on cushions and opened silk saris with their fingertips.

I thought I would keep the juicy scorpion on my thigh secretly, and wait until someone found it there, and lifted it off with his tongue.

*   *   *

Leo was my partner, to share our moments of discovery. He began with his story, beccause I didn't feel ready, I wanted to work out how I should talk to him.

'Well, my moment of discovery was in India. I was on this kind of tour, well just straggling around the country, hitching lifts, catching trains and sometimes buses. I was just watching this culture, like from a distance, thinking, it's cool but not for me. Well, there was a group of us and we hired a van and going along these roads, you should see the dust and the potholes, bumping along, the whole undercarriage creaking of this thing we had hired. The countryside was like really dusty and dried out, there were cows kind of scrabbling around in ditches with bones sticking out, real hungry, and women knocking clothes out in these really thin streams but real elegant they were walking out from these grass huts you could see right through with pots piled up and kids with no shoes playing outside. Then by the roadside we heard this real commotion, people screaming and shouting and a whole huddle of people around. We stopped the van, thought we should see what was happening, and in the middle of this crowd was an old man lying on the ground. Everyone around was shouting, jumping up and down, a woman there was like hysterical, but he just lay there with his eyes wide open and he was praying talking to himself like chanting under his breath with all this going on around him. I learnt he had been knocked over by a passing motorcyclist and broken something and they couldn't move him and everyone was going nuts but for the man himself. The guys I was with didn't want to get involved, it would have been reporting to the police and then to hospital, and then they might say it was your fault and all that stuff. So they pulled me away and back into the van and we were off.

But I couldn't forget that guy the way he made himself like real calm, and the way we did nothing and how useless it was all the wailing and screaming, how it helped nobody. I thought, yea I'd like to learn more about that way of being, like I could do that, just take away the pain he must have had - God, he must have been in agony, but taking away the pain like he did with thinking and praying and chanting.

Then after that I went to a monastery to learn Buddhism, and it began there, on that day and because of that man.'

'I know what you mean,' I said to him. And I thought, 'I bet you did some chanting to stop yourself hearing Isobel next door.'

Then it was my turn, and because I had got interested in his story, I had forgotten to prepare myself.

'I learnt about sex, in a school library book when I was fourteen,' I said. Leo stopped himself snorting like he did in the corridor at night, and instead gave his kindly day-time look.

'When I first saw it, I understood everything about women loving men. I thought I did. But it was only the theory. When I close my eyes, with Geoffrey, I try to be one of the women in the sculptures, and I try to feel that knowing look, to touch my head with red powder like the bride who remembers her lover.' Then I felt my whole inside burst up into my heart, 'but I don't feel that! I don't feel that with him.' I was shouting, and I couldn't stop myself, and I couldn't think why it should be with Leo and now. 'And I've seen how it is for women when they feel that, I see it turning their life over and over and I'm frightened. I'm frightened of what it does and how much it hurts. It's a spring, such a strong spring and I'll never feel it, I'll never feel it like they do.'

Leo put his arm around me and I didn't stop him.

'Why will you never feel it like they do?' he said, so close into my hair that my ear felt warm.

'I'm marrying Geoffrey and he will be my only man, and I never had that, I never had what they had, and if I did it would kill me.'

'Why would it kill you?' he said.

And it came out like a roar, I didn't know my own voice or which mountain it came from.

'It killed them. It killed them.'

And now I couldn't speak. I couldn't speak for the pain between my heart and stomach, like a string being pulled tighter and tighter. All I remember is Leo cupping my head onto his shoulder so I was in a cocoon of my hair, and he was saying,

'No-one killed them. They did it to themselves. They let it happen. But you won't. You're stronger than that. No-one could do that to you. You're strong.'

After that, I didn't know what to feel about Leo. I couldn't look at him, but when I remembered his breath against my ear, I felt my sari opening and my hips bursting out of their skirts.

I sat with Daphne at lunch. She was the only one who would let me be quiet, I knew that. Ours was the Heart table. The card said:

Your element is the air, your sense is touch, your animal is the gazelle,
your key words are universal compassion, unconditional, limitless, infinite.
May you find in your heart a broad ocean of nectar.

I liked the 'broad ocean of nectar' and I wanted that, I wanted to have a broad ocean of nectar inside me, and I wondered what it would feel like and whether there was anyone I know who had that.

Daphne was sitting at the table.

'You know, you are looking so bonny and blossoming these days,' she said to me.

'Am I?' because I really had no idea. In fact, I imagined I must be looking all pale and ghoulish because I never slept properly these days since grandma's visits, and I must have red eyes today.

'I think something here is doing you a lot of good,' she said,

'I don't know what.'

She laughed.

'I'm sure you don't need to know,' she said,'just you go on enjoying it.'

I saved some slices of cold salamis, a plate of rosti potatoes and onions, and two scoops of vanilla icecream for Isobel. She was packing, wearing a night-dress and a pair of bright white trainers,when I arrived at her room with the tray.

'Where are you going?' I asked her.

'What do you think? I'm not staying here. It's driving me mad being here. I hate this place. The food is disgusting.'

She sounded much better than this morning. I looked at the tray in my hands.

'Don't you want this?'

'You must be joking. I wouldn't touch that junk.'

'Aren't you hungry? You haven't eaten all day.'

'You sound like my father. He's always trying to make me eat. He's always trying to make me look like his pin-ups.'

She was throwing everything into her suitcase, even white slabs of hostel soap. Her arms scissored in and out like spider legs.

'There's no point you staying,' she said, without looking up. 'I'm fine, I'm looking after myself,' but everything was swilling around her so fast I didn't believe her.

'You're packing the hostel towels,' I gasped, as I watched the room move between her hands. She stopped, looked at me so strangely I backed away.

'Go away, I don't need you, get out of here,' she shouted, and gave my shoulder such a push the tray bounced up against my chest.

I walked out and slammed her door shut. A blob of vanilla icecream was making its way down the front of my summer dress. I felt my eyes pricking, but it was with shock, it was with humiliation.

Donald was waiting for me in the hallway. I was almost glad of him, I was almost glad of an hour on a boat. A boat seemed the only safe place to be. Donald was wearing an enormous rucksack with a steel frame and badges of the Alps stuck all over.

'What's in there?' I asked.

'Provisions. Lemonade, crisps, plasters and first aid.'

'That's mad. We're only spending an hour on the lake.'

'You must take these things seriously. Even an hour is a meditation.'

'But you don't need plasters and first aid for a meditation.'

However, Donald was insistent and he seemed to know what he was doing.

We walked silently through the streets I loved, the chocolate witches and street benches and shoe-shop doorway, the coffee shops with pink tablecloths and old ladies in hats eating Sachertorte with forks, the square that was back to normal now, with the fountain spitting joyfully and the icecream van back again with its stripey canopy. Though today I had died a little, it wasn't all over. Not at all. Not by a long long way. The boats were there, the sun shining on the green and yellow paint, and they were nosing each other gently against the pier wall.

Donald had set everything up with great care. The man in the boat hire recognised him, and our boat was ready tugging against its rope at the bottom of the deep stone steps. The boat hire man stood at the bottom of the steps and handed me into the boat as if it was a ballroom. Then he did the same for Donald, gently steadying his step as Donald began to slide across the boat's bow. In spite of that, when he landed in the boat, it dipped down so steeply he stumbled and then it dipped down even further so water slopped over the edge.

The seat on Donald's side was already wet, and when he sat down he made a face. Then he took off the rucksack and set it down, and realised it was set down in a puddle and put it on his knees and it left two wet patches on his trousers, so he set it down again under his boots.

'What's so funny?' he said.

The man hiring boats had a strange look on his face. He unwrapped the rope from a post and gave the boat a push. Donald set the oars in two handcuffs and began to pull. The boat began to rock back against the port, bumping into all the other boats tied up there.

'Nein nein,' the man shouted from the shore, 'ist de other way around,'

Donald looked behind him, as if there was something there that would help.

'He means you're rowing backwards. You have to change the oars around' I said.

'Let's change places,' Donald said.

So we got up and wobbled along the boat like tight-rope walkers, and Donald grabbed hold of me in the middle of the boat, I thought it was amorous but it was because he couldn't stand up straight. Then I was sitting on the seat with the wet patch and the rucksack between my feet, and I still had the oars there in their little handcuffs and Donald was sitting there on the other side with his back to the big smooth lake and nothing to do. So the next task was to lift the oars and pass them over to Donald. He leaned forward to pick them up as if they were really light or he was really strong, and I was struggling because they were long and heavy and I couldn't quite control them, it was a bit like ski-ing in air.

Then Donald got the oars into place on his side, but he was quite gasping with the effort, and it was difficult now for him to pretend he had done this lots of times before.

The boatman gave us another push away from all the other boats, Donald gave a pull on the oars which made him fall backwards, then another pull with more of the wood in the water, and we began to creak out into the open water. I liked sitting there with the view unwinding like a slow home video, gliding at that level just above the water where we could see our own reflection, and see weed and fish floating just under the surface. The people on the shore seemed like toys, their voices floating away tinkly and distant, and I dipped a stick into the water and watched the water hang on to it like hair. If I closed my eyes, I could pretend Donald wasn't there at all, and feel the sun making my skin smell sweet, and hear icecream van noises from the shore.

'Read my poem,' Donald said, as I dreamed.

'What?'

'In my rucksack. Open my rucksack and find my poem. It's for you.'

The rucksack was full of buckles, zips and drawstrings. You could never be robbed in a hurry with a rucksack like that. I pulled out a roll of paper.

'That's it,' he said.

'It's got wet.'

'Shit. Read it aloud, read what you can.'

I unrolled it and began reading.

'*If I something bot*'

'*If I were in a boat,*' Donald snapped.

'It's got wet,' I said again. It was true. The ink had run all the words together.

'*With you, if I something something*'

'*Were in a dream*'

'If I were in a dream,

I would land — I would something land—'

Donald leaned forward and snatched the paper out of my hand.

'If you're going to be stupid, I'll read it,' he said. His face was red, all his spots stood out. He smoothed the paper out on his knee.

'If I were in a boat with you

if I were in a dream,'

'You can't read and row at the same time,' I interrupted.

'I can. Listen.

If I were in a boat with you,

if I were in a dream,

then I will be the island, the palm of a hand,

you the treasure, the pot of gold.'

'It's a love poem,' I said. Even though I was worried about the boat going round and round in circles, I noticed that. I noticed it was a love poem.

'Of course it is. What did you think?'

'I didn't know.'

'Well you should know. I keep telling you but you never notice anything. Now listen.'

'Shall I row? Because we're going round and round in circles and I don't like it.'

'Well you read the damn thing then,' he shouted suddenly, and scrunching the poem up into a ball, threw it at me across the boat. It landed in a puddle at my feet. His face had become a dreadful kind of red, and he was puffing and gasping.

'Are you alright?'

'Yes,' he gasped.

'You're not.'

I stood up to move towards the middle, and the boat bent right over on one side.

'Sit down, for God's sake' he said.

'I don't like the way you look,' I said,

'Thanks a lot,' he replied.

'I mean you don't look well. That's all I meant.'

But I was half standing, half moving towards him, and it all felt rocky and unsteady. Standing in the middle of the boat, with the next ragged pull of the oars I fell heavily onto his knees.

'You're here, God, how did you get here?' he cried and, dropping the oars, wrapped his arms around me like a nutcracker. I screamed.

'What are you on about?' he said, and bunched his mouth up so hard and so suddenly against mine I could hardly breathe.

'Stop it,' I shouted, but in the 'o' between 'st' and 'p' he pushed his tongue into my mouth like a horrible wet silver fish.

'You're disgusting!'

'I love you!' he shouted.

'No you don't, you're just desparate.'

He squeezed my arm so hard it hurt.

'You're cruel. Do you know how cruel you are? Every day, you hurt me,'

'It's your fault. I never asked you to hang about me.'

By this time, the oars had begun lolling against the side of the boat, and were working their way out of their handcuffs. I leaned forward to grab them, but Donald's arm wrapped me round the stomach.

'You're mad. We're losing our oars,' and I watched it happen, the oars working themselves free, the boat bobbing amongst the weeds, the oars making their way in opposite directions towards the banks.

'We're stranded, we're stranded!' I screamed.

'This is how I dreamed it.'

'Oh shut up, I'm not staying here,'

and I don't know, something propelled me, something turned me into a silver fish, I propelled myself into the water and felt the weeds like hair through my fingers, and my hair fanning out around me and my sandals flapping through my toes, it all went quiet at the level of the water just the push push as I breaststroked towards the edge and the put put of my arms pushing out crescents and sending them rippling out to the edges. It was so calm I never wanted it to end.

A man with a dog collar who was passing pulled me out at the pier. Looking back at the lake, I could see Donald sitting there in the boat, his hands crossed on his lap, watching me with a strange mad calm, like a Lady of Shallott who had lost her way. I wondered what it was like to feel every day that someone hurt you. Then halfway down the High Street, something struck me which made me stop and think in the doorway of the Kuchenhexe tea shop. I always thought the people who did the hurting were people with rude smiles who lied, that people who hurt had monsters inside them and something outside which gave it away like long nails or yellow teeth or bottles of purple vodka. But that wasn't true. Anyone could become another person's monster, just because they felt differently, or didn't want the same things. Anyone could tread on someone else, on all the invisible threads they sent out. Without knowing you could trample them to pieces.

A note had been pushed under my door when I got back. It was from Isabel.

Laura,

I appreciate what you did, bringing me lunch, and I'm sorry for what I said to you. It wasn't you, it was me, I get like that, I can't stop myself. Often I do things and I can't even remember, people tell me the next day and I don't even believe that was me. Actually you were really kind and I never said thank you, but you were really good, I mean it.

I can't stay here, because it's got really bad for me. I know you know, but if anyone asks just say I had to go home. If my dad calls will you talk to him and tell him I'm on my way home?

My address is: The Cedars, Woodrow Crescent, Holly Woods, Sevenoaks, so write if you feel like it. You could stay if you wanted, but it's not that much fun at home.

Bye
  Isobel

Leo, Gloria and Daphne were already waiting in the meditation room for others to arrive. Leo was warming his hands over a candle and Gloria was shuffling the cushion around trying to get comfortable.

'Isobel and Donald won't be coming,' I said.

Leo looked up from the candle. You could tell from a flutter of one eyelash that he felt responsible, or aware, or involved, or something different to being a stone.

So we started without them.

I saw Isobel on the train with her suitcase full of hostel towels and bars of soap. Rosa was on the train with her Vilna fur-lined shoes, and Luba with her hair combs. I saw a line of men waiting for them the other end, standing in a line like wine waiters with silver trays. There was Isobel's father, but when I looked at him he smelt of whisky and sweet after-shave. Then there was Leo standing on one leg with his eyes closed, and Marek - but I couldn't see him quite clearly. Then there was Jacob, but it was my father Jacob with a hankerchief on his head tied at the corners, like he wears in the sun, to stop him going bald. When I looked closer at the women on the train, I realised I was there too, sitting in the carriage eating ice cream. I didn't recognise myself at first, because my hair was tied up with combs like Luba's, and I was wearing a long coat with a fur collar that belonged to grandma. Which man was waiting for me? Donald was in the line, and when I looked again, Geoffrey had appeared. He was holding a bridal veil, with one hand up inside the crown so the veil fell over his arm. I thought, 'why did you bring it to the station? It'll get dirty.' I was thinking about the veil, when the train began to arrive at the station, but it didn't slow down. It just went rushing on, and the women just sat there calmly, looking ahead with their hands in their lap.

'Open the window, go on!' I heard over my shoulder. It was Sean's voice, but I couldn't see him. He didn't seem to be in the carriage, but he was talking to me very clearly. 'Are you doing some penance or what?' he was saying, in that hills-and-valley voice.

I threw open the window, and put my head out. The train was belching out a grey exhaust that caught me in the face as it poured itself down the rails, the men waiting still in a line, watching as we streaked past. First they were left of me, with Geoffrey and the veil at the end, then they were right of me, with Isobel's father and the smell of whisky at the end, and their heads turned to follow us like a row of sunflowers, then they were a line of specks, and then nothing, nothing, we were out in the countryside with the rush of clean air and the tongues of green ribbon lobbing out over the fields.

The voice behind my ear was saying to me, 'No-one killed them. They did it to themselves. They let it happen. But you won't. You're stronger than that. No-one could do that to you. You're strong.' In the wind, I could hear a tin whistle playing a jig.

I was just exploring my picture in the train carriage, when the door of the meditation room banged open, and we all looked up, startled. Donald was standing in the door, like the ghost of Hamlet. Every part of him dripped. His hair dripped onto his nose, his nose dripped onto his shirt, his shirt was flattened in patches across his chest, his trousers dripped down to his shoes, his shoes were opened at the toe, his toes had gone sea monster green.

'What's this?' Leo said, unwrapping his legs.

'Ask Laura,' Donald growled.

Everyone looked at me. I didn't know what to say.

'I don't know how she can look so cool. She did it.'

'I didn't,' I heard myself saying, 'you did it to yourself.'

'I think it would be better, rather than arguing about it, for you to go and get dry,' Leo said, like a school teacher.

'I don't want to argue. I just want her to know what she did,' Donald said.

'Whatever she did, you're the one that is wet, and you are the one that should get dry.'

'I don't need to,' Donald said, stubbornly, and sat himself smudged and dripping, cross-legged on the floor.

'Well,' Leo said, 'it's as Laura said, if you get ill, it's you that did it to yourself.'

'I don't know, I think we should take responsibility if he doesn't want to.' It was Gloria. 'I'm going to go and get a towel.'

'Leave me alone.'

'No, you don't want to be left alone, otherwise you wouldn't be here.'

'Don't give me that stuff,' Donald snarled.

Everyone began talking at once. Daphne began saying,

'We all came here for a bit of peace, even Donald,'

Leo was saying, 'Well, let's talk about it. It seems some of us need to,'

Gloria was saying, 'it's all our responsibilities,' and I began saying, 'He needn't have got wet. He just let go of the oars,' but no-one was listening to anyone, and Donald was pretending to meditate with his eyes shut and the damp spreading in a circle all round him.

The phone went in the Yin:Yang room. To escape the noise I went to pick it up.

'Hello, hello, I need to speak to Isobel Haden.'

'Isobel isn't here. Who's speaking.'

'It's her father, Mr. Haden. She left a message asking me to ring urgently.'

'Yes, I'm her friend Laura. Isobel wanted to tell you she is on her way home. She left this afternoon.'

There was a short silence.

'Why's that? I thought the course finished on Sunday?'

'Yes it does. But she needed to leave early. Something came up.'

'So you're saying she's already left? She's already on her way?'

'Yes, yes she is.'

There was another silence.

'This is very awkward. This is really very awkward.'

I waited for him to carry on. There was nothing else I could say.

'Well, very well, I suppose there's nothing you can do,' he said, stiffly, and slammed the phone down.

When I went back into the meditation room, Donald was sitting up stiffly, meditating, with his fists clenched tight, and Gloria sitting opposite him with her eyes wide open, holding a towel.

CHAPTER ELEVEN

Friday night

I look in the mirror to see if Daphne is right about me being bonny. My hair has grown so long the colour seems to have run out at the tips. I coil it up into a comb like Luba,with one braid hanging down over my shoulder, and look at my face from side to side. Maybe I have Rosa's cheekbones after all, her gingery glow under the skin, and I have grown paler, milkier, since I was here. A layer has peeled off me. Wrapped in a sheet, I let it slide to the place where my breasts begin to rise, and the bones on my neck stand out like wings, like the neck of women on the escalators who advertise underwear.

I wish I was thin as a lathe, like Isabel with her elbows like blades: but I am dimpled like a baby instead, and I have to breathe in until I'm nearly sick before my stomach flattens. The women in the Indian carvings look down at the slopes they make and embrace them. They make pots and goddesses in their shapes. I look at myself sideways in the mirror and I could imagine myself as a pot, a gourd for carrying water.

These were the first night streets I had seen since arriving: the curtains were drawn across the tea shop windows, the chocolate shop shelves were empty and there were men standing outside bars in circles of cigarette smoke watching girls with pink cheeks sweep by swinging their hair and bags. I was different too, at night: I felt more dangerous in my skin, more prickling.

When I reached the lake I hoped Sean would not be there because my stomach was grinding: and I didn't know how to arrange my face so it would appear an accident that I had bumped into him, and I didn't know how to arrange my body so that it behaved like an engaged person.

So I didn't, I didn't organise any of it. He said I looked surprised and was it a mistake I was out at night, away from my penance school.

'It's not a penance. I like it. I think I do.'

'Well everyone to his taste, they say. Not for me, but sure there must be something in it for you. So what is it you were doing at school just now?'

I told him about our themes: journeys, rituals, moments of discovery, and he liked them. He thought the school didn't sound so bad after all.

His ritual was confirmation, and he said how little girls dressed up like brides in white lace. Then I described Leo and the strange noises I had heard on the balcony. He howled with laughter, then he said,

'Sure, it sounds like your priest is the lucky one, doesn't have to take the vows like our lot.'

'I don't know. Maybe he does. He just breaks them.'

He roared again, and I could see bits of spit coming out of him in the lamplight.

Sean looked like a tom-cat in the evening. The brown washed over him by the mountains looked leathery and grainy, and his teeth shot out blue stripes whenever he grinned, which he did often, whenever I said anything. If I sniffed I could pick up the smell of his soap and the warm parts of his shirt.

We walked round the lake and he said suddenly,

'And you know what I think?'

'What?'

'Tonight is your sabbath, your day of rest.'

I hadn't thought of it, but it was, it was that.

'Yes, I suppose it is. How come you thought of that?'

'Well, I was the fool not to know earlier. Should you not be doing something?'

'No, not if I don't want. At home they will be.'

'I suppose it's not fashionable to practise it, not today,'

'I don't suppose it is, but we do, my family and me. But I can't do those things on my own. It's a thing you do with your family.'

'What things would you be doing, say, if you were with your family?'

We sat on the wall, in the place where I had jumped in to escape Donald, and I told him about Friday nights, the night Grandma was the expert and we did what we were told, laid a white tablecloth and said prayers over the fruit of the vine and the fruit of the earth, divided the light from the darkness, sang a song to the Sabbath bride in spindly voices all ragged and out of tune, then tore the cakey bread into hunks and gobbled it down to drown the treacliness of the wine, then sunk it into the chicken soup bubbling with globules of boiling fat.

'I like that, the bread and wine, we do that too, how about that for a coincident. Just that yours is a Saturday ours is a Sunday. All that trouble just for the odd day, what d'you think? You know why we all wanted to be priests 'cos you get to drink all the leftover wine.'

.'How's that?'

'It's sacred wine, so you get to guzzle the lot if you're the priest, so no-one else gets their hands on it, and, you know, finishes it off for the wrong reasons.'

We both laughed, and his teeth flashed again tom-cat white.

'What about the grandma, any more visits?'

'Yes, every night. Each time she is younger and each time her story is more awful. Terrible things happened and I never knew.'

'Well I'm sorry. I'm sorry they were terrible, not sorry, you know, that you know. That's good, I think that's good.'

Our toes tap tapped along the paving stones and grew long in the lamplight.

'What, do you mean she tells you all that, when she visits?'

'She shows me. She kind of takes me there.'

'Well now, isn't that amazing!' he said, and he sat on that word, amaaazzing, spread it right across the long black slate of the lake.

I wanted to say, 'I'll never see her again, not alive,' but I couldn't, she stopped me, she stopped me in my throat and turned it round and round like custard. Then I felt his arms around me, his warm arms in the shirt I longed to touch and to smell, and I found myself hiding in it so he wouldn't see that my face had opened up into a wound, and the tears were spreading on his shoulders, soaking through and through so the pink of his skin showed through.

'I'm sorry I made you think about her,' he said into my hair.

'No, no, I want to think about her,' I said, and we stood in a heap together until I realised my shoulder was growing wet too.

'Why are *you* crying?' I said, and we both began laughing at how we rang from one another like two strings on a cello.

'I have my people too, you wouldn't want to know how many. Some in Ulster, some south. Only maybe you think real men don't cry.'

'No, I don't think that. Of course I don't.'

'It's not fair, what we have isn't fair.'

'I know that, I can imagine.'

'Och no, don't imagine because for sure it will be wrong. Now, far better, just give us a hug.'

I didn't know what it was, this electric layer that lifted off his words, as if there were another set of Laura and Sean, tiny ones in secret caves, exchanging messages inside us.

This was the place I had jumped into the lake, and I knew I had jumped in again. He stopped, just there where we were, where the boatman had handed us down into our painted red rowing boat.

'Better not, though. You're spoken for now, aren't you?'

'Yes, ' I said, meaning no.

'Course you are, a beautiful girl like you. Now, that's a lucky man that's found you and I hope that he knows it.'

'I think he does.'

'Now, if it was me, I wouldn't let you out of my sight five minutes, in case some wild Catholic whisk you away.'

Then he bent over so his mouth planted itself on my forehead.

'That's how I feel,' he whispered.

The scorpion spread its legs on my thigh.

So we had something to eat.

The room was steaming with sausages and strong cigarette smoke, and people squashed together at round tables. We found a space on a table that was already occupied merrily by a group of friends, and when we both looked harder, recognised the three musicians we had seen the night before. The three of them were sitting squeezed together, the flautist with her arms around the violinist, the guitarist holding a glass of beer with the froth sliding down his sleeve.

'I sure like your music,' Sean said to them, when they caught our eye.

'Well we're glad. You are English?' the guitarist said.

'I'm Irish, my friend here, she's English.'

'Oh, you build the bridges eh? We too, we build bridges.' He pointed at the two beside him and winked. 'This is Freddi, the nice young man, this is Claude his lady-love, I am Felix.'

We all shook hands round the table, and Felix had a strong warm handshake and looked straight into our eyes as if he was learning us, carefully and deeply. Without his skull cap Felix had hair like chicken down, almost pink from parts of his scalp reflecting into the blondness. It was the sort of downy hair you were afraid to comb in case it came out.

Claude was the sort of person who looked beautiful in baggy clothes, and the sort of person whose head was so perfect she would look fine with no hair at all. Her clothes were like dustsheets thrown over a work of art.

Felix, Freddi and Claude were the most surprising people I had ever met. Everything they said surprised me. Sean thought so too, I could tell. He was growing pinker and pinker, and sitting up straighter and straighter, and his eyes were growing bright and watery with laughter.

We learnt that Freddi and Claude had met playing music in an under-pass and both had nearly been arrested for disturbing the peace. Freddi and Felix hitchiked to Italy whenever their army papers arrived and Italy wasn't far enough so they were going to try Turkey and Kathmandu. Since Freddi and Claude had met they had only been separated for one night which Freddi had spent as a dare in a nuclear bunker under the Swiss bank. Felix had a good-luck cap which he always wore when he played the guitar, and which he had found in the middle of a field after a circus had packed up and left. In the field he had also found a spangled leotard, several syringes and a thimble which he used to store his gold tooth when he felt like removing it. The gold tooth was not firmly in his head because he couldn't afford the dentistry and he could (and did) roll it around on his tongue as a party game.

Felix had family the other side of the Berlin wall, and he said this year something might happen to the wall. What might happen? Wait and see what will happen, it starts already, he said.

They had busked on the Swiss-Italian border and seen Italians dump their rubbish on the Swiss side and the Swiss dump theirs on the Italian side.

The best acoustics for music were Milan station but the worst was in Pacino square because the cuckoo clock interrupted every quarter of an hour.

They sang a German drinking song around the table, holding up their glasses, and Sean joined in, humming and following the words from their lips, then I joined in and our song all ragged and slurry joined in with the smoke and bustle and laughter of the restaurant and no-one minded at all or turned a hair.

'Now your turn, sing an Irish song, we love this!' they said.

Sean blushed and said no and looked shy, said he could only whistle, wouldn't want to frighten away the other drinkers, sang like a dying crow but they could see he was delighted and just needed a little more beer and a little more time.

Then, without more warning, sitting beside me with his cheeks bright from the heat and the beer, he began like a whisper, like a swan gliding by, 'My-*y-y young love, she—e said to me*,' and we all went quiet, strained to hear the sound that wavered over the notes, that swayed all delicious and loose around the melody, and the words, the young love, *like a swan on the water* and when he ended, the words were perfect papery like prayers blown to the wind and I realised with a cold shudder that the young lover was dead, was a ghost, and he had spelled it out, slowly from the point of his tongue as if it had just happened, just *Last night she came to me/My dead love came in/So softly she entered /her feet made no din/and she stepped her way to me/these words she did say/it will not be long now/till our wedding day*

The others clapped and cheered when he finished, but I could hardly move because his face rung out like a lighthouse and the young lover blew cold around me and I was turned to powder.

Then they sang another, then I did, then another from Sean, then they taught us a song of the Italian partisans and I taught them a silly round they wanted to try. Then Felix felt operatic and began singing about fickle women, and Freddi wanted to be Bruce Springsteen in the tunnel of love. Claude laughed and looked serene and drank wine from glasses with long stems. Our faces opened out by the beer and wine and smoke and people at other round tables joined in and the barman smiled at us and didn't care. We sang until the bar cleared out and Freddi began to fall asleep with beery grunts and his head in Claude's lap.

'Freddi is a rude boy to snore so,' Claude said, patting his head on her knee.

'No, I had better leave now,' I said.

'Ay maybe we should. I'll be walking early in the morning, and not enough sleep to get me up a mountain,' Sean said, beginning to move.

Claude whispered, with Freddi's head in her hands,

'It has been our pleasure to make the music with you.'

'It was a piece of luck to meet you, we had a good time, all of us,' Felix said.

'I love your music. I've been watching you all week, the three of you.'

'It is lucky we meet you now. In two more days, we are no more here.'

'No more here?'

'Sunday we move on, we are away. You know, our life is on the road. We are off.'

'No, oh no. Where?'

'We try capital cities east, Vienna, Berlin, you know my home.'

'Berlin?'

'Yes, we go east, you know, on Sunday.'

We walked home, Sean and I, through the night streets. The beer was on his breath, and his face was light with the pleasure of it all. The sky had a see-through darkness and I knew I had lost Geoffrey now, I knew it, because I had walked out of my shape into another.

'It was the best night,' Sean said, quietly on the doorstep, 'and you're a grand girl, I'll tell you that. It was something, to sit with you round the table there and share the songs.'

'It was for me too.'

'Sure, you're my Sabbath bride tonight,'

'You too, it's the same for me.'

Then he reached for me and I reached for him in the light and there were no more edges between us and the smells I had searched on the air were in my hair and against my face, and all the sighs in me were seeping out and it was my tongue his tongue melting together and his fingers each one a separate pool of honey on my cheek on my neck and his skin warm under his shirt and leaping up into my hand as I held his shoulder in my palm and licked the bone of his neck and felt the cold of his silver chain against his skin.

It shocked me, made me tremble how it was to see happiness held out like a candy floss so bright you could touch it and to watch it open up and change and become a great opening tulip and inside my whole heart filling the space

'Shall I come in, Laura? Shall I stay with you tonight?'

and though I didn't say yes, I didn't say no, and when I looked next it was us, tiptoing past the porter under the wind chimes into the front corridor.

I was surprised that everything at the Centre looked the same. It helped me, that the corridors, and the open doors into rooms with scattered cushions, and the winking Buddhas, were the same, and nothing was rising up and shaming me.

'Oh Lord so this is where it all happens,' he whispered, as he followed me.

This is it, the balcony, the black ribbed rock and cool air and the bright electric geraniums and the place where people share darkness without even knowing it.

And then us, us sharing the balcony, a tiny space on it

we were wine, plum red

we were at the heart of the purple lake

every shape to cup and smooth and tunnel, stroke and fold and mould

his whole head against the moon breaking out, crying, as if a shower of gulls burst from our heads

all of that

his whole sweetness the whole mountain he had walked

all of him

all of me

yes

The sky was pale, and Sean had left, before I crept back to my room. Grandma was sitting upright on my bed. She terrified me, the shock made me cry out,and the shock of my own cry in the silent room frightened me again. She was turning the end of her shawl round and round in her fingers, staring out through me, through the door I opened.

'Where were you? We waited for you all night. I went to every place where you could be but you were nowhere, nowhere. It was cruel, to go like that and tell me nothing. No warning, nothing.'

She was a young girl, such a young girl. There was a girl's shine on her skin, but her eyes were red with rubbing and crying and sleeplessness.

It was a Friday night in late August 1939. Rosa was at home, in the small Polish village of Vigry.

* * *

Rosa set the table for Friday night. It was the same Friday she had had each week of her eighteen years, but tonight was more than all those others. Tonight she would play *hashem* , play the matchmaker, not in a fussy way like the *Shadchen-babushka*, but in a loving quiet way so no-one but she would know. She knew Elias and Lolinka cared for each other, the way Lolinka grew outrageous when they were together, the way Elias's face turned towards Lola's like a sunflower. They would watch each other from afar, watching each other's rise and fall of moods. After a ten months separation, there would be more to say, more to feel. Elias would bring back all the wisdom of the yshiva , the men's covey where he had lain hidden like a mole in a lair studying through his spectacles. Lolinka would bring all the stories of the ten months she had spent teaching in school, disappearing into the woods spending hours there even in the frost and when the pools were frozen over. There must be a story of what Lolinka did there, and how she kept warm.

As Rosa set the plates out she wondered about that, about Lola's secrets. Until now there had never been secrets between them. Lola had shared every book she read, and every thought she had. But in the last year, since Elias had been away, she had been more distant and more thoughtful, and Rosa had often caught Lola looking through her at something else beyond the room, beyond the village.

After ten years she was one of the family and only sometimes made Father and Mother fight.

'She has a mind of a man,' mother would say, 'and a heathen one at that.'

'She has a mind that does credit to man or woman,' father would say, 'and you should follow her example.'

'Follow her example and be a man's companion like an egg is to a candle.'

'She will be a companion any man will envy, and she waits her time.'

'Waits her time and the carriage passes, leaving her in the ditch with the mud on her.'

'She's twenty-one, mother, leave her alone.'

'Now look who's talking now, there's Rosa influenced by all your talk.'

'I hope she is,' and father would leave the room, slamming the door so all the dust lifted off the table and set them off sneezing.

But tonight Lolinka would be there to greet the guest of honour, Elias, returned from the darkness where men went to study and returned pasty and wise. He would have a world to tell, of the books he had read and how they had made him grow inside. Maybe, to see him, you would see how he had grown: maybe his forehead would be bigger, the way they say it is with wise people.

Rosa polished the knives and forks, covered the bread with the cloth embroidered with a loaf of bread just like the one she was covering. They had made and plaited the bread themselves, mother and Rosa, beating in eggs and flour, and she liked the way the bread came out yellow and fluffy like cake.

In the afternoon Rosa picked up the chicken fresh from the Grodscka house, and passed Lunke the stonemason riding out of the town on a droschka.

'Hello there, Rosa Klein!' he shouted.

'Are you arriving or leaving, Lunke the stonemason?'

'Arriving and leaving, you might say,' he said. 'Do you want a ride home? Come on up.'

He dropped his hand down, and it was chipped and nicked from cutting stone. He pulled her up onto the seat and she sunk her toes into the crackling straw and her nose into the hot steaming smells that dropped down the back of the carriage.

'Have you engraved a stone today?' Rosa asked.

'Just doing business.'

'Can I see your drawings?'

He reached into his coat pocket and took out a fold of paper. It opened, unfolded again and again into a large sheet that draped over his knee.

'That's not your usual kind of thing,' Rosa said, craning over it. Usually he did clasped hands, or piles of religious books, or a house with a lion's paw, for the stones of Jewish graves. They were beautiful graves, the only ones in the whole region like this, with images that told stories about the people they covered. But this drawing was of two people, a man and a woman, drawn from the back; the woman was laying her head along the man's shoulder, and the curve of her head was cupped under the curve of his chin so one line flowed into the next. It was drawn lightly and quickly with a pencil, and was full of tenderness.

'It's beautiful,' Rosa said at last, 'and strange that it's drawn from the back. I wish I could see the faces.'

'The lines could be the lines of any lover: but faces are more particular,' he said.

'Did you not want to be particular?'

'I did and I didn't. You see, it can be whoever you want it to be, can't it?'

Rosa looked again, and it was true: the two gentle heads, the tendril of hair falling over the woman's ear, could have been Lola and Elias, or a father:daughter picture of herself with Julius, or even her father and mother in happier days. Looked at like that, the picture was even more beautiful drawn from the back than it could ever have been drawn from the front.

'Yes, I see. I like it like that.'

Lunke bent his head around it.

'While the artist captures them he says goodbye at the same time: the two people are walking away from him.'

'Were they?'

'Ah now, you mustn't be too literal. You see, it would be no good if it told you too much, would it? Now you like it better, with a little uncertainty.'

Now Rosa, seeing herself in the woman's head, guessed the face of the man whose shoulder she leant on. She filled in the face with invented features, and she gave the skin weather and texture and roughness. The more she sat with Lunke, the more his picture became more real than he was himself.

Lunke took it back, folded the paper again into a tiny pat, leaned forward and tapped the driver on the shoulder.

'Drop the young lady off here.'

Rosa climbed down outside her house clutching the chicken, and the horse sidled off down the lane, the carriage rattling from side to side.

The picture made her feel tender and lonely at the same time, it made her jealous of the way Elias looked at Lola. When the knock came, and Elias appeared, it made her run to him as if he were a lover.

'Rosa,' he said. That was all. He stood stiffly within the door, as it opened straight into the steaming kitchen, with his hands pinned to his side as if it would poison him to touch her, and he issued his words like a lamp-post sending up a signal.

'Is this what yshiva has done?'

'I have been in the company of men.'

Rosa could not speak. For a while, Mother's chatter and clutter was merciful, and Father took Elias away to stroke the books in the library and talk gently into the shelves.

'Elias, have you been happy in that place?' Rosa asked at last.

'Happy?' he said, as if it was a piece of food on his fork, that he didn't trust. 'That isn't the point. The point is something else.'

'What is the point?'

'To see in every mite of dust a meaning.'

'Is that what you want to see, mites of dust?'

He turned his head, so she could have her own private look at the foreignness in his eyes and forehead.

'I feel the mite of dust is luckier than I am.'

But Rosa couldn't reply, because mother was clattering with the wooden spoon against the soup pan.

They were still waiting for Lolinka at the table when the sun went down.

'That girl!' Mother said.

She had taken her apron off, put it on again, unpinned her hair, pinned it up again, stirred the soup, picked up the noodles on the back of the spoon. The chicken had almost been stirred back to life in the soup tureen.

'What behaviour to be late on a Friday night, and now the light is coming down, we should start without her.'

'Certainly not,' father said.

Elias jumped up.

'Certainly we should if the light is coming down.'

'She'll be coming soon. She'll have got caught up at the school, maybe,' Rosa said. But it wasn't true, because there was no school on Friday afternoon.

Now everyone was pacing round and round the empty place at the table, except Luba, who wasn't troubled at all.

'What does it matter what time we light the candles?' she said.

'That's what comes of her head in a book like a fishball in the batter. She never comes out, not even for good manners,' Mother said.

'What nonsense. Elias is our real scholar, and he has the manners of a Mensch,' Father snapped.

'But now we should respect the evening and light the candles,' Elias said, and though he was only nineteen, he sounded more sure and more severe than any of them. They gathered around the table, over the white tablecloth growing grey in the oily light. Mother clicked the match into light, drew her shawl over her head and passed her hands flat over the candles.

*'Baruch ata adonai eloheinu melech ha'olam asher kidshanu
bemitzvotav vezivanu lehadlki ner shel shabbat,'*
Blessed are You Lord our God King of the Universe who makes us holy through doing His commands and commands us to light the Sabbath candles.'

and they all said, 'Amen'. Then Father Julius murmured the Sabbath prayer with his eyes closed, and Elias rocked with him back and forwards as if he was in a dark room alone,

'Lord I prepare to honour the Sabbath keeping faith with you and the generations that have gone before. I cast away any hatred or bitterness that lingers from the week that is past, so that my spirit may be at rest'

Then they heard something scuffling on the kitchen steps.

'It's Lolinka!' Rosa cried, and leapt out to open the door.

No, it was a neighbour's hen that had waddled it's way to the door dragging a clump of straw between its toes. Mother shooed it away, cursing Lolinka and the neighbour and the neighbour's chicken under her breath. Father carried on, his eyes closed, ignoring them. Through the door a first autumn chill came in and blew itself around Rosa's heart like a dark space around a planet.

After the blessings over bread and wine, they sat down. Rosa wanted to know about Elias's mite of dust, but every murmur on the doorstep or hen's cry made her jump and scrape her chair back.

'Now there must have been a mistake,' Father said, ' and it is no reason for this not to be the usual blessed sabbath. We will leave the empty place for Lolinka or for any welcome stranger who may pass. Let us say we have set a place for Elijah.'

But Mother was not amused, and Elias's spirit had bowed down and Lolinka's place was empty.

'Elias, tell us your news boy. Tell us what it is there in a real place of learning,' father said.

'Uncle, it's study. All I can say is that, morning, noon and night.'

'A blessed thing.'

'Maybe for some.'

'Now Elias, you are the great hope in the family!' father said, waving the chicken soup ladle at him.

'That is my problem,' he said.

He looked at Rosa again, and she mouthed to him,

'What's the matter?'

He mouthed back,

'I just can't do it. I just can't.'

Lolinka did not come for the chicken soup with matzomeal dumplings, nor did she taste the egg plaited bread sprinkled with poppy seeds. She was not there for the fishballs rolled in batter or for the chicken stuffed with chestnuts. And her place was empty still for the lemon tea in long glasses and the marzipan biscuits. Luba and Rosa cleared the table of breadcrumbs without her, and set the glasses down without bringing out an empty one for her. And Elias became quieter and quieter, the more Father begged him for details of his new life, and the more his misery spilled out like ink and stained them.

It was during tea the knock came and Mother and Rosa rushed to open the door. It was a little boy, the height of Rosa's knee, in a long man's jacket that spread round his ankles and the tips of his shoes with the toe peaking out.

'A message for Rosa Klein,' he said, holding a note out under his long sleeve.

She grabbed it. He waited on the doorstep.

August 1st 1939

Vigry, Poland but when you read I will be now in Vilna

Rosa,

I wish I could have told you another way, but I couldn't find a way to do it. No-one will understand in my family or yours, but maybe you will. I have left home to marry Lunke the stonemason. You know him, he visits our village to engrave the stones, we always liked him. But you know he is a gentile and no-one will ever forgive me for that so I have gone away, so as not to give you all pain. I was not happy to stay always in the village and with Lunke we will have another kind of life and live in the city. He is an artist and he reads poetry and philosophy like I do and like your father does. If the world was different we would all meet and I know you would like him, but that is not the way things are today. Lunke tells me things are not safe for you, his friends tell him things which make me afraid. Think about this, if you need to leave, take care and be ready if you must do this. I will always remember you with love and there will be a place in my home if you will accept us.

Lolinka

'Well?' Mother said.

'Lolinka, she has gone.'

'Shame on her! Shame on her!' Mother began.

'Shame, to hell! Where is she?' Father said.

'She's gone to marry Lunke the stonemason.'

Mother began wailing,

'Lolinka! Lolinka! And we always loved her! The hussy, the slut, the whore!'

'Shut up, woman!' Father yelled. 'There's nothing wrong with Lunke, he's a gentile, so he's a gentile, but he's a good man, he's a good man.'

'See what your books do? See what your learning does! Your books have turned her into a slut!' Mother began screaming.

And then Father with his tiny shoulders rode himself up and steered her like a cow through the open door, shouting

'Get out with your stupidity, let's have some people here who have a brain, let's have some people here who have a head, even a hole in the head is more than you have.'

The little boy still stood on the porch, his eyes wide like plates.

'Who are you?' Rosa asked.

'Lolinka teach me to read.'

'Here,' Rosa said, and gave him a handful of zloty from the drawer. She stood in the doorway and watched him run through the street. The night was black and had sucked out the last shreds of summer. She stood on the porch, hearing the rattle of carriage wheels, and the little boy tapping across the cobbles in his broken shoes. In the distance, she could hear glass breaking, shouting, the cries of chickens caught in fights on the porch.

'They're beating people again,' Father said. 'Come in, these days if we don't love each other, no-one will.'

The night had invaded them all. Elias sat where they had all left him round the table, staring out at the empty chairs through pinpoints of black ice and praying under his breath, again and again as if his mind had broken away from its anchor,

cast away any hatred or bitterness that lingers from the week that is past, so that my spirit may be at rest

cast away any hatred or bitterness that lingers from the week that is past, so that my spirit may be at rest

CHAPTER TWELVE

Saturday

Through the wall of my room, I could hear noises like a pool of hippos snorting underwater. They carried on, regular explosions, poum poum poum.

So I knocked on Donald's door. He said,

'Go away, Laura,' so I opened the door.

In the first second, I saw Donald sitting on a cloud. The next second I saw that the cloud was hundreds of snotty tissues, scrunched up into balls and heaped into the dents of the sheets.

'It's not healthy,' I said.

'What do you know about healthy? You were the one that made me ill in the first place.'

'I didn't. I wasn't the one that made you lose your oars.'

'You were.'

'Anyway, now you're ill you might as well get better.'

'What do you care?'

I picked up his waste basket and scooped all the snotty tissues into it while he sat and watched, sneezing into more tissues and scrubbing his nose like a carrot.

'Now what?' he said, as I stood by the door with the basket.

'Open the window and get some fresh air in.'

'You.'

So I did, while he just sat there. His head spun round and round watching what I was doing, as if it was on a stick.

'I don't know why you bother, when you don't give a damn if I live or die.'

'That's just stupid, you always go on like that. You always sound like you're writing a bad poem.'

'I could die here and you wouldn't care, at my funeral you'd just say, 'it wasn't my fault, I didn't throw him in.'

'I'll bring up your breakfast,' I said, and slammed the door behind me before he could.

I have walked from one shape into another, I have seen the moon explode behind Sean's head into a shower of stars. But no-one seemed to think I was any different. Even Leo seemed to recognise me and no-one heard the voice that wrapped me round and round: 'I am new, I am completely new.'

Daphne was my partner for 'sharing feelings'. I remembered that she had a story too and felt bad that for days I hadn't thought even once about her story.

'I have decided to let my son and his new wife have the farm to themselves,' she said. 'I have decided to leave it.'

'I'm sorry,' I said, because I remembered that the farm was her favourite place, her belonging place, and she had brought rocks with her as mementoes.

'I will be fine, I will buy myself a cottage somewhere nearby, I'll take one of the sheepdog puppies with me and start again.'

'You will be then, you'll be fine.'

'Yes, yes, but then, I don't really know, Laura, just how fine I'll be.'

Daphne had always been silvery and brave, she was the sleepy one who snored during meditations, and the one who said nice things about me. It was hard to understand that Daphne didn't only feed herself with her own wisdom but might need other people's too.

'It's a bereavement, to leave a home: that's how I feel just now, bereaved.'

She sat with her eyes closed, and I sat opposite watching. Her hands twitched slightly on her knees as if she was sleeping. I thought how unfair homes were: when you wanted to stay in them, you were forced to leave. And when you longed to leave, you were forced to stay. The moment you become happy in them, it is already leaving you. Pieces in a kaleidoscope are shaken up and you find a pattern you love, you see the tiny filings spin together into a sugary underworld and get sucked in through the cave door you can feel the blues become hanging glaciers and the spots become golden eyes on rock ledges and you're just saying 'yes' when it's all changed and you're on a pope's cloak and he's sweeping you through the temple with bags of incense blinding you.

'And you, Laura?'

Me. Well I never thought, last night, 'What next?' I didn't think at all, where it would lead and where it would not lead, and how the change in me could not be hidden but blazed out like a flag.

'Geoffrey is coming. In two hours he'll be at Pacino station.'

'And are you pleased? Are you looking forward to seeing him?'

'Yes,' I said, as if I meant 'no'.

'What will you do Laura, about what you feel?'

'I don't know. I just don't know what I should do.'

Daphne looked at me quietly for a while. Then she said,

'Maybe you won't need to do anything at all. Maybe it will just happen. Decisions often do, they just happen.'

Our theme for today was Completion. We drew the Yin:Yang symbols on big sheets of paper without lifting our pens: then we drew symbols of 8 and invented new symbols of our own where lines twisted amongst each other without a break. We made circles with our thumbs and forefingers, and practised making other circles with our bodies, finding new places to join up. I was in a strange luminous place like a paraffin lamp where sleep had lifted off me during those hours of the night, and I had stayed awake with Rosa. I could see how stiffly Gloria moved, and how her knees and elbows came to points: and how like a panther Leo still was, with his long thighs making circles with his elbows and his tongue licking his beard like a cat.

And then I noticed that Gloria had changed her velvet trousers and was wearing shorts that looked new, and had pulled her hair up into a pony tail that made her look almost like a girl. For a moment I missed Isobel, and worried about her father finding her inconvenient.

I found the engagement ring I drew on the first day, rolled up on rice paper in the corner of the room. I still saw it on my hand, it still split the light and it had one of the shapes Leo called complete: there were no breaks in it, no holes, not even now.

*   *   *

My completion story
On my eighteenth birthday, Tina and Polly took me to a pub.
'You're legal now,' they said. Tina and Polly had already been legal for seven months each. We went secretly, because Mother, grandma and Hannah would be shocked. Drinking for them was just something you did at ceremonies, with special sticky wine designed for you not to like it too much, like the priest's wine. Drinking for pleasure was something gentiles did in dark places which smelt and where children weren't allowed. People who drank became criminal and hit their wives.
So I went to the pub with Tina and Polly, because most things grandma and Hannah thought were wrong. Tina had given up cut up jeans and was now interested in body stockings with leather jeans and jackboots. Polly wore grunge and leant me some layers so I could be grunge too. We each wore five layers, all different lengths and different colours.
'You look like an old rag bag,' Mother said, as I went out.
I was pleased.
'Where are you going with the girls?'
'Polly's mother is having a bridge party and asked if we wanted to

share the food,' I said.

'I don't believe,' Mother said as I closed the door.

We met on the street corner where grandma always said bad girls met. Tina was looking very bad: she had spiked her hair with wet-looking gel that made her look slightly insane.

'Are you sure?' I said, when I saw her.

'What, the crucifix?'

'No, the hair.'

She honked with laughter.

'What would your grandma go for first if she saw me now, the hair or the crucifix?'

I looked Tina up and down. Grandma wouldn't know where to begin, that was the truth of it.

Pubs were where grown-up christians went. Tina said it was the best place to go because if you stood in one long enough you would see every single real man in the neighbourhood. I couldn't wait to try it, not to talk to them or anything like that, but just to look.

The pub was called the Prince Albert. It was brown, everything was brown, even the smell was brown. We sat on a brown sofa with knife marks in it, at a brown table with dark brown rings on it, and Tina drank something brown.

'Gowon,' she taunted, 'have a half.'

I had one, and sipped at it slowly from the top.

I didn't like the pub at all. The men at the next door table kept inter-rupting our conversation, and Tina began throwing her hair around, and then they lit cigarettes and puffed in our direction. When I tried to order drinks at the bar men in big jackets kept squeezing in front of me, and the bar man mimicked me, 'Oh, it's a half is it?' in a silly mincing voice that was meant to sound like me, and another man at the bar said to me, 'He's taking the piss.'

The men didn't look interesting at all. Some had yellow teeth and oth-ers had scratchy faces, most of them wore big straggly brown coats and some had yellow fingers. Tina looked at them under her fringe and over her beer mug.

'Are they meant to be better than the grammar school boys?'

'Oh they are, they're real,' Tina said.

'I think they smell.'

Tina and Polly laughed.

But I felt miserable. The men at the next table were smoking into my hair, and Tina was making stupid faces at a man with tattoes, and the men at the bar were mimicking me and doing strange things with their little fingers. Polly kept showing me how to hold the beer mug, with my fist wrapped round it like a potato. I didn't even like the taste of the beer. It fizzed on my tongue and made my eyes smart.

'This isn't much of a way to spend my eighteenth birthday,' I said.

'Least it's legal,' Tina said.

'Let's go back.'

Tina and Polly wanted to stay because they liked the man with tattoes, but I insisted on going. I hated the way the men at the bar were watching me, and the way something happened to Tina when the men showed their tattoes.

We stood on the street. Cars slowed down when they saw Tina, then sped up again as they got close and saw me. I was glad I was wearing five layers.

'What shall we do?'

'Fingals?'

'We got thrown out last time for being under twenty-one. They're checking real tough now.'

'Pizza?'

'I'm not hungry'

'Another pub?'

'Naa. They give me the creeps.'

We stood with our hands in our pockets. Then Tina said,

'There's a Trees for Israel disco up at the club. I know it's a bit desparate, but at least we'd get a good bop.'

'Won't Polly mind? Your mum belongs to the Christian Union.'

'Naaa. I'm nothing.'

So we went, crucifix Tina, grunge Polly and me.

The door opened like a cage onto a hot throbbing beast, its haunches flexing in the strobe light. Polly hitched up a layer of her grunge and threw herself into the red jaw with its tongue licking her.

'Come on,' Tina said, 'the guys here aren't so bad. Anyway, you can dance without one.'

I stood in the doorway and watched the limbs moving and the specks began dancing like pepper in front of my eyes. I thought I looked exciting, but really I didn't compared to all the other people. No interesting bits showed through my five layers.

There were some boys but mostly they were wound round girls, or standing up by the bar with glasses in front of them like riot shields so you couldn't get near.

I looked at them to see if they would look back, but the more I did the more they didn't. They weren't that good anyway. Most of them looked as if their T-shirts had come out the coffee grinder, and the ones that looked normal spoke through their teeth.

I stood there and I didn't care if no-one noticed me. It was being noticed that I didn't like. Boys with stupid teeth were laughing at me, and my clothes suddenly felt hot and heavy, and my knees began to feel baggy and my fringe began to grow so I couldn't see behind it, and suddenly it felt stupid to have long hair so long you could sit on it and no good at all unless you were thin enough to wear clothes made of bootstrings.

So I left. I just walked out the disco and sat on the table outside the door and pretended to collect tickets or look after the coats. Tina was too busy pumping her elbows in and out like a sewing machine to notice.

There I was, when Geoffrey the Pelter boy arrived.

'Come on, you've no need to wait for me,' he said.

It was a strange thing to say, since the last time we had really spoken was at his bar-mitzvah five years earlier. Since then, we had only been in each other's backgrounds.

He opened the door and pushed me in in front of him, before I had time to explain.

'Well I don't know about this kind of noise, it's not healthy,' he shouted at me.

I didn't know either. It seemed healthy for everyone else: just for me, it gave me a headache.

'I thought this would be a civilised do,' he carried on. 'It's brought Tina Henry out in a crucifix.'

She caught his eye and stuck her bottom out in his direction, all wrapped in leather jeans, grinning so her teeth and crucifix caught the strobe at the same time. He turned to me, and took me in, my hair, long and washed and shining, and my layers which were beginning to feel hot in this unexpected climate.

'Maybe it won't be so bad if we dance together,' he said, pulling me towards him. 'Maybe it will even be rather nice.'

While everyone jigged like puppets without strings, we danced a slow, awkward dance together as if we were at the wrong disco. Having him so close muffled the noise of the band, and if I tucked my head under his chin it hid the strobe lights, and he was like a wall between me and the monster.

'Never cut your hair,' he whispered through my hair. 'It's so lovely.'

'I wasn't going to,' I said.

He laughed, though I hadn't meant to be funny.

I didn't belong anywhere: not in the pub with Christian men with brown mugs of beer, nor at the disco where friends turned into flexing monsters and the music made you ill. But here, under his arm, tucked in like a blanket, he made a canopy where I could shelter and where the men with tattoes couldn't tease me.

*   *   *

After the class, I was called away to take a call in the Yin:Yang room.

'Laura?'

'Yes?'

'It's Isobel.'

'Isobel! Where are you?'

'Maybe I'll come back to Switzerland.'

'What do you mean? The course finishes tomorrow. What's the point?'

'I got no room here at the house.'

'What d'you mean?'

'Dad's girlfriend's daughter is in my bedroom and I hate her and she hates me. She's sleeping in my bed. Dad's schmoozing all over her to impress his girlfriend and I can't bear it. Maybe I'll come back to Switzerland.'

'There won't be anyone here, just - it'll be the next course. The advanced course.'

'Maybe I'll do the advanced course.'

'No.'

'What d'you mean no?'

'It's not a good idea. I bet your father's girlfriend's daughter won't be staying long. Your dad was expecting you home on Sunday. I bet she'll be gone by Sunday.'

'Yea, maybe she will.' Isobel said, and put the phone down.

I brought up for Donald a honey drink and a bowl of hot water with lavender drops for him to inhale. I decided that if he was nasty, I would just leave it inside his door and go away. But this time he wasn't nasty at all. He had dropped all his tissues into the basket, and was propped up amongst his pillows with his face all pink and serene. For a split second, I thought he was dead, until he put out his hand and groaned,

'The angel come to see me in my sick bed.'

'You seem better to me.'

'Oh, la belle dame sans merci, how hard she is.'

'You're meant to inhale this, not drink it. It's to clear your passages.'

'I wish you'd get out of my dreams,' he said. 'I keep dreaming about you and that girl who came to find you.'

I went to my room to get ready for Geoffrey. I didn't want to speak, for a while. I thought Rosa would keep her life separate from mine, but it was getting closer and closer, and I was afraid of what would happen next.

I wore jeans and Geoffrey's shirt and I had climbed inside my clothes to hide and had unwrapped myself from my hair so it didn't cover me like sheets. Nothing I felt about Sean showed on the outside, but it felt as if it did. I never intended to change the complete things between Geoffrey and I, but I walked as if I did. I walked from side to side of the road, bumping into people, as if I didn't know the way to the station: but I did. I hadn't been to the station since the day I met Isobel hanging onto Leo's neck like a fur: the day I met Sean and thought how a different person from me might love him.

It was the same station and I thought I might see myself there, look-ing surprised and new, carrying my rucksack and weekend hold-all with my initials LC. The person I was disguised as waited at the platform for the midday train from Zurich.

I saw its nose, sniffing out the platform. Then it laid itself out and waited for its coils to stop shaking and its wheels to stop hissing. Waited a minute while we all held our breath: then everyone spilt out, small, slate coloured. One of those shaken out will be the boy with the narrow shoul-ders. Even if I just stand here without moving, that boy will find me.

People all around me were being found and wrapping each other.

I had been here all my life without realising it, and that I would never be able to leave the station. I would watch myself coming on and off the train again and again.

And now here he was click clacking along the platform, Geoffrey who filled the canvas and had been as large as rice paper, lopsided, attached to a suitcase on wheels, and here he was just the same carrying the same ears and shoulders as if he had brought everything with him. Everything, Victoria Station, grandma, the youth club disco and Uncle Ezra, Hannah and Tina and Friday nights. He pulled them all on wheels along the platform clack clack. And the old Laura ran to meet him, and left the lights of the passenger ferry and the gulls circling under the mountain behind: there was a space cut out on the station where they had been.

'Laura, Laura,' he said, and he dropped the handle with the wheels, and brought his arms out with his elbows spiking out and squeezed me in a nutcracker hug that pressed my breath out against his shirt.

'Oh, I've missed you so much,' he said. And as I was inside his jacket and smelt the train in his hair and felt the squeeze in his narrow shoul-ders, I began to tremble and say,

'I missed you too, I missed you too.'

We walked through the streets, the suitcase wheels bumping on the cobbles, back into the yard of the Centre that was a converted school, under the wind chimes and along the corridor with the pyramids of burnt incense on the window sills.

'Funny smell,' he said, his eyes scrolling up and down the corridor like a school inspector.

Then we were at my door, and I had to open the lid and jump in.

'This is where you have been all week,' he said.

We had never been alone in a room like this, without some relation about to break in. But here, we could stay for two days without appearing, and it would be no more than what everyone else was doing. This was our first time: it was our first opportunity.

Geoffrey had thought the same thing. He put his suitcase on the floor. He uncurled slowly, like an astronaut, and his face changed in slow motion, from tired yellow to a red that began from the edges of his ears and moved under his eyes and widened his cheeks.

'We're alone,' he said, and waded towards me , and we were bumping together as if the walls were too near, and everything had changed about the things we knew. We were kissing but I was sucked into the furniture and became the bed and then I became wooden and flattened and crumpled like a sheet and he was something rolled over me like a blanket. Then he stopped, and pulled himself above me on his elbows, and said,

'This bed is bloody uncomfortable. How do they get to make beds like this? It's like a bloody convent bed.'

'Let's stop then,' I said, and I looked up so his hair filled all the edges of the room, and the thing that loved him ran down through the sheet, poured out like an empty bucket. Why am I in so foreign a land? Why am I not in the same land as you, where we used to be?

We uncrumpled ourselves and walked out to the streets, but there was a kind of armour-plating around us and we clanged when we touched.

'The streets smell of chocolate,' Geoffrey said.

'I know, they do,' I said.

I used to skip down these streets. I had run down them straight into the flat sky. But now beside Geoffrey I felt like the nutcrackers in the window, snapped closed, wooden.

'What a funny little place,' he said. 'Show me what you like about it.'

'I like the square. I like the lake. I like the mountain path. I like the musicians that play in the square, Freddi, Claude and Felix. I love them.'

He stopped and his toes were in a straight line, pointing up the street side by side.

'That's a lot of things to love,' he said. 'That sounds too much, to me.'

'No, no, how is that too much? When I show you those places you'll feel the same.'

But it was like throwing pennies down a well. They would never reach the bottom: it was so far down.

We found the square, and watched it from the pier wall, my favourite place to sit. An Italian family had crossed the lake with children in lacey dresses, and were promenading round the square attached to one another by the little finger in a daisy chain. At the head of the line was the oldest lady, tiny and bent in black, and at the end of the chain was the littlest girl, with brown curls all the way down her back. The group snaked round the square like one creature. Then the little girl broke away and went pad pad in her white socks to the fountain, throwing herself up into the creamy spray. The family stopped, scattered, the Mamma moved out, scolding, then the old old lady, half bent to the cobbles, traced the little girl's journey step by step to the fountain, waved away the Mamma, and bent slowly down over the spray herself.

'That little girl gave the grandma a good idea,' I said.

'She splashed her white dress,' Geoffrey said, because yes, the grandma had stood up and was wiping the silver sparks from her mouth while the family waved their arms about and worried about lace, and the silver washed down onto grandma's collar and onto the little girl's, one only inches taller than the other.

'Laura, tell me about your week, whether they've treated you well there.'

'Treated me well?'

'Your room looks a bit grim, and that place smells funny. Have you been OK?'

'Of course. I've been fine. I didn't even notice that my room was grim. Is it?'

'Why don't you pack up today and we can go off somewhere, and be on our own? There's no point in staying, is there, if it's a bit grim?'

'It's you that said it was grim. I don't think it is. Really Geoffrey, I want to stay a bit, until the end.'

'What's the point? You're not learning anything.'

'How do you know? You never asked if I had learnt anything.'

'Well have you, have you learnt anything?'

'It's not like that. It's not learning, like in school.'

'What is it then?'

'I like the way it makes me think about things. I can't explain.'

Geoffrey made a noise like a horse spitting out a turnip.

'They've got you hooked,' he said.

I leapt up, to show I was free. The only strings around me were his suspicions, and they stuck to me like a sticky web.

'You don't even know who 'they' is,' I snapped.

'I don't really want to know.'

'You're just frightened. You're frightened it may be something interesting and you're missing out, and you're getting left behind.'

'Oh I don't think so,' he said.' Anyway, I don't know why you're so bad-tempered, when I've arrived just for you, and I only want to look after you and make you happy. I knew that course would be bad for you, I thought it would make you miserable. No wonder you feel bad.'

'I don't feel bad,' I shouted, so loud my voice bounced off the cobbles and up the wall and back to me; and the Italian old lady turned round as if I had called her name.

'My God, you're in a state,' Geoffrey said. And I began to think, maybe I do feel bad, maybe I am in a state. He wrapped me in his jacket and my head pressed against the buttons of his shirt leaving dents in my hair, and I began to sob as if I did feel bad, even though I didn't, not in the way he thought.

'Oh my poor Laura,' he said, rocking me, his hand on my head, as if I was his little sister having a tantrum. 'Let's just be happy, let's be nice to one another.'

When I came out of the cave, the place in his jacket, I decided not to talk again about what I had thought or felt this week. I decided to take Geoffrey somewhere else I loved instead.

'I can show you a mountain,' I said. 'It's more than pretty. It's marvellous. Will you come?'

He did, he came with me. He walked behind me peck peck like I had walked behind Sean, up behind the wooden houses to the place where the lane drained away into a trickle and the fields moved in like great plates. There they were, the sheer drops yowling down into plugholes, and climbers on the rock pouring themselves into hairline cracks like tendrils of ivy.

We took the low path where we wouldn't get bowled over by staircases of scree, bowling along, the champagne wind, the fields a line of plumped cushions. And then we turned a corner and there they were, a crowd of blacknosed sheep tottering in dainty stilletoes, crowded across the path like headmistresses at a bus-stop, elbowing and nuzzling each other out of the way. They sucked forward, a fur-coat army with kiss-curled foreheads battened down. They were quite firm, quite unmoving, this was their path, they had always been here, teetering among the scree and rocks and feeding on the underwater streams where crops of grass burst out. They had a warm stench, they busied and jostled us like rude teachers, I could feel their breath down my cheek. Geoffrey froze.

'Just move out the way,' I said.

'Where?'

'Out the way.'

'There's no room.'

'I mean off the path. The rest of the mountain.'

'It's dangerous off the path. Everyone says mountains are dangerous off the path.'

'Then let's just go forward, and they can move out the way.'

'They won't.'

'They will. They're good on the mountain passes.'

'It might be dangerous.'

'What do you mean? They're only sheep.'

'But they're animals, you never know what they might do next.'

'They're going to eat grass next.'

'They might not.'

'What do you want to do then?'

'Go back.'

'We've only just begun.'

'What if the mists come down and trap us?'

'The mists are stuck in the valley, you can see them rolling about below.'

'That's just not logical, to say that mists are stuck in valleys. You should know your facts if you're up in a mountain. They're dangerous places, they're no joke.'

'Oh no, we'll be fine. There's hours more daylight.'

'Daylight isn't the point. You're not listening to what I'm saying.'

He was behind me, just a few paces, frozen, watching the sheep as if they were wild elephants, letting the landscape shake out around him unseen.

'Oh stop it!' I said, 'stop fussing.'

He stopped, a few feet below me, and shouted

'I'm not fussing, I'm just looking after you.'

There was no point. No point at all. I let my legs fold me down to the tufty ground and threw myself along the grass and pushed my face up into the sky so the air breathed out of me in cold puffs. The sheep tossed their curls and wobbled past me on their high heels.

'You see,' I said, 'They're not interested in us at all.'

'Look,' he said, 'you're tired already.'

'I'm not. I'm waiting for you.'

He folded down to the grass beside me. I felt his fingers dangle down into my hair, and I moved out of his reach instinctively, before I could stop myself.

'You've changed,' he said, 'something's different. You're so bad-tempered with me. You never used to be.'

I let the sky rub itself all over my cheeks.

'I thought you would like it up here.'

'Oh I do, I do,' he said, 'but I just want to be safe.'

'You worry so much.'

'I have to,' he said.

I sat up and saw his eyes pulled together in a knot at the centre of his face.

'Why do you have to?'

'I've got used to worrying.'

'Why?'

'Maybe because of mother. If she's frightened or unhappy, she makes us all go crazy. She drives dad away, sometimes for months on end he disappears.'

'I know, I know he does. She is like that. Poor you.'

We sat for a moment and I thought how poor he was, and he was, but that didn't make me love him or want his worry.

I saved the mountain for another time. I would go back. Whatever happened, I would go back.

So we walked back, me in front with my head down and the picture of him screwed up inside it, him behind with his head down watching his steps one by one as the ground changed from grass to dust to tarmac.

The lights in town were coming down, and we were hungry. The cafes had spilled out onto the square. We chose a table near the lake. The waiter lit a candle between us.

'You are beautiful in the candlelight,' Geoffrey said.

He leaned over to kiss me, and a puff of ice rolled between my cheek and his lips. We both waited to see who would speak.

'What's happened?' It was Geoffrey.

The gulls moved above me in slow motion like seasickness. It was one thing to know in my secret places that I had left him. It was another to leave him actually, really, all the broken bits, the pieces.

'Nothing,' I said. Because I had shown him what had happened, and he hadn't understood.

I do live every day with everything I know inside me. I do live with him inside me, directing me, guiding me quickly away from people who might hurt me, places where I might get lost, or cold, or dirty. But I don't know. I don't know any more, if I wouldn't like to try it differently now. I'd like him to wait at the edge of the lake and let me throw myself off.

'I thought we were happy. I'm sorry. I thought we were happy. You should have told me,' he said.

He stared, stared out across the lake looking for a boat. He stared straight through the gulls, strutting across his gaze with their noses in the air.

'I could be more happy,' I began, 'I think I could, if you let me stretch out more.'

'I don't know what that means,' he said desolately. It was so cold, I shivered sitting so near his words.

'Tell me what that means. Does it mean other men, is that it?'

'No, no,' I said, but I couldn't think what I meant. And it was true. Sean was not there. This was not about Sean.

'You're shivering,' Geoffrey said at last.

He took off his jacket and hung it over me, slowly, tenderly, as if I was still real.

'Say something,' he said at last.

I was too tiny, too far away.

'I can't' I said.

All my pieces were uncoupling: the piece that was him, and all the other pieces that held him in place. They were falling apart.

'When you think of yourself,when you see yourself —older, when you see your— future, do you see me? Am I there, when you — think of yourself?'

But we couldn't look at each other, because then he couldn't ask me and I couldn't answer.

I huddled into his jacket. He looked out to the mountain, searching for his path. A few centuries passed and I grew old. My hair grew white and I began to wrinkle. I had no future: it was over. My future grew mouldy and dropped into the sea. Next time I sit in this square, I will be a ghost, invisible. I will have to build a person out of the scraps that I find: bits dropped by the gulls, bits I pick up round the hot dog stall.

'No,' I said at last,'no, I don't see you.'

He stood up, he seemed to wobble, I couldn't be sure, he moved one foot, he filled the whole sky. Stop him now but I was too tiny just an ant. Stop him going there is nothing else in the cave nothing nothing no candles no people no kisses no weddings no birthdays no family photos no mazeltov no please god by you no future no future stop him don't go don't go

He waded through the cement of the square. I saw him move getting smaller not believing as I watched not letting him go as I let him go, sitting there sitting there letting him go until he wasn't there the square didn't hold him only the smell of him on the collar of his jacket

CHAPTER THIRTEEN

Saturday Night

The waiter bought two fried potatoes and onions. I ate mine. Then I ate his.

I was still alive, because the food was warm as it slid down me and I could feel its route, winding round and round and breaking up into scraps.

When Geoffrey had his bar mitzvah the gold thread of his cap shone in the chandeliers. I knew before he did that the kerby grip was working its way out of his hair.

I knew that he was wrong about the sheep. The sheep just wanted a quiet walk and a nice patch of grass. I knew before he did, that what he had was an attack of vertigo.

Geoffrey was afraid at the disco. The disco and the mountain, both made him panic. Geoffrey feared the new: it was not an adventure, not a task, it was a monster. It was a loaded gun. It was not he that protected me from the monster, it was me that protected him.

I never saw it before so perfectly.

All these things I knew made him part of the routes inside me.

I didn't know any other ones.

I walked back to the Centre, and all the parts of me led me there, with myself dragging behind.

Under the door there was a note.

Laura,

I have checked into the youth hostel. I would like to have my suitcase and jacket, if you could please bring them round.

I don't know what has happened. Before you left, we were happy. I wish you had never gone away. I thought I could look after you and make you happy, but it's not what you want. I don't know what it is you do want. I thought I understood you, but now I see I don't at all.

I came all this way, for you to tell me this. I can't believe you have done this. It makes me feel ill thinking about it. Why didn't you tell me before I came?

Geoffrey

I pulled the suitcase along the cobbles just like we had done this morning. It was like taking a naughty dog for a walk. It lolloped from side to side.

Geoffrey's suitcase.

I cried, thinking of everything inside it. His shirts which he had ironed himself, folded up: all of them with long sleeves and buttons, none that were made for climbing mountains or being splashed with water.

White regulation underpants with aertex holes. I would have bought him unregulated ones after we were married.

Spare glasses in a leather case. Total protection suncream. Athletes foot powder.

Maybe when I saw him again at the youth hostel I would love him and want to live with him forever and have his children.

Or maybe not.

I didn't know.

The youth hostel was on the path up to the mountain, amongst all the gingerbread chalets.

I wheeled myself in behind the suitcase.

'Geoffrey Pelter. I want to leave this for Geoffrey Pelter.'

'You can find him yourself, Fraulein, in the men's dorm room 4 first floor.'

The room was full of blonde wooden bunks. No-one was in the room, just Geoffrey. He was sitting on a bottom bunk near the window with his head in his hands and his feet turned in like a puppet.

'Geoffrey.'

He looked up. His face was puffed and moist like an open mouth. I knew in the first second that I felt sorry for him. I felt very very sorry. I felt so sorry for him it almost felt like love, the way you ache, the way you remember them as children.

'Change your mind. Tell me it's not true. Tell me it's a nightmare,' he said.

'I can't.'

'Tell me what has changed, what have I done wrong.'

All my words closed up into a tight plughole.

'Nothing. It's not because of you.'

'Tell me what they said to you in that place.'

What I wanted to say dried on my tongue and came out in pieces of air.

'Nothing.'

He pushed me away. I pushed myself away.

'Don't treat me like an idiot! You HAVE changed and you won't tell me why. When you left a week ago we were planning our wedding. You loved me a week ago, and today you don't. What am I meant to believe, that it was all just a joke to tease and humiliate me?'

'None of that is right. It all sounds right but none of it is. I didn't mean any of it to happen. It all just happened and I don't know how and I couldn't stop it. I didn't even know for sure until I saw you again.'

'Oh thank you oh thank you so much. I come all this way, I rush to be with you, and you say, I've seen you, I'm not so sure. I can't believe it. I can't believe you could do it.'

'What have I done? I haven't done anything.'

I was fighting for words, there was not a word I could think of that I meant, everything I felt had turned into a pea.

'I just feel different, I can't help it, I didn't want it, I wish it hadn't happened, but I do, I feel different.'

'You say that, but I've no idea what you mean. What do you mean, you're different? What do you mean, you've changed? How? Is it what they've said to you? Is it some man you've met?'

He blustered about, he blustered about all over everything I felt.

'I don't want to be organised any more. I don't want to be organised to live near mother and work with Uncle Ezra and like kitchens and cooking and choose the holidays you want and avoid mountains and avoid strangers. I don't want my friends to be called freaks, and the things I learn to be called dangerous. I don't want to do everything right because you tell me so. Do you understand, I want to be free! I like what I can see there, I like it, I'm not afraid of it, I don't want you to stop me!'

I was a windmill, I felt my chest opening with the wind and whirling round and round, and the air rushing through me like butterflies.

Geoffrey sat on the bed with his mouth open.

'I don't know what you're talking about. Free?! I never stopped you doing anything. I never stopped you coming here, you did it, you did exactly what you want. You always do exactly what you want.'

But I was sobbing with frustration, and he was heaving as if he couldn't breathe.

'You all stop me, it's not just you, it's Hannah, Mother, grandma, you all crowd me in so I don't know what to think. I don't know what's mine and what's yours and what's theirs. I don't know who people are that I haven't been introduced to. I don't want to be looked after, I don't want to make a little house with you, and only let people in who you like and never leave it but when you allow me to. I don't know what it is I want to do, but why should I know? Why should I know now what I want forever, and tell you and ask your permission? Why can't I not be sure? Why can't I ?'

It felt better, oh yes, the air came rushing out.

'I don't know what you're talking about. I never said anything about you being sure or not sure. You've been with a bunch of feminists. They've brainwashed you.'

'You won't listen! You won't listen to me! You find some label for everything I say, so you don't have to believe it's me talking, you don't have to listen to what I say. You treat me like a little girl and you do the thinking for me. You don't believe I can have a single idea of my own. It's bad for me, don't you see, I start to believe you, I have to get away.'

We had run out. There was just my ring, his ring, still on my finger. I had worn it for two months, the symbol of the circle.

'Do you want this back?'

'What would I do with it? What use is it? There's no-one else, I haven't got anyone else. Of course I haven't.'

I was shaking when I left the room.

But the wings, the butterfly wings, were in me, and there were breezes in my halls and passages and windows opening sucking out the darkness.

I opened another button on my shirt and walked down the youth hostel stairs past the man with the jowls at the reception desk and into the porch.

I want to walk through the door. I want to say goodbye.

The ring winked on my finger.

I worked it off my finger and walked back up the stairs. Geoffrey was standing where I had left him, staring at the back of the door.

'Here is your ring,' I said.

So I sat in the path amongst the buttercups growing electric in the dusk, and scribbled a note.

Dear Sean,

I never was so happy as last night when we were together.

Also I want you to know that my boyfriend came today and I broke off my engagement. I never thought this would happen. When we were together on the train I never in a million years would have guessed that would happen.

Please could we meet to say goodbye? I just want to say goodbye because you helped me make up my mind, though it just happened, I didn't realise it had happened until it did.

If you have time would you meet in the square just in the place where we first met, tomorrow at 12.0? I hope you will.

Laura Cherry

Then I left it at the desk with the man who had shown me the way to Geoffrey Pelter. He gave me a terrible look, as if I had sold my body. But

I didn't care.

When I got back to the room, Donald opened his door.

'I've been delirous.'

'You're not better then.'

'No, I'm worse, and you were out all day. Someone came to look for you. She kept knocking on my door.'

'She?'

'Yes. She. She said you would know who it was. I didn't know you had so many friends in Pacino. You've only been here a week' and he closed the door.

I stared at the back of his door. Then I banged.

'What did she look like?'

'Reddish hair, pale, funny clothes, looked about sixteen or seventeen. Didn't know you had friends that age.'

'What did she say?'

'Did you want to come for a picnic in the forest. Did I want to come.'

'Did you want to come?'

'Of course I said no.'

And he closed the door for a second time.

She was there, so young a girl I drew breath to see her, with her mad bright smile and her brown summer dress and a picnic basket.

'I asked Elias, Lola, I hope you don't mind, do you?'

'I'm not Lola,' I said, but it was strange, she was seeing me but another one behind me, inside me, through me. She was looking, but just beyond where I might have been.

'Oh go on, you're always so mysterious. The droscky is coming for us. You won't have to sit next to Elias, if you think he's a bore.'

'I don't think he's a bore,' I said, but I don't know why I said it, because I didn't know.

It was late summer 1938, and Rosa was eighteen and at home in Vigry.

*   *   *

Rosa went down to Grodscinski the butcher's to pick up a chicken for the picnic. Marek, the butcher's son, was alone behind the counter. He had grown taller than his father in the last six months, and his beard was beginning to grow. On her last trip to the butcher's, Mrs. Klein had said, 'Ooh what a handsome boy he's become'. Rosa didn't agree: or at least, she chose not to notice.

'I'd like the best chicken you have,' she said.

'What if there's a forfeit for the best chicken?'

'What do you mean, a forfeit?'

'Nothing's for free in this world.'

'Of course not, I have zloty.'

He came round the counter, wiping his hands on his apron. She stepped backwards, and he stepped with her, pressing her against the counter opposite.

'Well maybe zloty just isn't enough, and from someone so pretty especially.'

'Keep your stupid chicken,' Rosa said, and pushed him so fiercely out of the way he struck his hand on the counter.

An hour later, Luba went up to Grodscinski's for the chicken. She returned, pink and smiling.

'Marek's coming with us on the picnic,' she announced.

Rosa was not pleased.

'How come?'

'I invited him.'

So it was done, and couldn't be undone.

It was already quite late for a picnic: the air was picking up a streak of autumn chill. Rosa and Luba filled the basket and covered it with a folded tablecloth: boiled eggs, bread in a long yellow plait, salami like a blood red kiss, a tub of sour cream. The rest of the basket they could fill with mushrooms, sneaked from under damp leaves in the toes of trees.

Luba spent all the time they were baking bread, plaiting her hair in front of the mirror and curling it over her head with combs; then trying on Rosa's dresses, and mother's, to see which suited her best.

'Why do you care so much? Who are you trying to impress?' Rosa shouted at her.

'Oh you, you just like to be a schoolmarm' she snapped back.

'I like to be with sensible people who have more thoughts in their head than what colour dress to wear.'

Lola arrived out of breath, with her hair falling out of its pins and a book in her pocket. She jumped up into the carriage while the horse cocked its leg by the tree and sent out steaming pats.

Elias had been sitting in the carriage for ten minutes already, narrow and pale and his fringe had grown too long. He looked at Lola through his fringe and watched the tendrils work their way down her cheek.

They clopped down the cobbles leaving the pats behind them like a row of steaming stepping stones.

Marek was waiting at the end of the lane with a whole roast chicken in a pot. He threw his leg over the carriage and jumped in.

'Phew, this horse stinks!' and they were off, sidling out of the narrow lanes and into open forest, picking up speed and rattling over the potholes that were beginning to fill with fallen leaves.

The droscka driver was whistling to himself, the basket was bouncing on the floor of the carriage, when Marek shouted,

'Put us down! Let's walk from here!'

It was a good place, Marek was right. The trees formed cool corridors with long slices of shadow and in between there was a silver hair of water to roll in and wash feet in and beyond that a long flat plate of water with the sky shining on its back. They planted their picnic in the toes of a tree and pulled off their sandals so the dust painted dark rings round their toenails on the way to the stream. Marek climbed trees, crashing and snapping against the lower trunks that had no footholds, trying to impress, to leap above Rosa, Luba and Lola, surprise them like a forest wolf. Rosa felt the warmth beat through her dress, the bursts of water like silver fireworks as she lifted the stream on her toes. Lola followed the footprints of wolves, some still frozen at the bottom of ancient black puddles. They played hopscotch with the light crisscrossing through the trees, where they had walked in winter and watched the men fishing through cracked ice over the frozen pools. Luba ran under the trees, watching Marek like a monkey, catching the branches and tufts of emptied nests he found her.

Elias tried to cross the stream to a dry patch, his trousers rolled up above the ankle, wobbling from stone to stone holding his pockets like a skirt.

We spread, Rosa thought, as if the wind had thrown us, we find our place, earth, air and water.

When they were hungry, each one found an arm or elbow of the tree roots that fitted them perfectly, and organised their bodies into the space and opened up the baskets of bread rolls and salami, turnips and eggs.

'The forest is my favourite place,' Rosa said.

'It's my favourite place sometimes,' Lola said. 'Sometimes I don't like the spirits here.'

'What spirits?'

'Well sometimes I feel the good things from the maples and birches and larches. Sometimes I feel the bad things from the wolves and poison mushrooms. The poison ones sometimes look not so different from the good ones.'

'Why should that worry you? If you know the difference, you'll not eat the poisonous ones. And if you don't know, then better not eat either,' Rosa said, careful and scientific.

'It's not that, it's something else. You know, if we ate poison in the forest it would go on just the same and not mind one bit. Bad things could happen and nothing would change here.'

'I like that. I think it's good that nothing would change,' Rosa said, quietly, turning the earth over with her toes.

'It is good , but it's blind, you know, it would turn away and not see us.' Elias pulled himself up onto his elbows.

'What strange things you two talk about.'

'Well, you do too, men can read strange things we girls are forbidden to read. You know, Elias, we could have a pact. What do you think?' Lola said.

'What pact?'

'I'll tell you girls' secrets, and you tell me mens' secrets.'

'What mens' secrets?'

Marek laughed rudely, a plump chicken leg on the way to his mouth, 'Elias doesn't know men's secrets.'

'I don't mean those, stupid,' Lola rebuffed, quick as a bullet.

'I mean the ones he'll read about when he goes to study, but you wouldn't know about those, Marek Grodcinzky.'

'I wouldn't much want to. '

'Oh who cares what you would want? Now, as for what Elias will learn at the yshiva, now that's different, and I bet they'll tell you girls are too foolish to share them. But you will, won't you, if we have the pact?'

Elias looked at Lola as she sucked the end of a blade of grass and her hair tied loosely with string began to unwind and her sleeve was tipped off by her shoulder, pushing it out bare and brown into the sun.

'Yes,' he said, so he could see her teeth when she smiled.

She laughed and threw her head back so he got extra delights, watching her hair fall back along the furry part of her neck.

'Yes, let's have the pact,' he said, and it seemed a thrill, to say the words that clinched them into some kind of future where there would be confidences between them.

'We can start today,' Lola laughed. 'Tell us all about it, promise, tell us what you learn.'

'I promise,' Elias said.

'Do it solemnly, promise solemnly.'

'Course,'

'Say it.'

'I solemnly promise to tell you everything I learn.'

'Yes, Elias!' Lola said, and kissed him on his white forehead. He blushed right through from his heart to his ears and through the long tunnel of time between them.

'Do you want to go away and study?' Rosa asked Elias.

'I think I do. I think it will make me a better person.'

'Oh no,' Luba said, 'how would studying make you a better person? It would make you an old person like the rabbi.'

They all screeched with laughter.

Rosa looked at Elias, pale as a thumbnail and it was true, she could see him grow old like the rabbi, and never let his feet dangle in the water and never throw off his shirt so the sun beat him in the chest.

'What book have you brought, Lola?' he said. 'You've always got a book.'

'Pushkin. I like his poems.'

'If I lie here, for our pact, you read me one, will you?' Elias said, and settled himself into the grass with his head at an angle so he could look up at Lola sculpted in the sunlight.

She read carefully, as if she was writing the poem as she went along. It had the feeling of a thought made for the first time, in the moulting forest of late summer 1938.

> *'What comfort for you in my name?*
> *It will die like the sad plash*
> *Of a wave breaking on some distant shore,*
> *Like the sounds of night in a dense forest.*
>
> *On the pages of your album*
> *It will leave only a dead sign,*
> *Like the vague traces of an epitaph*
> *Carved in an unknown tongue.*
>
> *What comfort for you? Long forgotten*
> *Amidst the storms of new emotions,*
> *It will not offer to your soul*
> *Pure and tender memories.*
>
> *But on a silent day of sorrow,*
> *Speak my name in your grief. Just say:*
> *There is a memory of me, there is*
> *In the world a heart in which I live.'*

Nobody said anything, for a full few seconds when Lola finished, and laid the book back down on her lap.

'That's a bit miserable,' Luba said, eventually.

'You didn't say to read a happy poem. It just opened on that page.'

Elias had grown quiet, looking at Lola from below with his head in the grass.

'I think it was beautiful. It was beautiful, the way Lola read it,' he said, in a small voice.

'Well, it was a bit miserable.'

'Poets are miserable, quite often,' Rosa intervened, helpfully.

'You lot don't understand,' Lola said, 'that happy and sad are the same thing.'

She stood up, to break the shadow. She wandered out towards the lake, and Elias watched her shape grow transparent and disappear.

'Lola is the lonely type,' he said as he let her go. 'I wish I understood her.'

'Not lonely, I don't think it's that,' Rosa said. 'She's just different from other people, she needs to do that on her own.'

'She is different,' Elias said, his voice growing heavy and secret, 'she is more wonderful than anyone else in the world.'

They stayed in the shade, side by side, while Marek, already tired with sitting and tedious talk, pulled out a bottle from his pocket. The liquid inside was purple and stunk like paraffin.

'Don't tell,' he said, pouring it into his mouth, gagging, and trying again.

Then he and Luba went off into the forest and Rosa heard shrieking and laughter, the sound of cracking branches and splashing streams, and pebbles plashing and falling. Marek and Luba played like children.

All the eggs and chicken legs were eaten, and the dishes were packed back in the basket, and the shadows were getting longer and the sun sinking before Lola returned; her hair was loose over her shoulders, her eyes with bright moist rings around them, and her skin warm as a cherry.

'I'm sorry, the time just went,' she panted.

Her whole skin looked dipped in and out of the silver, the lake hanging over her like a veil of fat silver beads. Elias was alarmed, to see her so bright.

'Where have you been?' he said.

She pulled a piece of paper from her belt and unfolded it. It was a scrap of paper, maybe picked up from a leftover picnic, but on it were faint lines in soft pencil. Rosa and Elias craned their heads and narrowed their eyes to interpret the drawing.

'Oh,' Rosa gasped, as the shape began to grow firm out of the page. It was the head of a young girl swimming, her hair fanning out all around like a silken shawl, and tangled in it, spirals of bindweed and cloverleaf lilies. The whole was understated, in just a few soft lines that hinted at the silkiness of the hair, the lightness of the water, the tangling of the weeds.

'Who did it?' Elias said, tightly.

'Is that you in the water? ' Rosa said.

Lola folded up the paper carefully, corner to corner so it sat in the palm of her hand, where she held it on the walk home.

'It might be,' she said carefully.

They walked back, slowly, along the paths, Elias near Lola where he could smell her and where he could put out a finger to touch her, Lola quiet, the lozenge of paper in her hand, her eyes searching between the trees for something that was no longer there, Marek jumping and shouting like a young monkey, much the worse from his foul vodka, Luba trailing him, her cheeks pink as if they had been pinched and kissed.

'You said we would share secrets,' Elias said quietly. Lola touched her lips with her finger and tossed her hair so the drips wove down her neck and made her shiver.

Rosa felt uneasy. Since the Pushkin poem, there seemed to have been a shadow and she hadn't washed it off, as the others had, and she wasn't sure if she liked Lola's picture.

They walked back to the droscka in a line. They had walked further than they thought and had further to go to meet the road when they came upon a man, standing in their path. He was planted there like a tree and at first he was that to them, a tree, a part of the landscape, a part that was there and could not hurt them. But then the moment slid so quickly into another so quickly like blinking he grew from a man a shadow into a thing bigger than the forest bigger than all the past that held them together all the things that had made them grow up carefully and with prayers he became the thing that war is he became hate they had never seen it never before looked like this into its face and it was bigger than them it was not them it turned them into nothing and as this happened he lifted his arm lifted it like a javelin thrower they saw his arm tighten along the sky its shadow tighten the fist opening so the palm the fingers panned out flat as a starfish, and some animal in them pulled them down to the tree roots as something spun out through the air from his open palm a stone the size of a pumpkin grazed the space which their heads emptied a second ago, and he ran forward, picking up stones as he ran, pounding them out back into the air back into the spaces they emptied as they ran.

Yids vermin rats scum they didn't hear they didn't think they didn't see on and on it went on and on a drone of hate. Rosa closed her ears so they were black inside with just the pounding the pounding of his fists against the walls and she closed them up tight to seal him out seal her in as it pounded

pow pow pow pounded

his hate his face pulling them in like a plughole whirling them up together mixing them up into a scum

They ran all the way back to the road, letting the last pieces of salami and muslin basket covers float off the baskets and land among the tree roots.

Elias rocked in the carriage, his eyes closed, his fingers turning the button of his shirt round and round, round and round, rocking, praying through his closed teeth

Hashem God be praised, be praised for this day that you have saved us you have saved us

Hear O Israel O Israel Hear Hear Hear O O O Israel blessed be blessed be O Israel

and never opened his eyes, all the way home never saw anything but the black inside his head.

Marek stood on the carriage, let it throw him like a drunk from side to side, throw him heavily edge to edge, bruising him

I'll kill cut strangle meat cleaver axe chop tear cut

I'll kill him God hashem be praised with a meat cleaver Hear O Israel Hear O Israel kill chop axe hallowed be thy name

Luba sobbed into her dress.

It's all over, Rosa thought. It will never be the same again.

'It was too cold for a picnic,' she said, quietly.

'Yes,' Lola said, as if she knew.

One week later Elias left for rabbinical training at the yshiva. Lola and Rosa helped him with his bags onto the cart as it smelt and rattled in the street, and waved him off, shouting, 'tell us all about it. promise, tell us what you learn.' They saw Elias disappear round the corner, sitting up with his back straight against the seat and his face pale and transparent as a piece of muslin.

*　　　*　　　*

'Poor Elias,' Rosa said, 'do you think he'll be alright? He'll miss us, I know he will.' She was wringing the sleeve of her dress round and round in her fingers, looking out through the window into Pacino as if he might still be there.

'He's not there any more, Rosa. He's gone now, he's on his way. I'm sure it'll be alright.'

'He's so delicate. I don't think they know how delicate he is.'

'You'll see him again.'

'Of course I will. I'll see him soon. It'll go so quickly, ever so quickly, and then I'll see him again.'

I ran after her, but she melted into the twists and turns of the corridor, her yellow dress flickering on and then off like a flame.

And bumped into Leo.

I smelt him first, the sweet jasmine smell of incense on his skin, then the campsite smell of damp blanket.

'Well well,' he said. 'If it's not my mystery girl, the sleepwalker again?' he said.

'No it's not, it's not the sleepwalker, I'm not sleepwalking.'

'I apologise. I'm sorry it's a problem.'

'It's not a problem,' I continued, 'it's just wrong.'

'Well fine, fine. Thanks for putting me right, and let's get to sleep. You and I don't seem to get too much.'

'Where are you going?' I said, without knowing where I said it from, or why.

'Now that's a question. Where are you going?'

'No, that's not fair, you always throw questions back. You first.'

'To my room, fair lady.'

'Then where have you been?'

'With Gloria.'

I didn't really care any more, what Leo did. Only I thought he should care.

'It's Gloria now?'

'Well since you asked.'

'Now you've dumped Isobel, now you've ruined Isobel, you just move on, don't you, you just move round the circle and see who you can pretend to help. Why do all the women fall in love with you?'

'Do they?'

'You know they do, because you like it. You encourage it. You pretend it's all for their own good, but it's really for your good. '

'Have you fallen in love with me?'

'No, certainly not.'

'Then it's not true, is it, that all the women do?'

'All the stupid ones, that can't see what you're doing.'

'Where does all that anger come from?'

'Where does it come from? It comes from you.'

'I make you angry. Why's that?'

'Because you're a cheat and you're dangerous. Nobody is really special to you. You make everyone feel special, but nobody is special to you really.'

'Am I special to you?'

'No. I don't care about you at all. You use clever games and slogans to stop yourself feeling bad. You hurt people and find clever ways not to feel guilty. You could never understand a person really, because you only think in slogans, and you could never care about them because you would always care more about yourself. Do you know what you did to Isobel?

Do you know how desparate she was when she left here?'

'Isobel is the only one who can help herself.'

'I bet you didn't say that when you got her to fall in love with you. I bet you didn't mind at all being her hero, because it was useful to you, because you're afraid to be alone in the dark aren't you? You're afraid to be alone?'

Leo was getting angry now.

'Look little girl, I'm off duty now. If you want a truth session, I'd prefer you give it a go when these things are scheduled, rather than 3.0 in the morning when I'm not too bright. But one thing you can go away and think about, is whether you haven't got it a bit wrong about people doing things to each other. I didn't get Isobel to fall in love. She did it herself. She's not a puppet.'

Then I took the corner of his blanket and pulled it so it unrolled weave by weave a mountain unwrapping leaving him raw and cold with his silver shoulders and dark strange nest of hair shivering in the corridor the incense and pillow smell coming off his skin and his jaw just opening in an O of surprise.

'Oh don't people do things to each other?' I said.

I ran down the corridor and looked at the clock.

He was right. It was 3.0pm.

Lola's poem was in my diary.

'What comfort for you in my name?
It will die like the sad plash
Of a wave breaking on some distant shore,
Like the sounds of night in a dense forest.

On the pages of your album
It will leave only a dead sign,
Like the vague traces of an epitaph
Carved in an unknown tongue.

What comfort for you? Long forgotten
Amidst the storms of new emotions,
It will not offer to your soul
Pure and tender memories.

But on a silent day of sorrow,
Speak my name in your grief. Just say:
There is a memory of me, there is
In the world a heart in which I live.'

CHAPTER FOURTEEN

Sunday

Sunday, our last day. A week since I arrived. Seven days and seven nights, and on not one of them have I rested. No, for seven nights I have hardly slept. There has been too much to do.

Donald said he was still delirous and had strange dreams and fevers. The doctor came round with a thing in his hand like a gun and felt him all over under the sheets. Then he said, Donald had constipation of the lungs and prescribed him things to breathe and swallow and other things to go up his nose. I stayed in the room with him, and it was true, his head was hot and when he fell asleep he groaned. I missed breakfast to stay with him, then went on to the morning session.

As I turned to leave, he said,

'I dreamt about you just now.'

'You did?'

'Yes, that's what I said.'

'What happened?'

'I was in a cart with a big black shape pulling it. I couldn't see what, it must have been a horse, it smelt and rattled and I was just rattling on into this darkness with you waving and shouting.'

'What was I shouting?'

'You were shouting, 'tell us all about it, promise, tell us what you learn.'

'Then what?'

'That's it, that was it. Weird isn't it?'

I felt as if I was catching Donald's fever. I could feel the space between my ears pumping in and out as if it would pop.

'You had your hair up in combs.'

'Are you sure it was me?'

'I thought it looked nice. You should do that.'

I looked at Donald. He was pale and fragile and his loves were hopeless and he wheezed whenever he tried to be alone. Rosa had mixed him up with Elias and mixed up the dreams.

I went on to the morning session, the last one of the course.

Even though I now knew all about Leo, he was just the same with me, as if nothing had happened, distant and religious. He made a comment about the 'survivors' and it was true, there weren't many of us left and even those of us who were there looked as if we were really somewhere else.

We built a circle with objects that were our selves: Daphne's rocks, my picture of the engagement ring, Leo's china Buddha wearing a green loincloth, and Gloria brought the bottom of her jeans which she had cut off above the knee to make naughty shorts that showed her bottom. This was what she felt about her ex-husband. Then we had to put in the middle our Life Enhancement diaries and find someone to share ours with. By mistake Gloria and I picked one another's, so I ended up having to hear about her diary and her hearing about mine.

She read to me long passages in her diary about how she didn't feel angry any more with her husband and how she had shouted at cushions instead and it had helped and it had made her see that really the sad person was her husband for not being her husband any more and one day he would see how sad that was even though now he grinned a lot and had a thin girlfriend and spent lots of money. I listened, but felt quite sick. When it came to my turn to share the diary, I panicked. I couldn't share all these thoughts with Gloria. I wanted to throw you into the sea: I'm sorry now, as I write inside you. It seems very disrespectful: but I felt quite ashamed of you suddenly. It got worse: Leo joined in. He went on about a problem I had with trust, and how it was good to share things if they were painful. I said it wasn't that things were painful, but they were confidential. And then I got so infuriated with him, that I burst into tears. Leo tried to hug me, and I got even more furious, cried even more, got furious with myself for crying. What I hated, was that I was doing everything Leo had wanted of us: feeling angry, crying, shouting, getting confused. It felt like his victory, and I was furious with him.

Before the Closing Ceremony, I went to see Donald. He was sitting against the pillows with one of the bottles up his nose.

'I'm going to stay here until I get better,' he said. 'The doctor said to.'

'Will you be OK?'

'I might make a friend in the Advanced group.'

I sat and listened to him wheeze.

'I had another dream.' he said, 'It must be this linctus stuff he made me drink.'

'What was it?'

He picked up the bottle.

'Honey and eucalyptus.'

'No, stupid, what was the dream.'

'Even now you're abusive, you don't deserve to get mixed up in my dreams.'

'I'm sorry. Please tell me, Donald. Actually you don't know how much I like hearing your dreams.'

'Well you know this morning I told you about this other one with you wearing hair clips. There was more of that, I had been in this rattling cart hours and hours and could see nothing, you kept bobbing up saying 'tell me what you learn, you promised'. Then I was in a room and it was like a monk's cell, with no light, only books. I opened the books and I couldn't read them. You know how you look at a strange language. I looked and looked, I could see the words but I couldn't understand them. I squeezed my eyes and rubbed them and pulled the books up to my nose, but I couldn't make sense of a single word. But what was strange, I felt that the words were absolutely precious, they were so important, they were my only food and drink and if I couldn't understand them I would starve. It was terrible, I have never been so frightened.'

'Elias at the yshivah,' I said.

'But it was worse. The next thing, I was throwing the books onto a fire, a great fire out in the yard and there were other men like me with white faces piling books on too and sobbing as they did it. And what felt so bad, they were sobbing as the books burnt, but I felt glad, I felt relieved. It was madness, I didn't know what was happening, even in my dream it was like I had got into the wrong place and instead of a joke it was becoming more and more of a disaster. '

'Oh Donald, I can't believe you had that dream.'

'I don't know, just because you were in the dream I thought I would tell you. And you said in the dream, 'tell me what you learn', and that was it.'

'Maybe you couldn't see properly and no-one had realised. Maybe you needed stronger glasses.'

Then I hugged Donald.

'I'll read your poems, Donald, if you send them to me,' I said to him.

'Will you?'

'I promise. I'll give you my address.'

At the Closing Ceremony, we had to say one thing we appreciated about each person in the group, even about the people who weren't any more in the group.

Daphne: I appreciate her cornflower dresses and the way she made me think about my wedding and see that it would be a black wedding, a burnt offering, that I was not ready.

Leo: I appreciate that he showed me how silver and brave are a man's bones in the dark even when you don't love him.

From Donald I learned that even unexpected people have something to tell you if you listen to them.

From Gloria I learned that slogans about recovery get you nowhere if you are not recovering, and that trying too hard isn't always the right way to do it.

From Isobel I learnt that even people you don't like have reasons for being the way they are, and knowing the reasons may make you like them a little.

From Geoffrey I learned that you don't love the people you ought to, and sometimes you don't love the people you think you do.

From Sean I learned that you do love the people you oughtn't to, but there is always a good reason for loving them. My reason for loving Sean was that he took me to the mountain top.

These are the things they appreciated about me.

Daphne appreciated that I was the same age as her new daughter-in-law and it helped her to feel kindly towards her and imagine her taking over the farmhouse and being a friend.

Gloria appreciated how innocent I was because she didn't think girls my age could be so innocent.

Leo appreciated how brave I was, much braver than I appeared, and he had learned a lot from me.

Then we hugged and it felt less strange and it felt more real and I didn't get caught in people's hooks and scarves but smelt the soap on their skin and picked their hairs off my T-shirt, short silver ones, curly black ones from Leo's beard.

It was over, Life-enhancement was over and now it was my own course I was starting.

I went to meet Sean at twelve o' clock. I didn't know if it had worked, the note, and it felt too soon after Geoffrey to meet someone in the square and be happy. I was grieving because Geoffrey was, and I felt free because there were no more rules left to break and I felt the heavy thing pressing on me where Rosa had left in the night.

Even though I just wanted to say goodbye to Sean I was making up stories with him and other places where we might meet and imagining his office with the high window and the boarded up street in Belfast where he lived. Then even though I tried to shut down the film, it went on, how I would meet him at the airport, no, at the station, at the harbour, he would come by boat, and we would find a place, a park a hotel a student room a little home by a lake a mountain in a city centre and close the door and how the hours would be the hours and hours the stroking cupping moulding smoothing sighing crying the stars again breaking out the cry of gulls, and then his jokes and his white teeth and his black fringe and whistling and as I walked he was walking inside me and I inside him

Then vaguely, slowly, I looked at the world I was walking in and it became apparent that Pacino was not the same as usual. The streets were full of people. In fact, I could hardly walk on the pavement and had to walk quite often in the middle of the street, jumping out of the way of bicycles. While I was thinking about Sean, I trod on a lady with large hair who smelt of perfume. She went 'tsk tsk' and threw her hair around. I didn't care.

I arrived at the square just before 12.0 but I didn't recognise it. It had completely changed. There was a solid line of stalls all with different coloured stripes and smells from sausages and onions, chocolate and chestnuts, goats tied up in a pen, hot leather and bunches of enormous cut flowers, and all the noises were mulched together - a musical round-about going round and round with giant yellow teapots, the lake ferry making loud steaming noises, goats eating paper bags - and the people and stalls and sellers and animals were completely solid so the fountain had disappeared, the other side of the square with the wall and the gulls had disappeared, the ice cream kiosk had disappeared and I couldn't even say where it had ever been.

What do I do? What do I do? I waited, watched all the new people pouring into the square from the corners and the lanes and the main street, then I began pushing into the crowd to get to the lakeside of the square but fell over a crate of chickens. Everybody was having a lovely time, except me. Everyone was blowing up balloons or picking up chick-ens by their necks, and I felt miserable and wanted to tread on them and puncture their balloons. So then I pushed my way back out of the crowd into the street, and now it was even more chaotic, because a group of clowns had arrived in big yellow pants and all the children were crowd-ing round them screaming.

There was no square. It was the first time I had ever seen Switzerland dirty, and it was the day I was to organise my future with Sean.

I stood in the centre of the square with children and dogs pressing around me, spun round and round so the lights stretched out like stream-ers, and the clock in the square did its whirligig for 12.15 and then 12.30 and he was not to be seen.

So I walked up the trail to the youth hostel and there was someone new at the desk, a large lady with moles and a mouth pushed out into a snarl. I said,

'Did Sean Kelly pick up my message?'

and she wheezed and snorted, and said, 'Ja,' then, 'Nein' and produced my message from behind the desk, still folded just as I had left it.

'Is he still here?' I asked,
and she wheezed again and her mole sprouted hair, and she said, 'Ja,' then
'Nein' and produced the visitors' book and scrolled down to his name,
'Checked out 11.0am'.

Now, I've gone home, back to where I always was, and it's no place for
me and no place for you. And it's no place, neither, for you to change it.
This one you have to leave to me, and look to your own life, for you to
change if you so want it.

So I didn't get a chance, not even a chance to say goodbye or to invent
a new magic place in north London or Belfast or the Makilecuddy Reeks.

I walked back with the note in my hand.

I never was so happy as last night
I never thought this would happen.
It just happened, I didn't realise it had happened until it did.

I was thinking all these things as I walked through the gates of the
Centre and down the tea-shop street, the Kitchen Witch and chocolate
cockroach street, when someone said to me,

'Oh hello, it is Laura,' and I leapt as if Rosa had touched me through
the tunnel of time, and flustered because none of my feelings or clothes
were organised and thrilled because it might be Sean. But when I looked
again through all that confusion, I saw a kind welcome funny face with a
gold tooth and embroidered skull cap and it was the friendliest kindest
face of the day.

'Where you go?' said Felix.

'To say, to see Sean.'

'Your Irish friend?'

'Yes, yes.'

'But he isn't there.'

'He isn't there?'

'No,' I said.

Felix looked at me tragically, then he said,

'You have a cup of coffee.'

'No.'

'I mean, I invite you.'

I walked beside him, with my note in my hand.

'You know what was my job before playing on the street?' he said.

'No,'

'Feeding mice to snake in the zoo.'

'Oh my God.'

'So for you it can't be so bad as that.'

It was true, losing Sean wasn't as bad as feeding mice to snakes in the zoo.

We sat round the round table at the Schwend where people were still eating sausages and drinking beer, just as they had done all those nights ago and I held the mug between my hands to warm them even though I wasn't cold, it was comforting like a bag of fish and chips.

'Today is my last cafe in Pacino,' Felix said, and grinned so his tooth bobbed. 'I have,' and he glanced at his watch, 'ninety minutes before the train.'

'Oh, so you don't have long' I said miserably.

'I have,' and he looked at his watch again, 'ten minutes I can be with you'.

'Where are you going?'

'Innsbruck, then Vienna, then Berlin for November.'

'Berlin for November? You seem to just make things up as you go along, but really you are so organised.'

'We must be organised, we are a business.'

'How do you do it?'

'We are like birds, we go south in winter to get more hot.'

'Berlin is more east.'

'For Berlin we go east and east for a while, then south and south.'

'You'll go further east? How will you do that?'

'We will see. We will see if we can do that.'

'How far east?'

'Maybe Berlin, Gdansk, Vilna, Moscow.'

'Really?'

'It is our plan. We learn new songs as we go, and live cheap, and do the odd job.'

'It must be wonderful to be like that.'

'Like that? We are how we have to be.'

'Yes,' I said. 'We are how we have to be.'

Then I thanked him and he grinned and gave me a kiss on the cheek, and I said,

'Do you need a singer?' and he said,

'We play always first in the main square, then we move into the side streets.'

When I went back to the Centre to pick up my suitcase, Gloria was there dusting the wind chimes and setting them up for the next group.

'Just giving Leo a bit of help,' she said as I passed.

First I dropped in to see Donald.

'People have been coming and going all day to see you,' he said. 'Where do you meet all these people? I don't understand.'

'Who?'

'One dropped a note under your door. Then that lady came with a fur coat on, hasn't she heard of animal rights?'

'No,' I said.

The note under my door was in scribbly pen.

Lady Laura Cherry.

Dear Laura

I hope you did not think I took advantage of you in any way or made it bad for you to see your boyfriend today. I never wanted at all to make things worse for you, only to make them happier.
I think you are a great girl, I think you are one of the best ever, and beautiful, and I will never forget you. I never thought this would happen, that I would feel this and get carried away. Please forgive me and forget me.

With all my love and I hope you will always do the things that make you happy

Sean Kelly

I sat on the bed with the note open on my lap, and the bed stripped, the cupboards empty, my bag with its labels sitting waiting for me to go, when there was a knock on the door. What happened, she walked in before I had time to open it.

'I've found you at last, dear Maya Abelhofer, just like in your photo. I've come to thank you.'

I said nothing, frozen, though she smelt sweetly of perfume and looked soft, gracious, fuller and more beautiful than I had ever known her, her tiger collar nestled up like a halo round her soft chin.

'Drowned in the cold cold lake. Dear Maya, do you know in a way you were lucky, luckier than others, to be in your own home in a place you had watched from childhood through every season, and do you know, for me you were always nineteen. Poor Maya, it was not your life to live: it was mine and I thank you. It was a good life, and you gave it to me.'

She took my hand again and the cold made me gasp.

'A hundred men and women helped to pass your papers from you to me through the secret borders. I have every one of them to thank. They made me a secret tunnel to pass through. But you were the one most of all I wanted to find. Is it here, then, Pacino?'

'Yes, Rosa Klein, this is Pacino.'

'You must think I was very bad not to find you. I never did find you, you know. I don't know where you were at all, that Phonixstrasse 90. No-one knew it. Was it a place at all, Maya Abelhofer?'

'Yes, I think it was,' I said, but only because I was not myself, I was frozen into Maya in case I woke her from the dream.

'But I went to the lake. You...well you would know it wouldn't you?'

'Yes.'

'When I looked in it I saw your reflection: yours and mine, they are very alike, don't you think? I think of you, you know, in that lake. I came to say goodbye. I have completed everything now that I must do. I cannot stay here without you. I'm going to go north, that's where they tell me. There are trains north. That's where I will go next.'

She looked at her hands, turned them over as if they were new to her.

'They tell me it's nice north, across the sea, but a bit cold.'

'I'm sure it will be.'

'Maybe I will find some of my people over there. I can't be sure, maybe some have reached that place too. Do you think so?'

'Yes,' I said, 'I do think so. I am sure.'

Her eyes opened up gold as tigers.

'I am so glad, so glad I found you. And now I must catch my train.'

Then she leaned over and kissed me on the cheek and her shadow crossed my face and with it an arc of perfume.

Your grandmother passed away today at 12.0 noon.

I stood with my bag, and my note, and the pale face of Rosa and the pale face of Donald and the tears of Geoffrey. Because no-one could hear now, because no-one now was trained to give hugs, because everything had gone, even Rosa's journey was nearly complete, I sobbed, I sobbed from the bottom of my empty heart, I sobbed to fill all the caves that had cracked open and crumbled, the dark nun sacrificed at the wedding altar and the engagement ring I had unwound from my finger so nothing shone any longer, sobbed sobbed at the thing she had shown me that place with its lost people that lost place with its frozen ponds and stone kitchens those people I had met and not met and would never meet and then I sobbed at the empty places they left and the empty page I had made without Geoffrey without grandma without Sean without anything I knew and I knew it had all changed and

nothing now nothing I touch stands still

I looked through the window, the sky cut in my wall and the butter-dish bed the convent bed and all the pieces whorled round in my head

until I knew what to do next.

She passed away peacsfully in her sleep

If Rosa could not find Phonixstrasse 90 than maybe I can.

I left my bag with the porter. Leo was just leaving in his van to take Gloria to the station. I'm sure she would help him change gear in her cut-

off jeans, and the farewells at the station would be tragic, and his eyes
would empty out as soon as the train had pulled out, waiting for the
arrival of the Advanced group on the next train to fill them up again.

Phonixstrasse was on the map of Pacino but it was out beyond the
youth hostel. I began the walk, then jumped on a tram that wound up the
path in the right direction with a metallic bell and piped announcements
at each stop. Old ladies in hats sat in rows, staring forwards as if it was
illegal to look at each other.

Phonixstrasse seemed to be a field with a few scattered houses here and
there, designer villas dropped down with their backs to each other so none
were overlooked. To walk from one to another took some time, and num-
bers were hidden so I felt like a thief snooping behind gates. But none of
these were right, none would be Maya Abelhofer's home. They all smelt
new, and their lines were new all of them built in my own lifetime. In one
front garden, a large blonde lady was organising flowers in a box.

'Ja?' she said.

'I am looking for number 90, nommer neunzig.'

'Neunzig?' the lady said suspiciously, standing up and looking me up
and down, moving slowly down my hair to my jeans and bare ring finger. 'Es gibt kein. There is not a number 90.'

I began to walk away, she bent over her flowers again, and as I was
behind the wall, she stood up and waved across the field to an old grey
walled building like a fortress the other end of the field.

'Go there if you want,' she said.

I walked there slowly, so its greyness grew bigger and more gnarled
and more fierce and its walls loomed up and covered the winking of a few
windows behind it.

Barmherzige Schwester it said.

Sisters of Mercy.

Phonixstrasse 90

It was penance school alright. I thought of what Sean would say, if
only I could tell him. This was it, this was where my grandma was des-
tined if she had arrived, this was the place that was to welcome her. Was
this the little price she would have had to pay for finding her benefactors?
A small matter of conversion?

I sat on the grass in front of the closed gates. If I had been Maya and
this was my address, what would I have done? I would have jumped in
the lake, I would have climbed a mountain with a rebel, I would have
jumped on the first train going east, going west, going anywhere there
was life. What would I have done, Maya Abelhofer? Anything but rot
behind grey walls.

We buried her quickly. We said goodbye quietly.

It was clear what I must do. It was clear what I must not do.

The next train to Basel was in two hours. I had time to collect my bags, write a letter home, and buy a railway ticket.

I am so sorry I was not with you all for the funeral. But I said goodbye to her in my own way. And she to me.

I had a few days before my money ran out, and by then I would have met up with Felix, Freddi and Claude, and begin to earn money singing in the squares and cafes. Then I could work, anything, in the bars, in the cafes, and travel with them back through the eastern tunnel.

I was thinking that, when the train reached Basel.

It stood, snorting and steaming, while its back and front and middle were locked and unlocked and cleaned. The front of the train was in France, the back was in Switzerland.

There wasn't much time to make the change. I bundled my bag off the seat and onto the platform. It was wide and loud and confusing, and everyone was milling dazed across the wide sooty tracks. Streams of dust moved slowly between lights like tiny motorways.

I stood under the boards and Europe clicked on and off in black letters: Orient Express to Istanbul, Venice, Vienna, the Simplon Express, the gateways beyond the Wall, Berlin, Budapest.

Yes.

I pushed towards the east as the crowds unrolling from the warm dragon pushed in the opposite direction to pick up their connections to the west. We were all pressing somewhere new.

'The way to Oostend, England, can you help me?'

'Yes,' I said.

It was a young girl, with a pale heart face and a long coat down to her ankles that she would look gracious in when the journey had rolled off her.

This way, that way, over there, that platform, that train, keep to the end, the middle, the end of the train, hold on to your visa, your passport, your cash, hold on to the old photographs.

She went on towards the west with a square suitcase in her hand with steel corners, and her hair bobbed around her neck above her brown coat that was a little too big and that tucked under it all the layers of the winter.

I went on towards the east. I found the carriage and felt the pull of fear as it moved in the opposite direction to the one I had first intended, and I knew there was no return.

Berlin in November, then Gdansk, Vilna, maybe Moscow.

I will sing in the main squares and walk in the forests.

By then grandma Rosa will have finished her journey, and I will have started mine.

Vigry Christmas 1989

In the middle of the field was a wall. It was impossible to ignore because the rest was so flat, a snow desert, and so far from anything standing that man had made. It had wandered in from a town, and stayed there.

I took to the field. Every footstep piped down into a tube of snow, and I loped towards the wall, the wall loped towards me, my boots picking up giant moulds of snow with each step.

Nearer to it, the stone sent out a layer of heat. I scraped the frost from the surface, and as it lifted onto my glove, images hoved into view under the cobweb of snow. Each piece was covered with tight stone scribblings, Hebrew words, some Russian, names and pictures. There was half a Rachel with her last letters butted in beside an Avram, and an Eva with a wrist cut at the hand, a Jacob with a lion's paw on his head, and a Rebecca with half a holy book.

It was a wall of tombs, broken tombs that had been snapped off like teeth and crisscrossed in together. This had been the cemetery, this field: all that was left a single standing jigsaw puzzle of people and their picture descriptions.

If you looked hard, you could see the faces there of people you had heard of, buried behind the symbols. I drew their carvings with my finger in the frost , the carvings they should have had: books for Julius Klein, a loaf of bread for Mother Klein, spectacles for Elias, a quill pen for Jacob Tabaschky, a goblet of wine for Marek, a marriage canopy for Luba. And for Lola, hands clasped across a continent, maybe: a forgiveness.

If you tried hard, there in the field, they could be by your side.

'Was it here, then? Is this your home?' I said.

She was a little girl beside me, maybe seven or eight, her chin a tiny pale point in the frame of her coat.

'Oh we come here for picnics.' she said. 'There are trout in the lakes here, you know, and I do love talking to the fishermen. Don't tell mother though.'

She pointed at the stones in the wall, the clasped hands and holy books.

'I wish I could draw pictures like that. Lunke makes them, you know. I talk to him when he comes to the village. He talks to me about things.

No-one else does, only father. I wish I had a best friend I could talk about things with.'

'I'm sure you will, one day soon.'

'I wonder what they would say, if I went with you on the droschka to Vilna?' she said. 'I know just where the carriage stops, by the barn. Don't tell. Don't tell that trout farmer lady. She would tell on me, I know! If I had a best friend, we would never tell on each other,' and she touched her hand to her small child's heart that was full still with the bloom of trust.

She pointed along the spidery line I had drawn in the snow with my footprints.

'You've made footsteps for me. I always like to walk in people's footprints,'

and she took to the field, hopping from piped print to print, her feet tiny in my big galosh puddles, hopped, hopped, sending screams of laughter out into the white sky, her face full of glorious conceited hope. When I looked again, it wasn't laughter at all but the wind whisking up the birch branches.

I picked up the snow she had trodden in. It crumbled into air in my hand. A new layer of snow flaked down and peppered the stones, sitting softly in the cracks which spelt names and covering them as I watched.